Lady Scandal

A FURIES NOVEL

OTHER BOOKS BY WENDY LACAPRA

Lady Vice

Lady Scandal

A FURIES NOVEL

WENDY LACAPRA

Entangled Publishing, LLC
2614 South Timberline Road
Suite 109
Fort Collins, CO 80525
Visit our website at www.entangledpublishing.com.

Scandalous is an imprint of Entangled Publishing, LLC.

Edited by Erin Molta
Cover Design by Kelley York & Liz Pelletier
Cover Art by The Killion Group Inc.

ISBN 978-1-943336-78-4

Manufactured in the United States of America

First Edition July 2015

All right, Rev., this one is just for you.

Chapter One

Earl Baneham's Rules for Winning

"REVEAL NOTHING OF YOUR INTENT."

Lady Randolph, née Lady Sophia Baneham, stood silent and still in the Dowager Duchess of Wynchester's parlor while recalling the first rule printed in her father, the Earl's, secret and much-coveted book, *Earl Baneham's Rules for Winning*. She knew every rule by rote, though she had sworn for the sake of conscience and soul never to learn them by heart.

Tonight, however, she would call forth the darkest part of her being.

The mantel was cool under her palm; cool as the poker in the fire was hot. With her eyes fixed on the flames, she spoke to her friend Thea, the current Duchess of Wynchester.

"Go to bed," she said. "Lord Randolph will come for me. When he does, I must meet him alone."

Thea made a sound of distress. "I cannot leave you." Her skirts rustled as she paced. "You were there for me when

I left my husband. You were there for Lavinia when she left hers. We are the Furies and we have remained united through heartache, scandal, and near-ruin."

"This is different, Thea." The roots of this fight stretched down deep into deadly Baneham secrets.

"The dowager," Thea's cadence slowed with frustration, "shared her home with us so we could remain together."

Sophia turned, reached out, and cupped the duchess's cheek as she would have a child's. Her impending separation from the Furies thrust a dagger into her heart. The Furies had been her solace and her strength, but her reprieve had ended.

Associates of her father's greatest enemy, Kasai, had been seen on English soil, fulfilling her father's prediction that the man would not relent until he had devastated the lives of every Baneham. And, if being hunted by her father's enemies was not bad enough, tonight she had discovered she had tied herself—for better or worse—to a deeply duplicitous man…a spy who'd trained under her blackguard father.

Both the other Furies would take up her fight, but the vengeance sworn on her house was hers to face alone. She rubbed Thea's cheek with her thumb and sighed. At least she need only endure Thea's persistence, since Lavinia, recently exonerated of her estranged husband Lord Vaile's murder, was currently enjoying the much-deserved attentions of Maximilian Harrison, her beloved, within the neighboring mansion.

"Listen, dearest," Sophia said. "Randolph married me under false pretense. I alone can force him to reveal the reason behind his deception."

"*Force* Randolph?" Thea snorted. "He could heft you

with one hand."

"True. But I have this…" Sophia bit her lip and sent Thea an affected smoldering look, "and, should sensual distraction fail, I have this." She curled her fingers around the poker's handle and stoked the fire. "Randolph is just a man. And like all men, his power lies primarily in my acceptance of it." She set back her shoulders. "I will convince him I will not leave him and then cajole him into revealing his secrets."

Thea's eyes widened. "But you *are* planning to run, aren't you?"

Sophia's smile stalled beneath her eyes. "A Lady does not *run*, Thea."

"But *you* are," Thea insisted. "You are planning to take the gold we made from our gambling salons and leave Randolph for good."

And Thea often accused *her* of being able to read minds.

"Do you think I," Sophia widened her eyes, "famously enamored of silks and comfort, would flee into the night in *this* storm?"

Thea swiveled toward the window with a scowl. "This *storm* is nothing more than a squall—the worst will be over in minutes." She turned back, eyes hard with stone-solid resolve. "Tell me the truth."

"I can tell you only this," Sophia said with a hard look of her own, "I do plan to go into hiding. I have good reason."

"Oh, Sophia," Thea's distress sang through her words. "You will return, won't you?"

"I do not know," she confessed.

She was in danger. *Mortal* danger. Three years past, her hated father, Baneham, had been murdered and the deed had gone unacknowledged, unprobed, and unpunished.

This morning she had unwittingly married his protégé. And, shortly thereafter, learned that the men who had murdered Baneham were once again on the hunt.

What hope had she against such power?

"I have been through every possibility, and the wisest choice—for now—is for me to flee." Flee like a gazelle into the brush, hoping the lions would turn on one another in a battle to rule the pride. "Try to trust me, Thea."

Thea put a hand on her hip and considered. "What will Randolph do if he realizes you are about to flee?"

"Randolph will not harm me in the middle of Mayfair." She lifted a begrudging brow. "He is too cunning for such a lack of subtlety."

Thea cast a skeptical glance. "I trust your greater understanding of the man, but I will ready two footmen. If you need them, call. And promise not to leave before we talk."

"I will promise." She would *never* leave Thea without a goodbye.

"I *still* have a terrible feeling," Thea said.

Sophia squeezed Thea's arm. "Goodnight, Thea."

"Goodnight." Thea strode across the room, but paused in the doorframe to glance over her shoulder. "May fortune be with you, Sophia."

Sophia forced another smile. As her friend disappeared into the dark hall, she turned back to the flames and her smile disintegrated. Fortune would never shine long on Earl Baneham's daughter.

Baneham's greed and dishonest dealings while in diplomatic service to the East India Company had made him an enemy of a man known as Kasai—the Butcher. After Baneham's final return from India, he had given Sophia a warning: *Kasai will come for us and kill us both. Or worse, he will kill me and take you so deep inside the desert you will never be found.*

She had thought Baneham mad. Within weeks, however, he was dead. *Murdered.* Since then, three long years had passed without threat to *her* life, and she had grown soft enough to believe herself free of her father, free of his corruption, and free of his enemy's intimidation.

Until tonight, when not more than a league away from the dowager's home, Lavinia's Max Harrison, who had been imprisoned by Kasai and had survived his brutality, had identified Kasai's jackal henchman. Here, in London.

She should have known better than to let down her guard. She would never be free of her father's enemies. Just as she had never been free of his influence — even when he had been continents away.

Hadn't she thought herself free when she married her first husband, only to lose him to her father's influence and, later, to death in a pointless duel?

She stared at the shining-new band hugging her finger, shame weighing heavy as a boulder in her chest. Now she was married again. Closing her eyes, she wished away the memory of the vows she and Randolph had exchanged this morning, hours before she had learned of his true character and associations.

If she had been properly minding her weaknesses, instead of gazing into Lord Randolph's winter-grey eyes and marveling at his masculine perfection, she would have recognized the devil as a "graduate" of Earl Baneham's corrupted coterie *before* she had taken his wager. A wager that, when she lost, granted him her hand.

She wet her lips as she speculated. Who had Lord

Randolph become since Baneham's death? And what was his current aim? At best, he could be a mercenary in service to the East India Company or a spy in service to the crown. At worst, he could be selling his services to the highest bidder—possibly even Kasai.

As a former student of her father's, Randolph's loyalty would always be to his own gain.

She splayed a hand over her stomach as she inhaled through pain and fear. Through the exquisitely fitted silk, she felt the smooth edge of her busk—tough bone beneath beauty.

No matter who he was, Lord Randolph had chosen the wrong woman to deceive.

She would outwit her father's enemies *and* break free from the corruption, blood, and lies that had tainted her father, and now tainted, by extension, any proxy. Violating her marriage vow was a smaller price to pay than the loss of her life.

Outside, a coach rattled to a stop. Through the drumbeat-fall of rain, Randolph's voice penetrated the walls. He had come to claim her. *His wife.*

She removed the poker from the fire and set it to the side of the fireplace—the last step in a night of mad planning. Moments later, the mirror above the mantle reflected his entrance. She met his gaze in the glass.

With a Bridewell-heavy *click*, he closed the door. Strain, no doubt born of his part in the night's mission, had etched a crease into his brow. Even so, his broad shoulders and sensual-even-in-fury lips caused her wayward heart to lurch in the usual way.

"The mission has gone to hell," he said. "A possible

traitor has disappeared with an associate I thought I could trust."

Randolph's rolling baritone seized Sophia's heart in a vise grip and twisted.

Stay calm. She had her own two-fold mission now: extract information and survive.

Slowly, he pushed a hand through his damp hair. She smothered her longing. So what if his locks fell about his shoulders in lovely, thick waves of sand-blond beauty? Being a fine specimen of a man did not make him any less dangerous.

If Baneham's specter hadn't risen, however, and if she still believed Randolph to be the lazy rogue he'd acted, right now she would be welcoming his return by smoothing her fingers through those waves, pressing her palm against his chest, and lifting her lips to his—just as she longed to do.

Pity she had to leave him, really. The kind of pity that blasted a gaping hole where her stomach had been.

He sauntered toward her while his predator eyes studied her face. "I inquired after your friend. The dowager's butler informed me that Lady Vaile is resting."

The butler did not know Lavinia had used a secret, swiveling bookcase that connected this house with the next to join Max Harrison in his bedchamber. Nor did Sophia care to inform Randolph of the truth.

Randolph may have dishonestly earned her confidence by testifying on Lavinia's behalf when she had been falsely accused of murdering her husband, but Sophia refused to be again fooled. Randolph had never cared for her or her friends. He cared for nothing but his own mission—and what his true mission was, only he knew.

For now.

He stopped walking, unsurprisingly, just beyond the reach of her poker. "You would have been proud of the way Lavinia goaded the real killer into revealing the truth. He died by his own hand." Randolph's monotone suggested familiarity with gore. "I would have returned Lavinia to you, if an agent of mine had not gone missing. I know you must have been worried."

She narrowed her eyes, her expression revealing just what she thought of his concern.

"Speak, Sophia," he ordered. "Say *something*. Anything."

She clapped her palms together and concealed her shaking fingers by tucking her hands beneath her chin. "What do you wish to hear?"

"I know you are angry with me," he said with an edge of impatience, "and I am sure your pretty head is full of dark delusions. But the past does not affect what is between us. We have our marriage to consider now."

The word *marriage* bounced off her gut like a coward's blow.

"I am not angry" —she was furious— "and my *pretty head* is not full of *delusions*." Not anymore.

He resumed his slow prowl until she felt his heat against her back. *My. Had he always been so tall?*

"Play ice-hearted queen, if you must," he said, "but look me in the eye when you lie."

"With pleasure." Her skirts swished as she turned. She fit between his shoulders like a small painting fit an over-large frame, but victory did not always go to those with a physical advantage. She granted him the most dazzling of her smiles, a smile she used to knock men on their heels.

Weaving a purr into her words, she added, "Then again, what does a hard look in the eye mean, one liar to another?"

Randolph had sense enough to step back.

"I did not tell you of my past connection to Earl Baneham," he said low and quiet. "But my deception was for your protection."

She hated hearing the Earl's name on his lips.

Earl Baneham. Her father. Or, as they'd called him when he worked for the East India Company, *The Ruthless*. The Earl had taken pride in his reputation, and had insisted that any man he mentored show proof he possessed the same quality. Her gaze dropped to Randolph's clean, gloveless fingers. She did not want to know what atrocity those hands had committed to gain access to her father's lethal—and very secret—club.

She sidled away from Randolph...and closer to the poker. *Information.* She needed information. "How long did you work for Baneham?"

"There are few who assisted the government in the same capacity as I, who had *not* worked with your father."

"Not an answer."

He sighed. "I began assisting him during my grand tour."

Five years? How could she have been so blind? She kept her dry, rough eyes wide open.

"Tell me," she asked, "how well did you absorb the Earl's tutelage? Did you memorize his book of rules?" She wagered he had a copy of those rules in his pocket. "Did you believe, like his other starry-eyed students, that he held every answer to questions of power and authority and governance?"

"He was wise and effective," he said.

"More like brutal and cold-blooded. I *do not* need a lecture on the earl from one of his lackeys."

He stiffened. "I was hardly Baneham's lackey."

"To the Earl, *everyone* was a lackey."

"Oh?" he asked. "Why then, did he trust me with his most valued possession?"

"His most valued *possession*?" Her voice edged up like a cocking pistol.

"You."

The single syllable exploded in her mind.

"So, I am a possession the Earl could *will* to a particularly esteemed devotee?" She bared her teeth. "A possession from the Latin *possidere*—to be master of, to own."

"A possession from the Latin *possidere*—to have and hold." His smooth voice rolled over her fury. "I would protect you with my life, Sophia."

How did he make his lies sound smooth and genuine? How did he keep his gaze intent and sincere? Bitterness practically wafted from hers just as the heat wafted from the fire.

Ah, he would be dangerous to someone inexperienced with a heartless man. But she was the daughter of a killer.

"However angry you are at me," he continued, "you cannot doubt my ability to keep you safe."

Safe? She was not safe and never would be.

"No, Randolph," she said quietly. "I do not doubt any of your abilities."

He narrowed his eyes.

She was not lying. She did not doubt he was fully prepared to carry out whatever mission he had undertaken. What she did not know was *who* he was working for. Death lurked in the shadow of every night, biding its time, and waiting. Trusting the wrong man would leave her dead, just as it had her father.

"You would protect me like you protected the Earl?"

She placed a sweaty palm against the side of the mantle, inches from the poker's handle.

His eyes glittered. "Baneham's death was ruled an accident."

"I grant his broken neck could have been caused by a stumble. But a knife to the back?" A vision of the blood and the Earl's unnaturally bent body flickered in her mind and she swallowed the aftertaste of sick. "Cook was not careless with her cutlery."

"By whatever means," he said, "Baneham is dead. What concerns me is you."

She only *considered* grabbing her weapon. Her wrist was in his grip before she saw him move. He wedged himself between her and her only physical defense, pinning her arm against the mantel as he kicked aside the poker.

"I will not let you go." He kept hold of her wrist and rested his other hand on the mirror, just beside her shoulder. "Bet against me and you will lose."

"Will I?" She would win because she had to win. "Men have placed bets in the thousands when we faced each other over cards. I have beaten you before. With odds against me."

"I am not your enemy," he said. "Trust, at least, in that."

She laughed, dry and brittle. "You cannot honestly expect me to trust you."

"Perhaps not," he said, nostrils flaring, "not yet. But mark me well, Sophia. I expect you to honor your wedding vows — or, if you wish to think of our arrangement in less personal terms, pay the debt you accrued when you lost our wager."

Flesh to flesh, his hand burned where he held her wrist. He radiated feudal-like dominance. Of course, obedience was what he expected. *Compliance. Deference.* So far, she had been an easy mark.

"I should have seen it in your eyes," she said. "That little spark of fury. The thrill that leads you from chase to chase, never caring who is crushed."

"All is fair in love," he started.

"And war," she finished, squaring her shoulders and ignoring the pain that shot up her arm. "Mark *me*, Randolph. I would never have agreed to your pitiful wager if I had known the truth. You presented yourself as a man of leisure. A rake without a care in the world but for seduction and gambling."

"Deep inside, you knew who and what I was."

No. She had been utterly blinded by a silken-voiced seducer who had stirred needs she had not indulged since her husband's death.

"When I agreed to our wager," she said, "I expected to win."

"Only a fool gambles what they cannot afford to lose." His hard-edged gaze softened, as if she had come into focus in a different way. "You are no fool."

A fool she must have been.

During the Furies' scandalous and illegal gambling soirees, Randolph had begun a campaign of small, seemingly innocuous contact. He had, however, laced each touch with suggestive intent—his palm lingering at the small of her back, his fingers flitting briefly against her shoulder and then "accidentally" brushing her neck, his hand covering hers, hot and firm, whenever she had been obliged to take his arm.

…The same hand he would later use to hold her still while, against her ear, he described shocking carnal intentions in thrillingly wicked detail.

The night he had issued the wager, she had thought

him exactly like her first husband: a rake with weaknesses she understood. A rake who would leave her secrets—and her heart—untouched, while bringing a permanent and passionate end to her celibacy.

The ghost of his kiss pulsed against her turncoat mouth.

"Tell me truthfully," he said, as if sensing her thoughts, "you never once imagined how intimacy would be between us."

The skin at the base of her throat quivered as the air between them heated. *Such fine lips*. Firm and dry and, she wagered, expert in coaxing a woman to heights of abandon. When he had won, she had not felt as if she had lost. She had been eager to join him in bed and learn which of his imaginative intentions he would first indulge.

"I am not your enemy," he repeated softly. He placed his cheek against hers and whispered, "What I am, my dear wife, is potent and primed to satisfy *all* your erotic desires."

With languid skill, he drew his knuckles up and down her arm. He had stripped her bare using her bone-deep fear, and now he flayed her using her lust. The back of her throat dried as, conversely, her mouth watered. She should push him away and slap the arrogant assurance she imagined in his cursed grey eyes, but her free hand remained limp and heavy at her side, warmed by his finely-muscled thigh.

"So-phi-a," he whispered her name in a blasphemous incantation. "You hunger for me the same way I hunger for you."

His breath tickled her cheek, heightening his magnetism—the irresistible draw she had felt from the moment they'd met. He placed a kiss on the outer corner of her ear, another on her jaw, and a third on her mouth's trembling edge.

She strove to remain still. "Are you so expert a lover you can tell the depth of my attachment from a few careless kisses?"

Slow, as if he were painting a delicate line, he ran his thumb across her bottom lip.

"Careless kisses?" he questioned, voice smooth and gentle. "Is that all they were?"

"I never succumbed," she mouthed with little breath.

"You *succumbed* entirely." Triumph glinted in his eyes. "You may have refused to be my mistress, but you are now my *wife*." He mocked her voice. "*I am many things, but I will not be your whore.* If I snared you by deceit, the web was of your own making."

"Never," she said.

He snorted. "Chastity outside marriage is a charmingly provincial rule for a woman known as Scandal."

She squeezed her eyes shut and turned her head, biting her lip hard enough to squelch the tingle left by his touch. He'd hit close enough to the wellspring of her pain for tears to threaten.

Provincial indeed. She had not believed in love, nor, truthfully, in marriage. The Baneham household had been a mockery of both. She was aware enough to understand that, like her father, her passions ran to excess. But where her father had longed for power, Sophia longed for touch. Yes, she flaunted most of society's rules, but she had kept one—only for protection. Without that rule, she'd foreseen a spiraling descent into ruin.

"You have used my weakness. You have used my integrity. I should have known you would use *any* violence to force me into submission."

Quick as she had found herself trapped, she was released.

Her eyes flew open as he kicked the poker. The heavy brass rod hit the far wall with a startling clatter. Breathing heavy, he clenched his fists. She braced for a Baneham-esque roar of pure rage. None came. Instead, he stared at the poker until his breath slowed and his skin returned to its usual pallor.

"I am exhausted." His shuddering sigh was thick with resignation. "My men are scattered in pursuit of a traitor I allowed to slip through my fingers because my thoughts were fixed on *you*." He paused. "I had, however, no cause to insult you. And whatever you may believe, I do not want you to fear me."

She lowered her hand from where he had kept her pinned.

He closed his eyes and stretched his neck. "…As for using your weakness, my strength in these past few months has not been exactly augmented by having a near-perpetual cockstand."

Shame heated her cheeks—a pale cousin of the way his shocking words had once warmed her blood.

He reached out—palm exposed, grey eyes fathomless. "Forgive me, Sophia. Let us begin again."

Unlike a student of the Earl to admit a wrong and then to ask forgiveness.

Down through her fear, down through her anger and hurt, *something* existed between them. Shared recognition, perhaps…and palpable need. If she could trust him, she would have an influential ally…and the comfort of his bed.

She blinked.

Damn him. He'd done to her as she had intended to do to him. She sliced away thoughts that could lead to affinity.

Giving in to the urge to trust him would put her life at risk. Even if she could trust that Randolph meant her no harm—which she could not—she would never again live her life subject to the whims of a man who had pledged himself to power at the expense of all else.

The Earl had been charming too, when the need arose. And he had been directly responsible for her husband's death and indirectly responsible for her mother's…not to mention the deaths of countless others.

"Nothing," she said, "can change the fact you deceived me."

"I crafted an image that served my purposes." He let his hand drop. "Do you not do the same?"

"What do you mean?"

"To the *ton*, you are known as Lady Scandal—Reigning Queen of the Furies."

"That was no crafted image. I am a Fury."

"You? A degenerate scandal?" He chuckled.

The bastard.

"You should know," she countered, "you attended the Furies' illicit gambling parties."

"You really *do* think me blind." He shook his head. "The Furies' gambling parties provided the means for you to support Lavinia and Thea after they'd left their husbands."

"An obvious enough assumption," she said.

"The genius of your deception," he continued, "lives in the invitation lists themselves. You knew your father's killer was out there—knew Kasai could send him after you. The greater the number of powerful men you placed in your debt, the better protected you hoped you would be."

Chapter Two

Earl Baneham's Rule's for Winning

"DECEIT IS ALWAYS NECESSARY."

The thrill-like terror of exposure surged through her veins. How had he seen what everyone else had failed to see? She had *wanted* to help Lavinia and Thea — her love for them was true — but she had *needed* to keep both friends and enemies close.

Too close, as it turned out.

"You have guessed," she acknowledged, "my means and method, but you can hardly compare my deception to yours."

"*I* never placed the lives of my innocent friends in danger," he said. "Oh, save your indignant glower. You know you were spared for a reason — you have something Kasai wants."

And how — *how* — did he know what, until now, she had only *suspected*, unless he worked for Kasai?

"Earlier," she said, "you did not admit Baneham was murdered. Are you saying you have known all along?"

"Officially, your father's death was ruled an accident," he said. "But I grant the timing is suspicious. If Baneham left something behind—anything—that could help lead me to Kasai, you must let me know. You can trust me, Sophia. I am the only person you *should* trust."

Trust him? Why? So he could then ensure she was silenced—forever? She kept her eyes widely innocent.

"You have lounged in my study." *Good God*—had he been searching for Baneham's papers since he had wormed his way into her home? "You *know* I kept none of Baneham's effects." Although she had certainly searched for anything that could have offered protection.

"Playing naive, are you? Again and again I have watched you twist men around your little finger." He lifted her hand from her side and kissed the finger he had maligned. "Your machinations will not work with me, however cunning you were to place the most dangerous men in London in your debt. Your father would have been proud."

He said it as though she should care. "I would scorn the earl's pride, if he still lived."

Randolph cocked his head. "He loved you above all else."

"Yes. The love of *The Ruthless*." It was her turn to laugh, the sound like a rock dislodged, cracking against a mountain as it fell. "How lucky I am."

"He asked me to protect you," Randolph said.

"He died," she said, "*three years* ago." And she had been left alone and confused as powerful men tried to make her believe his death had been an accident. "If Baneham did entrust you with my care, you have been dreadfully negligent."

"I may not have been by your side, Sophia, but by remaining in India and engaging Kasai, I *was* protecting you."

"And now his agents are here. As you are. The timing fascinates…"

"For God's sake, Sophia. Now you are being ridiculous. I came back for you. Kasai has lost his largest sponsor—France. He is desperate. He will come looking for what he believes is his."

Oh God. She felt her face drain… she had known Kasai had sent emissaries to England, that alone had been enough for her to plan her flight. But she had not known of Kasai's desperation.

"It looks dire, yes, but we will prevail," he said, "I promise."

The skin on her neck prickled. *Now.* Instinct commanded. Now was the time to make Randolph believe she was fragile and about to break.

"I want more than anything to believe you." Her laces squeezed tight as she inhaled. "I am terrified."

He frowned. "Of me?"

Of course. "Of Kasai."

"I will take care of Kasai," he said, fiercely sincere. "I *vow* it."

Again, the earl's arrogance. "Did the earl truly believe you could keep me safe?"

"Yes," he said.

Oh my. His eyes truly gleamed when he smelled prey.

"Come, Sophia," His voice liquid and warm, like heated chocolate. "Let me look after you. You are no longer alone."

How could he taunt a parentless widow with the promise of kinship and belonging? If she'd been anyone but Baneham's daughter, she may have broken, in truth. Instead, she forced out the tears lingering behind her eyes. And, damn Randolph's corrupted soul, once they started she could not make them stop.

They bathed her eyes in a salty relief—years of pent emotion, finally free. A performance, yes—but her sob wrenched loose the hurt that necessity had kept frozen.

"Ah, Sophia," Randolph stepped close and cupped her cheek. "There is no need to cry. Come. Let me make amends."

She leaned toward him as if pulled by an irresistible force. "Oh, Randolph."

He smiled—indulgent, exultant—and then gathered her into his arms.

Why did his embrace have to feel warmer than the finest wool? Why did she fit so comfortably into the crook of his arm?

Steel yourself and don't be fooled. He only wishes to slake his lust—the tingling sensation returned in her neck—*and then finish his mission.* Should something happen to her, would anyone even think to blame her new husband?

"I will," he said, "take you home."

She pulled back and looked into his eyes, clouding her intent with shades of the truth—her concern for Lavinia, her promise to Thea. "I cannot leave the Furies tonight. Thea is distraught and Lavinia is…still recovering. I have assured them both I would be here."

His eyes ran over her face, searching. A knock sounded on the door.

"Yes?" Sophia called.

"I beg your pardon my lady," the dowager's butler said, "but a letter has been delivered for his lordship."

She slid out of Randolph's arms to collect the sealed letter. "Thank you."

The butler nodded and then disappeared.

She ran her fingers over the folded parchment, expecting

Randolph to demand the letter.

"As my wife," he said, "you are free to read my correspondence."

She gave him a curious glance—what game did he seek to play with such a gesture? She broke the seal and quickly read the lines. She raised her brow.

If the letter was genuine, Randolph was in the employ of the same man who had disguised her father's murder. If his gesture had been meant to inspire confidence, he had failed.

"The Under Secretary of State," she handed him the letter, "requests your immediate presence."

He ran through the terse contents. "Damnation," he cursed. He re-folded the paper and tucked it into his waistcoat pocket. "I had hoped he would be satisfied with the records he wanted, but left my direction in case."

Meaning Randolph had anticipated the prolonged argument they'd just had. She could not count on him to underestimate her.

"Rest," he said, "and tend to your friend. I will return tomorrow afternoon. You will remain here?"

"Yes, I will remain here *tonight,*" she said with a slight frown. *Despite the summons, he'd capitulated with too great an ease.*

"I have men watching the house." He cleared his throat. "For your protection, of course."

Ah. She smiled—he thought her little more than his prisoner, then. "I would expect nothing less."

His men did not know about the secret passage from this house to the next—which she would use, though to do so, she must disturb Lavinia and her lover, Max.

Randolph ran a knuckle down her cheek. "Thank you." His gaze searched hers, pointed and earnest. "From the start you have known we were made for each other."

A bitter truth existed in his words.

"Perhaps," she said. "We are both spawn of the Earl—one in spirit, one in flesh."

Randolph's fingers left a brand beneath her chin. He lowered his head and gently brushed his lips against hers—a chaste kiss belaying the blackness in both their hearts.

"I am glad you did not run." His voice, though pleasant, held a hint of warning. "Though I would have found you, no matter where you went."

"I know," she said. *You would have tried.*

She remained still as he released her shoulders. Still, as he bid her good night. Still, as his footsteps sounded on the marble hall.

But when his coachman's whip sounded in the late night air, she pressed her shaking hands to her closed eyes and forced the fear back down into her heart with deep, determined breath.

She was strong, strong in the way only a woman whose experience of familial love had come from a ruthless criminal could be strong.

Randolph would try to catch her. He would fail. As much as she hated herself for it, she *was* her father's daughter.

• • •

Earl Baneham's Rule's for Winning
"DUAL ALLEGIANCE IS FATAL."

With aching limbs and sweat-stung eyes, Randolph marched toward a reckoning with England's Under Secretary-of-state, who dually served as spymaster.

A reckoning he hoped would end more in his favor than

the battle with his wife.

He had begun the evening confident he could, as ordered, secure brothel records damning men highly placed in Pitt's newly-formed government; confident he had, by marrying Sophia Baneham, ensured the protection of his mentor — her father's — youngest and only legitimate descendant; and confident he would soon, through Sophia, have the means to destroy his mentor's deadly nemesis, the infamous Kasai.

Then Sophia had uncovered his past connection to her father. And next, his agent had turned. He should have predicted his agent's sedition. He should have known Sophia would unearth his secret. He'd been dazzled by her charm before he'd glimpsed the shrewd mind beneath the beauty. And then...

Well, then he'd been *entranced*.

Sophia — sensual, witty, sly — was indisputably his to protect, now. Setbacks or not, he must win this deadly game.

He stepped over the body soaking in a crimson pool, narrowly avoiding the blood seeping into the brothel floor boards. The Under Secretary looked up from the papers he had been examining. His wig of white curls appeared out-of-place in the scene of carnage.

"This is one unholy mess, Randolph." He was not speaking of the body.

"I am well aware."

"I understand," the Under Secretary said, "one of your agents has gone *astray*. Have you located the woman?"

"No." Simple answers must serve — at least until Randolph's blood cooled and he could finally *think*.

The Under Secretary folded his hands behind his back in mock deliberation. "Men at the highest levels of the East

India Company lauded you for your brilliance and cunning. Yet, you placed an untrustworthy agent in a key position, allowed her to steal the records I hired you to secure, and then you *lost* her?"

In fact, he had. He ignored the question, and instead followed the secretary's accusation to the inevitable conclusion.

"The records," he said with bitter realization, "are missing as well."

"Yes." The secretary shoved the sheets off the sideboard. They scattered into the air the way leaves scattered in a squall. "What was left here incriminates no one of importance. The vital records are gone—and along with them, proof of perfidy capable of, once again, toppling Parliament. By God, Randolph, we just suffered through an election—the country cannot bear further instability."

Behind the Under Secretary's anger, Randolph smelled fear—fear he could use. The Under Secretary himself, or someone very close to him, must have been implicated in those records.

"You will have your *vital* documents." Randolph steadied and lowered his voice. "The resolution to our problem has merely been delayed."

"*Our* problem?" The Under Secretary snorted. "Why should I allow you to keep your position? Sources tell me you compromised the mission with other priorities. They say on this day, the very day our work here was to be complete, you put to use a special license and were married—by the Bishop of London, no less." His eyes narrowed. "How is the new Lady Randolph?"

Devastatingly beautiful and utterly furious.

"I had to take action," he said, "to secure Baneham's

daughter."

And yet, his marriage *had* compromised the mission. That he had done so in response to a greater threat did little to deaden defeat's burn.

…*Never admit defeat.*

A rule from Baneham's book came to mind—with a consequent soothing effect. Slowly, the night's shattered pieces reconfigured. The developments did not necessarily spell disaster.

He would fix his mistakes. He would find Helena, his missing agent. Though his wife had hurled insults at him with hatred and disgust, he would protect Sophia at all cost, even if he must protect her against her will.

And, he would accomplish his ultimate goal: to put a definitive end to Kasai.

The Under Secretary drummed his fingers on the sideboard.

"I find myself at a loss," he said. "How do the late Earl Baneham and his daughter relate to your mission?"

Randolph studied the Under Secretary, a man renowned for his effectiveness. How much did the Under Secretary know about Kasai, Baneham, the East India Company, and the atrocities committed in the name of profit and revenge?

"When the Company warned you one of their enemies would attempt to buy Montechurch's brothel records, they told you little, I expect, of the enemy."

The Under Secretary raised an imperious brow. "They told me he has been a thorn in the company's side since the days of Clive."

"*Thorn*?" Randolph made a sound of derision. "He is so much more than a thorn. Kasai is not his name—no one knows for certain who he is—but they know enough of his work to call him a word meaning butcher."

The rat-a-tat of the Under Secretary's fingers grew more pronounced, accenting his impatience.

Randolph took a step closer and continued, "Kasai is brutal. He is without loyalty to any country or king. Chaos brings him wealth and opportunity to feed his well-documented thirst for blood."

"I have heard, of course, of Kasai," the Under Secretary said. "An ambush he planned led to the death of the Duke of Wynchester's brother."

"The same ambush survived by Maximilian Harrison—the duke's confidant and former judge of Calcutta's high court."

The Under Secretary shook his head. "*I* had to convince the enraged duke he was needed here—not in India trying to hunt down a shadow."

"Kasai is responsible for Wynchester's brother's *alleged* death," Randolph clarified, "among more burning atrocities."

The Under Secretary froze, head cocked. "Did you say *alleged* death?"

Randolph nodded. "This morning, two survivors of that massacre identified Lord Eustace, the duke's supposedly dead brother *and only heir,* as the translator traveling with Kasai's emissary—the man attempting to buy the records."

Calculations shifted in the Under Secretary's gaze the way counting beads slid across an abacus rod. When the Under Secretary's finger-drum resumed; Randolph sensed the mental equation had not been reconciled in his favor.

"The records are likely with your missing agent," the Under Secretary said, "which means Kasai and Lord Eustace, if he is indeed alive, remain the Company's concern. *Not mine*."

"The *Company's* concern?" Randolph held the Under Secretary's gaze, direct and secure. "A menace is now on English soil. A menace you cannot begin to fathom."

"I have dealt delicately with France, Russia, and Prussia," the Under Secretary said in a vinegar-drenched tone. "I believe I am capable of identifying the priority."

"Kingmaker-games," Randolph said, "are undoubtedly essential in the power-jockeying between nations. But Kasai is not a nation. …In some ways, he is worse."

"How?" The question was sarcastic. "His greatest weapon is the disruption of Company profits."

"Kasai has set Mughal against Mughal. He thrives on chaos and incites internal divisions that result in bloody battles."

"Perhaps he can play such games in India." The Under Secretary sniffed and stood tall. "*We* are a civilized nation."

Arrogant bastard. Randolph inhaled slowly. "Kasai's attempt to buy these secrets is not a chess move against the Company. The Butcher has set his sights on England."

"The Company told us the records could injure their allies in Parliament—among others."

"Exactly. Those records are a means for Kasai to gain influence in Parliament."

"If you are right…" The Under Secretary words faded like snuffed tallow smoke and the darkness behind his eyes deepened in the absence.

Randolph smelled blood—and not from the body on the floor. "Kasai wishes to take down our government. If you do not believe me, consider this: Last year's Treaty of Paris put an end to French support of Sultan Tipu, one of Kasai's many employers. He no longer has the means to drain the Company using his army of mercenaries. He will turn, instead, to the source of the Company's power."

"Where is Kasai's emissary now?" the Under Secretary asked.

"Dead."

The Under Secretary's face grew red—a stark contrast to his wig. "Why? And by whose hand?"

"I do not know, but Eustace and my agent are headed north—and I have to assume one or both are working under Kasai."

"Why would he have his own man killed?"

"I intend to find out. I have assigned a man to their trail, a former soldier intimately familiar with Kasai's methods. They will be apprehended; the records will be retrieved." *And Sophia will be safe.*

The Under Secretary's eyes narrowed. "You have not explained the connection to Baneham and the new Lady Randolph."

The look in the Under Secretary's eyes suggested he knew more than he was admitting.

"In the final year of Baneham's life, the Company charged him to discover Kasai's true identity. Attempts had been made before, but not by anyone of Baneham's level or experience. Baneham sent his only female agent—his illegitimate daughter Helena—to infiltrate Kasai's camp, and then he led an attack. The attack failed. Only he survived. He was sent back to England to heal."

After that night, Baneham had not been the same. He had returned from the battle suspicious and threatened. When Randolph had been alone with Baneham, Baneham had raved that there was a larger plot afoot—raved about timelines, sapphires, and traitors. Officials in the Company had believed him mad. *Randolph* had believed him mad.

"What happened to the illegitimate daughter?" the Under Secretary asked.

"I made it my mission to rescue the woman." He lifted one brow. "I *thought* I had earned her loyalty."

Light dawned in the Under Secretary's eyes. "Baneham's bastard is your missing agent, Helena."

"Yes."

The Under Secretary's eyes narrowed. "And the new Lady Randolph? How does she fit?"

Randolph felt the darkness gathering in his chest—the putrid result of a wrong he'd spent the past year trying to atone. "Baneham repeatedly told me Kasai would aim to gain influence in England, and part of his plan would involve making Sophia his prize. Kasai wants Sophia. I have her. She is the key to breaking up this plot."

The spymaster rubbed his forehead. "Recover the documents, the agent, and the duke's brother. I want to speak with Eustace Worthington."

Thank the fates for one small favor…

"…As for Kasai's personal vendetta against Baneham," the Under Secretary continued, "Baneham is dead. That particular game has come to an end. Lady Randolph is irrelevant."

"With all due respect," Randolph said. "Death did not end Baneham and Kasai's rivalry." Randolph had ensured that Sophia was indeed less relevant, now married with her fortune protected, but Baneham had believed Kasai would attack him first and *then* come for his daughter. "I would not have leg-shackled myself on a whim."

The Under Secretary snorted. "Half my men attend those gambling parties Baneham's daughter and her friends host—what do they call them? Lady Scandal, Lady Vice, and Duchess Decadence? I am not fool enough to believe you failed to note Lady Scandal's famous charms."

Warning shivered in Randolph's spine. "To question my allegiance is to question my honor."

The Under Secretary hit the sideboard with his flattened palm. "The mission will come first—I will have your word on this."

Randolph put the full force of the vow into his eyes. "The mission will always come first."

In the excruciating silence, the Under Secretary deliberated.

"I must go against my inclination and trust you…" he started.

Randolph exhaled.

"…But fail again, and I will assume your loyalty is not with the crown."

Randolph nodded. He took his leave before the spymaster could change his orders.

Strange quiet haunted the courtyard behind the brothel. Hints of dawn lightened the cloud-covered sky. He paused at the edge of the street, where a few lit lanterns cast a faint glow.

He had never before failed in a mission. *Never.*

Clearly, he had been off his game and there was only one reason.

Sophia.

Before they had met, Randolph had thought of Sophia as an evil-made-necessary—a means to probe the secrets Baneham had left behind. But then she had turned her cornflower blue eyes on him and *everything* had changed.

…Hours after returning from India, he arrived at a Fury soiree—uninvited. Lady Sophia's footman stuttered under his glower, but the man refused to grant him entry. No one could be admitted to the soiree, the man insisted, without approval of the hostess, even if accompanied, as Randolph was, by the hostess's cousin.

He remained in the hall, suffering the indignity of his wait with hands clasped behind his back. The entry was hardly what he had expected of Baneham's home. The man had been the epitome of male. These furnishings could only be described as—he suppressed an inward shudder—dainty.

He peered into the rooms beyond. The dandies within did nothing to dilute the feminine air. The library was a rainbow of velvet jackets and frothing cravats, topped with clouds of fluffed white wigs. Even from the distance, the scent proved this the motliest male collection of Eau du Cologne enthusiasts ever assembled.

"Cousin Charles has brought me a gift, I see." Her voice sang over his veins the way the wind sang against lines of a hoisted sail—the song sank all the way into his cock.

He turned.

The voice came from a petite, provocatively curved woman sewn into her pink silk bodice—he could think of no other way the fabric could fit so tight. Her hair powder was laced with a matching pink hue. She looked like strawberries and cream and, if he was permitted a taste of her lips, he was certain she'd be as mouthwateringly sweet.

Her gaze dropped from his face and traveled boldly down his body.

By Saint George, he wanted a sampling of her sweetness.

"Lord Randolph," he said, "at your service."

Her faint smile implied a flirtatious scold. "You do not have an invitation, Lord Randolph."

"Soon remedied, I hope. I am recently returned from the continent." She did not need to know which continent—nor how recently. "I have heard your soirees are the must-attend events for any London rake worth his salt."

"Do you fancy yourself a rake, then, Lord Randolph?" She sounded hopeful, blast her sensual voice.

He leaned forward and whispered, "Issue me an invitation, sweetness, and I will provide any proof you may require."

"No proof is required…" a faint, secret smile teased her mouth—both challenge and invitation, "…at present."

It had been lust at first sight. She lit a carnal fire in his blood and the resulting burn was hotter and deeper than any he'd known. He'd pursued her with both the urgency of his mission and the force of his desire. She had held herself aloof for months, but, in the end, the lust running between them had been a grinding stone to her resistance. And now?

Well, once her rage had passed—a slow smile spread his lips. He would make sure they picked up where they had left off—her seduction.

He would draw in Sophia. Sophia, in turn, would draw in Kasai. Nothing angered a man like an enemy's possession of something—or someone—the man considered rightfully his. All he need do was master his own intoxicated response to her touch.

He pulled out his hair-tie and shook out his locks.

The road out of the city called to him with a Siren's persistent pleading. *The Under Secretary is right. Lust has blinded me. I must join my men in pursuit of Eustace.*

No. His most trusted men were already in pursuit. He'd make a few necessary arrangements and, by tomorrow afternoon, he would collect his wife. If he played things right, he'd put an end to Kasai and Sophia would be his prize.

He began the long, ill-scented trudge through vile lanes. Though vermin infested streets beneath his bloodied boots portended doom more than auguring triumph, he did not credit omens and augurs.

A clatter of rain erupted yet again, quickly strengthening with a force so great it would have given Noah pause.

Chapter Three

Earl Baneham's Rules for Winning

"BE PREPARED. AND IF YOU CANNOT BE PREPARED,
PERSEVERE."

The stage clattered on, the din of London's shopkeepers and merchants slowly receded, and the view changed from house-row to hedgerow. Still listless, Sophia drifted into a dream.

The closed carriage became an open, airless plain and thudding horses' hooves became thudding soldier boots—an army marching through hard-packed desert sand. This army was not dressed in the smart military attire of the dragoons. They were dressed, instead, in white...all except for their leader. He bore an executioner's black robes and hood.

She wanted to run, but her feet were buried in the sand and covered with stones. She screamed, but the sound was lost to the wind whipping the executioner's garments into demon-wing frenzy.

He looked down on her from atop his horse; his voice

was a rolling baritone she knew well. *Randolph*.

"For crimes committed by the Earl Baneham, I sentence you to death."

A polished sword caught the light of the sun as he lifted it high. Glittering, it fell. Her eyes flew open and she gasped.

"Madam!" her fellow traveler exclaimed. "Are you quite well?"

"Yes." She blinked. "I beg…your pardon." Her voice scratched like a garden hoe through her throat.

She lifted a small mirror and angled it to see the rear of the carriage, checking to make sure she could not see a lone rider with an all-too-familiar shape. The jumbled reflection showed nothing but a slow-moving farm cart, pale gravel, and mottled green hedge.

The man's gaze grew speculative. "You would not be checking for the law, now would you?"

"My mistress warned me not to speak with strange men," she said in the accented tones of the servant class. With as much dignity as her disguise allowed, she shifted her shoulders and returned her gaze to the window as if offended by his presumptuous intrusion. "If you must know, I was not looking for some*one* but some*thing*. I have little trust in the straps holding my valise. I just dreamt it had been lost."

Out of the corner of her eye, she took note of the man's long, assessing glance. Finally, he settled back into the bench. Perhaps he, too, had something to hide.

She cursed the siren call of sleep. She may not need to fear judgment for Baneham's crime, but her current danger was real.

She snapped her mirror shut and leaned back into the bench, ignoring the way the horsehair stuffing bit into her back. She dreamed of traveling in her plush landau, and would have even preferred a newly constructed Royal Mail coach—mail coaches moved more quickly than private coaches, and they also had the benefit of an armed guard, thanks to Mr. Pitt and his recently-authorized routes. Her landau was out-of-the-question and the Royal Mail only left London in the evening. Timing had made discomfort an imperative.

As much to discourage further conversation as to ease the sting of weariness, she closed her eyes, took a deep breath, and recounted her protections.

One, Randolph would be at a loss as to how she had escaped the building...unless Thea or Lavinia told him about the secret passage to the old Wynchester mansion.

But no, they would *never*.

Two, he would waste essential time questioning every hackney driver in the vicinity of dowager Emma's house while she put ever more distance between them.

Three, even if he somehow discovered her direction, he would have no idea where she was headed.

A sick feeling accompanied the rogue thought that the Earl would have been proud of her preparation and quick thinking—just as Randolph had intimated the night before.

She tightened her grip on the leather strap, still warm from the morning sun, and concentrated on her breath.

In—slow like a full-measure note strung hard across a violin string. Out—quiet as a rabbit hidden in brush. Within the movement of her breath, she spoke silent reassurance: *Randolph will not find me.*

Three times she repeated the phrase, and three times her assurance failed.

Randolph was Baneham-trained. He would have informants in places no one would suspect. The moment she let down her guard was the moment she would lose.

Randolph and Kasai hunted her. She must reach the one place neither would ever look. God help her, even she would not seek herself where she was headed.

She glanced out the window. When would her time in hiding be over?

She was nothing more than a pawn. If the search for her grew too cumbersome, the combatants would likely return to their true aim. If she was lucky and smart, the hunted could become the hunter.

She suspected, as did Randolph, that Baneham had left something hidden. Something, besides her own life, that Kasai wanted.

Once she was certain Randolph and Kasai had given up their search for her, she would assess. If Kasai was still a threat, she would find, or pretend she had found, whatever it was he wanted, and then she would reel in her father's killer.

If Randolph had been involved, he would pay. If not…

There was not any cause for an "if not." Randolph *had* to have been involved. He *said* he wanted to protect her against Kasai, not deliver her to him, but if true, why had he taken so long to return? Why would he have concealed the extent of his dealings with her father? Why would he have spent so much time drawing her into a false trust?

No, he saw her only as the key to Baneham's lost information. Once Randolph had what he wanted, he would deliver her to Kasai or dispose of his unwanted bride in his own way…

She shifted, hot from the added padding she wore and

sweat-drenched with a rush of fear.

I am disguised. I will prevail.

The padding she'd added beneath her servant's clothes concealed her true age and shape, but her odd behavior had placed her at risk and she needed to stay unremarkable.

Someone a man might forget if he was, say, questioned by an enraged peer.

When she changed out of this disguise and into the next, she would not miss the padding. She wished she could have made a believable man. She imagined slipping her legs into buckskin—smooth and fitted. But no, Thea had been right. She curled her lips into a wry smile, thinking of their last conversation.

"Promise you will not try to disguise yourself as a man," the duchess said.

"Why not?" she asked.

Thea raised her brow. "You know you couldn't stop the feminine roll of your hips if your life hung in the balance."

The duchess was, simply put, right.

As long as Sophia could remember, she had loved the heady power of being a woman. Loved sending smoldering glances, loved sweeping her lashes down in breathless anticipation of a wayward touch.

Such interests—and the desire to get away from her father—had led, as they often do, to her early elopement.

Her first husband had no title. Yet she had taken a great pleasure in his freckled shoulders, the hot look in his bright eyes, the way his hungry hands had passed over her flesh like wind on the surface of the ocean. They had little in common but for the depths of carnal joy—which might well have worn thin, if the earl had allowed him to live.

The memory of the pleasure they had shared was why she had fallen so deeply under Randolph's spell. Marriage to Randolph may have seemed a simple solution to her lonely state, but it had been a carefully laid trap.

Her mind traveled back to the first time she had allowed him to linger after a soiree, and join her as she entered the night's draw into her ledgers.

…Heavy-lidded, he lounged on her settee. His extraordinary eyes drank her in as if she were the first sip of wine from a vintage cask, and he an exacting vintner.

"When," he asked, "are you going to come to my bed?"

Sophia glanced up from her calculations. "I have told you, Randolph. I am not that kind of woman."

"And yet you have invited me into your inner sanctum. What will the servants think?"

"My study hardly rises to sanctum-level." She lifted a brow. "And my servants are loyal and discreet."

"What of your fellow Furies?"

"Must you even ask?"

"Then how about the last of your guests, who likely noticed I remained behind? Aren't you concerned they will gossip?"

She peeked at him through her lashes. "My guests are not interested in gossip. They are interested in dissipation. Besides, Lady Scandal must maintain a certain reputation."

"And so the truth is finally spoken." He placed his hand over his heart. "The lady uses me."

"Perhaps." Sophia rested her chin on her fist and sighed,

admiring his form. "Then again, maybe I just like to look at you."

He groaned. "Just one small indiscretion. You would enjoy the lapse." His voice deepened. "I swear."

"Of that much, I am sure."

He laced his fingers together and placed them behind his head. "Shall I deepen your certainty?"

"You may try," she replied, "so long as you stay where you are."

His right leg fell to the side. "Turn your chair and face me."

Her heart did a fluttery little dance as she turned. "Yes, my lord?"

"Ah," he said as if sinking into warm water. "A yes from your lips is straight from my dreams."

"Then you," she quipped, "have been asking the wrong questions."

He closed his eyes. Sophia studied the seam on his breeches. He had an excellent tailor.

"Some men," he said, "are seized with the need to sail unchartered waters, desperate to be the first to set foot on virgin land."

"Is that the reason you travel?"

"I said some men. Not me." He opened one eye. "I find virgin places over rated. I prefer places long-settled. Places that have had time to cultivate beauty and grace."

A blush traveled up from her chest to her cheeks—not a mad rush of heat but a gentle warming. "And what do you like to do when you travel to such places?"

"I like," he whispered, opening both eyes, "to enjoy the view."

She swallowed. "I am sure you have enjoyed many a pleasant view."

"None so affecting," he said, "as the one before me now."

"Randolph—" she said in warning.

"As promised, I have not moved."

"Very well," Sophia said. "Go on."

"Where was I?"

"You were speaking of a view."

"Ah yes. I enjoy a view, but what excites me most is the many diversions such cultivated places have to offer." His gaze traveled over her body as if she were a table of sweets and all he need do was make a choice. "Gardens, for example."

"Travelers are often not permitted to indulge in such diversions."

"If so, I would ask the monarch for special dispensation in the name of knowledge." His smile was faint, and his breath slightly shallow. "She would agree, of course. I have a way with women."

"Do you?"

"Yes. And then I would begin an exhaustive exploration."

"Exhaustive?"

He nodded. "Every enthusiast of travel knows, one must explore with all the senses—scent, sight, sound, touch, and, my favorite…taste. I have a weakness for anything sweet."

"Some fruits are forbidden."

"Within your garden, I would devour every fruit—forbidden or not."

Sophia's blush deepened to a smolder. "I am not sure I could survive such an exploration."

"I would temper your ability to resist."

"How?"

"I would untuck the inciting bit of gauze peeking out from your bodice—"

"Fichu," she interrupted.

"—and I would use it to tie your tiny wrists behind your back."

Sophia gasped.

"With your permission," he said gravely, "of course."

"And then?" she asked, having intended to tell him to stop.

"And then safe from hands threatening to betray your body's need, I would release your hair from all those troublesome ribbons and pins."

She inhaled.

"Your locks," he continued, "would weigh heavy in my hands. They would move like silk through my fingers and I would let them fall against your breasts." He tilted his head to the side. "Each light brush of hair would tease your skin."

She swallowed, but her throat was strangely dry. She rested her hand on her neck. "And what would I be doing?"

"You would be raising your face in the hope of being kissed."

"A service," she said, "I am sure you would willingly provide."

He shook his head; his eyes remained wolfish and fixed. "Not then. You see, without the fichu, that lovely, fitted bodice would be ever so slightly loose. And those beautiful breasts of yours would be a temptation more irresistible than spun sugar."

She meant to say, "oh," but her lips parted, only to freeze in silence.

He continued, "I would edge the soft fabric down until I freed each darkened nipple. Naturally, your back would arch. I would welcome each jutting tip with a kiss, feeling your sighs against my skin."

He stretched out his other leg and dropped one hand to the top of his thigh. How could he lay there, stretched out as if he hadn't a care in the world—lie there blithely, as she burned?

"I would stroke beneath the curve of your breast as I learned your taste and preference—would you prefer a gentle lick, slight graze, or something harder? You would not need to speak. I would know when your peaks grew hard inside the softness of my mouth."

As if compelled by some unnatural force, Sophia's hand fell from her neck to her breast.

"Would you not prefer my tongue?" he asked with a low chuckle.

"Fiend," she said, but not with anger. She straightened her back and folded her hands firmly in her lap. "Go home, Randolph. I have had enough of your teasing."

He stood slowly and bowed. "Sweet dreams, sweetness." He smiled. "Until next we meet."

She placed her hands over her heated cheeks, and forced her breath to slow.

The carriage lurched and swayed as the driver turned into their destination, a posting stable yard.

She checked the mirror—still no sign of Randolph. She clicked it closed and dropped it into the pocket beneath her skirts.

A horse neighed and the carriage rolled to a stop.

"Right." The clerk leaned over to glance through the glass. "Reprieve at last."

The sound of the stair squeaked as the coachman let it down and opened the door. Without a glance to the clerk, she took the coachman's hand and descended, putting distance between herself and her memories.

First, she intended to hire a post chaise with the story she was making arrangements for her elderly aunt whose walk was stiff and slow and more than a little hunched. Then, she would have a bite at the inn and find a tree against which she could rest. Once fed, she'd darken her tresses and remove the padding beneath her dress.

She would make certain her "aunt" caught the coach on time.

• • •

Earl Baneham's Rules for Winning
"IF YOU MUST MODIFY YOUR PLAN, DO SO INTENTIONALLY."

Randolph scowled as he rounded the corner of a busy London square. He ignored cheerful bird-chatter in the branches, sun-lit shadow patterns on the walk, and cart wheels' rattle on the rain-washed streets. Instead, he headed with single-minded resolve toward the dowager duchess's home.

He hoped his formidably reluctant wife had kept her word, because the fruits of this morning thus far had been setback and adversity.

Though Maximilian Harrison had appropriate skill and ample cause, he had declined to join in the pursuit of Eustace and Helena. Randolph had been counting on Harrison's help, but the foolish man had refused.

Randolph suspected Harrison's refusal involved Sophia's fellow Fury, Lavinia, Lady Vaile—known as Lady Vice to

Sophia's Lady Scandal. Why would any man deliberately choose female folly over the opportunity to exact revenge?

He could not understand. Nor could he understand women in the least. Not that he had ever tried. He had been content to let them occupy their world without interference—case in point, his mother and much older sisters—so long as they did not interfere with his.

Where Sophia was concerned, respectful indifference was not possible.

Last night, he had improvised a plan: Nurture her concern for her friends and keep her arguing. Once she lowered her dammed hackles, he had planned on replacing "arguing" with "in bed." Not his best plan, admittedly. Of course, everything had gone to shit.

Apart from throwing her over his shoulder and waking half of Mayfair to scandal, he had to give in to her request to remain the rest of the night while he met with his superior. He hoped his concession, however involuntary, would earn him some advantage. Even a slight easing of her distrust would help. The distraction of his marriage had cost too much already. A price he would have refused, if he had not fallen for her...

He froze mid-step.

Have I fallen for Sophia?

No! He would swear on the fiery pits of hell that he had not. Not in the traditional sense.

Dreams of pleasuring her in ways so intimate, they would make a high-priced courtesan blush, filled his nights, but those dreams were simple lustful wanting—basic to the nature of man. He was not fool enough to develop an attachment capable of compromising all his plans.

He shook his head as if he could banish the idea.

He admired Sophia's wit. He lusted for her body. That was the sum. One did not develop an attachment for a pawn when one was held in check by a madman.

He resumed walking at a slightly slower pace and quickly spotted his man. The fellow fell into step at his side.

"Any trouble last night?" Randolph asked.

"No one's come or gone."

Thank heaven for small favors.

"Keep watch," he said. "We cannot have her leaving out the back while I come through the front, can we?"

The man gave a discreet nod and fell away, leaving Randolph to stand at the foot of the dowager's steps, staring up. He took a deep breath and climbed the stairs, two at a time. The butler opened the door before he had a chance to knock.

"I have come to see my wife," he said, dropping the hand he had raised to click the knocker.

"I suspect you have," the butler replied, face as bland as his voice. "This way."

Something in the butler's lack-of-tone made icy fingers trail up Randolph's neck.

The servant stepped aside to allow him entry to the sitting room. Just as the night before, the white marble mantle was there. His palm-print on the glass was there. Even the blasted poker was still there.

Sophia, however, was not.

Lavinia, Lady Vaile, and Thea, the Duchess of Wynchester stood at the far end of the room. Apparently, they intended to use the settee as an embattlement.

"Where is my wife?" he asked, voice astonishingly even.

"Lady Sophia is not present," the duchess said.

"I can see Lady *Randolph* is not present." He took two steps forward. "Where is she?"

Lady Vaile's grip on the settee tightened. "We do not know."

"You do not know," he repeated, not recognizing his own hoarse voice.

"We would not tell you if we did," the duchess added.

He took another step and the duchess held up her hand. "Think before you act, Lord Randolph. Strangling a duchess is frowned upon."

The haughty harpy. No wonder the duke and duchess remained estranged.

"Thea," Lady Vaile scolded with a brief shoulder nudge against the duchess. She cleared her throat. "Lord Randolph, Sophia has gone. She did not tell us her destination, nor did she say how long she would be absent."

"What *did* she say?" he asked.

Lavinia visibly swallowed. "...she said she had good reason and we should give her our trust."

"*Trust?*" he echoed, dumfounded.

"Yes," the duchess chimed in, "*trust*. A concept of which you are undoubtedly unfamiliar."

Ah. So she had told them she had been deceived. But how much had Sophia revealed? He dispensed with artifice. "My men saw no one leave this house."

Lavinia blushed. "Your men do not know this house's secrets."

Thea put her hand on Lavinia's arm. "All he needs to know is that she is gone."

A bubble of which he had been unaware suddenly burst inside his chest, sending rivulets of cold fear through his veins. This was not rage. This was *terror*.

"Listen," he rushed to the settee and took Lady Vaile's hand before she had time to pull away. "Sophia is in danger. *Great* danger." Gone was the flat tone and he did not recognize his own near-panicked voice. "You have to tell me everything you know. *Now*."

Lady Vaile opened and closed her mouth without speaking.

"Randolph, this display is beneath you," the duchess said. "You tricked her into marriage. Sophia left you for good reason. She has every right to be furious."

He ignored the duchess and kept his eyes on Lavinia's contracting brow.

"She promised me," he said, "she would remain here."

"If she promised," Thea replied, "she did not promise what you think she promised."

His gaze snapped to the duchess. "Should I require a damned barrister every time I speak with my wife?"

The duchess arched her back. "Your anger would be justified…If. You. Had. Not. Lied."

Randolph released Lady Vaile's hand and curled his into a fist. If he allowed the fire in his chest to meet the ice in his veins, they would explode into frothing rage.

But…such excess would not retrieve Sophia.

The closest thing he had to information was standing in front of him right now. Had Lady Vaile and the duchess been men—or even women in the same line of work as he—he would have known how to proceed without question. But these were *ladies,* however society-scorned.

He pulled a breath through his anger and fear. In the brief reprieve, he reached out to Thea and Lavinia with his mind, almost as if they were imaginary doors and all he need do was run his fingers along the edge to locate a weakness he knew existed.

Love.

Sophia loved them and they loved her. They would protect her.

A swift rapier of jealousy stabbed near the vicinity of his heart, followed by a renewed gush of fear—alone, Sophia was at risk. And he needed her safe and he needed her here in London if his plan to draw in Helena and Eustace was going to work.

Right now, Lady Vaile and the duchess were protecting Sophia. All he needed to do was convince them she faced a greater threat than he. A threat she could not conquer on her own.

…Which happened to be the truth.

He settled his gaze on Lady Vaile, the one he judged would break first, if either of them broke at all. His first parry: convince her he was a man in love. Even if he didn't get valuable information, he would need her as an ally if he found Sophia.

When he found Sophia.

"What will it take?" he asked, addressing Lady Vaile.

"Are you insinuating I can be bought?" Lavinia asked.

"No." This exchange would fester like a lead-ball lodged in muscle, but there was nothing to be done. Sophia had already vastly reduced the value of the commodity formerly known as his pride. He took Lavinia's hand from the back of the settee, inhaled and fell to his knees. "I am asking if you need to see me *beg*."

The gasping sound, he assumed, had come from the offended duchess. But Lavinia's eyes had grown soft, and soft was what he needed.

"Even if I did know where she was headed," Lavinia said, "I could, perhaps, be persuaded to pity, but not to betrayal."

"Brava, Lord Randolph," Thea said, "I *almost* believe your distress is in earnest." She tugged her gloves, straightening the seams. "We know nothing. And, even if we did, we would not involve ourselves in affairs she saw fit to keep private. Sophia believed she could fend for herself and your broken heart is none of our concern. Come, Lavinia."

Time for assault number two.

"What if," he asked, "I told you I am not the only one who wants her found?"

The duchess froze.

"And," he continued, "the others who seek Sophia have devious and possibly deadly intentions."

Both ladies turned to stare.

"*Please*, Randolph—"

Lavinia placed a hand on Thea's arm, silencing Thea's sarcasm.

"Wait, Thea. What if Sophia is in danger?"

"Nonsense," Thea said.

"This morning," Lavinia spoke to Thea, "she told us she has been long-prepared for the possibility of flight."

Randolph's neck hair stood on end. What had Sophia planned? She may think she understood base corruption, but she had no idea of the fate she could expect if she fell into Kasai's hands.

Lavinia turned her guileless, pale brown eyes on his. "And last night, you said Kasai would come for Baneham's daughter—and Sophia appeared to understand."

"Yes," Randolph coaxingly conceded. "Kasai is a much worse threat than I. That is why I visited Harrison this morning."

Lavinia frowned. "Kasai—the same Kasai who imprisoned Max?"

"Yes," Randolph said, "and the man who killed the duke's brother, Lord Eustace."

"Randolph," Lavinia asked, "what would a man like Kasai want with Sophia?"

He should have known the simple recitation of a threat would not be enough for these ladies. He weighed his options— Baneham was dead. Revealing his involvement with the East India Company could harm no one.

"I will tell you. And then…" He pursed his lips as if angry at his own weakness which, as it happened, was not entirely a ploy, "…and then you will help me."

"Speak," Thea crossed her arms over her chest. "I am *dying* to hear your convoluted explanation."

"Lady Vaile, I plead my case to you. Sophia is angry because I did not tell her," he swallowed, "about some significant associations in my past."

"Mistresses aplenty, no doubt," the duchess quipped.

"I wish this was a matter of simple jealousy." He didn't have to force a wry grimace. "I was an associate of her father's."

"Earl Baneham?" Lavinia asked.

"Baneham worked in diplomacy for the Company. He and Kasai developed a rivalry," he said, although *rivalry* barely captured their deadly entanglement, "and Kasai has sworn to possess or destroy anything and everything that belonged to Baneham—and was likely behind her father's early death."

Lavinia's sharp intake of breath was comfort to his ears. "Baneham was murdered?"

"I beg you," he tightened his fingers around Lady Vaile's hand. "No matter how clever Sophia is, she cannot beat Kasai alone. Surely Harrison has told you some of what he suffered at the hands of Kasai."

"Yes," Lady Vaile breathed, "he has."

"The man who tried to blame you for murder was, on the same night you chose to confront him, attempting to sell very damning information about some of the king's key allies to emissaries of Kasai."

He held the duchess's gaze. Thea's piercing blue eyes shot daggers. *And now for assault number three.*

"The man negotiating the sale on behalf of Kasai was an Englishman unknown to me until Harrison and his friend Sullivan identified him as Lord Eustace."

Thea paled, blinked, and then paled even further.

"That cannot be." Her tone was not that of a grieving sister-in-law. "Eustace is dead."

"Eustace is alive," Randolph said.

The duchess lifted her fingers to her lips. "Where is he?"

"I am not sure," Randolph said. "He is on the run—voluntarily or involuntarily—with a former agent of mine who may be working for Kasai. I need to find Sophia…before they find her."

"Does the duke know?"

"No one but Harrison, his man Sullivan, the Under Secretary, and I, know the Englishman traveling with Kasai's emissary is, in fact, Lord Eustace."

Thea grabbed his arm. "The duke must not know of this."

Her vehemence shocked. "Wynchester will find out… eventually."

"Eustace's return could ruin him."

Randolph lifted a brow. "And you?"

Thea made a fist. Her eyes held all the answer he needed.

"Sophia is intimately connected to Kasai, and Kasai to Eustace. Help me find Sophia, so we can break this plot."

Thea searched his gaze. "Swear on your life you will not harm Sophia."

"An oath I can easily take," Randolph said.

Her fingers bit into his arm. "Swear!"

"I swear on the Randolph title," he said, "*and* on my life. I *will not* harm my wife."

Thea grasped his other arm. "Now swear you will find Eustace—and until you find him, you will not breathe a word of this to the duke."

"I am doing everything I can to find Eustace," he said. "Speak with Harrison. He will explain."

Thea took a shuddering breath. "Sophia left through the mews behind the old Wynchester house."

"Private coach?" he asked.

Thea shook her head. "Hack to a stage. Sometime after dawn and before noon."

"Where is she headed?" he asked.

"That," Thea replied, "we do not know."

They had given him something, at least. He did not waste time on farewells.

Chapter Four

Earl Baneham's Rules for Winning

"IF YOU CAN, SPLIT THE ENEMIES' RESOURCES AND ATTENTION."

There was something to be said for meat pie. Sophia inhaled the warm aroma of boiled mutton, pretending the scent was beef.

Beef, served with a spot of sugared tea and some fresh, rich cream.

There was also something to be said for deceiving one's self in order to survive. She twisted her lips into a wry grimace. She'd been rather brilliant at self-deception of late.

She retrieved a spoon from her reticule, preparing for the dubious pleasures of traveler's fare.

"Coo," breathed a young woman sitting opposite.

"Beg your pardon?" Sophia asked, affecting her servant's accent.

"That is a fine piece," the girl said.

"Me Mum's." Sophia's smile hid her full set of teeth. "The last I have of her."

Not true. She had commissioned the engraved cutlery herself, but sympathy could draw in the young woman. The earl always said, if you formed a kinship with a thief, they would find stealing from you more difficult.

The young woman cast another longing glance toward the spoon. If the girl could see the gold sewn into Sophia's stays and the jewels lining her hems, Sophia wagered she would have fainted straight away.

The stranger sent Sophia a half-smile before she wiped her hands on her apron and reached for her lone piece of crusty bread.

Sophia frowned.

The Earl had *also* said a thief would immediately seek to draw you into *their* confidence. The two statements were somewhat contradictory, and she had never noticed. She studied the hapless traveler with more tender eyes. The poor young woman was not a thief; she was, simply, hungry.

"I am happy to share," Sophia offered.

Dark eyes met hers, distrust lurking in their muddy brown depths.

"Why would you share with the likes of me?"

"We traveling women must stick together." With each stop, Sophia had planned to work down the alphabet, changing names. She held out her hand. *Stop two.* "I am Mrs. Bradford."

The young woman took Sophia's outstretched fingers with a grip made faint by either shyness or hunger.

"I am Polly," she said.

"Pleased to meet you, Polly." She ignored the slight grumble of her stomach and pushed the meat pie across the table. "Here. You take this."

The look of wonder on Polly's face as Sophia handed her the spoon was enough to shame her for weeks. She groused internally about the loss of her tea-and-cream when, in all likelihood, poor Polly could not remember her last hot meal.

"Me thanks, Mrs. Bradford," Polly said. She took a bite, closed her eyes, and beamed ecstasy. On her fifth bite, she stopped and pushed the bowl back toward Sophia.

Sophia shook her head no. "You finish."

"Oh," Polly's eyes widened. "I cannot. You will go hungry."

"Never you mind," Sophia assured, although Polly spoke truth. Sophia could not order more. A flash of extra coin would just invite trouble, and she was doing her best to appear nothing more than a servant traveling from one post to another. The apple she had eaten in the coach would have to do.

"Take me bread, then?" Polly offered.

Sophia smiled, genuine. "Thank you, Polly."

With a quick prayer the bread did not contain anything that would make her sick, she took a bite. The rough, dry crumbs rolled like pebbles through her mouth. She chewed carefully before risking a swallow. More rock than bread, she decided.

"Are you far from your destination?" she asked.

Polly glanced up. Distrust lingered, then her eyes fell to her pie.

"You need not say, of course."

"I am heading to London," Polly said, "in hope of work."

"Do you have family in the city?"

Her slow nod turned to a sorrowful sweep of her head. "No."

Sophia's heart squeezed. So, Polly was on the run, too.

Yes, Sophia may have left behind luxury and beauty and ease, but she was not completely on her own, unfunded.

How lucky she was.

The thought stunned. Yes, she — daughter of *The Ruthless* with a killer on her heels who may or may not be receiving aid from her husband — *was* lucky. She was lucky because she had resources. And, more importantly, she had friends.

She started to speak, but the door opened and a gust of wind ripped through the crowded room. Sophia's neck hair went rigid. Without turning, she knew. *Randolph had come.*

Surreptitiously, she glanced toward the door. Randolph's pale blue eyes brimmed with fury as they traveled through the room. She bowed her head, praying her drab costume, padding, glasses, and mobcap would buy her time.

"Welcome, Sir," the innkeeper drawled. "Is there something I can get for you?"

"I seek a woman."

The innkeeper's face hardened. "I do not run that kind of establishment."

Clamor followed, with patrons jostling to take a verbal jab at the newcomer. Sophia's insides turned to mush and the single bite of stale bread threatened to reappear. She lifted her eyes and met Polly's round gaze.

"Trouble?" Polly asked.

Sophia nodded. *Trouble* was not quite sufficient a description.

"Follow me," Polly said under her breath.

Polly rose like a wraith and wound through the crowd, silent as smoke. Sophia followed, moving with equally deliberate steps as if she knew exactly where she was going and was in no hurry to depart. For once, she was glad of her diminutive height. The two yards to the kitchen felt more like leagues, but the commotion provided an excellent cloak.

Sophia doubted her luck would hold.

Never admit defeat.

The rule came to mind with an accompanying wave of nausea. She was not, and would not be, defeated.

She followed Polly through the kitchen, out a side door, past the stables and into a small alley.

"Thank you, Polly," she said, grasping the young girl's boney hand.

"You are most welcome, my Lady."

Only then did Sophia realize she had dropped her accent.

"I hate to ask," she said carefully, "but I must trouble you once again."

"If I had something to give, it would be yours."

"What I need is not material," Sophia said, looking the girl up and down. Yes, the girl was thinner and younger, but they were nearly the same height—and shared the same flaxen hair.

"You can help me by becoming me."

Sophia expected Polly to back away, hands flailing. But she did not.

"I do not understand," Polly said.

"The man back there will stop at nothing to find me. Someone will soon send him in our direction." She removed a few coins from the pocket hanging from her waist just beyond a slit in her skirts. She pressed the coins into Polly's hand.

"What is this for?" Polly asked.

She took Polly's hand and led her behind the hedgerow where she had concealed her valise. She pulled out a pouch embroidered with her initials. The sack contained a modest but pricy traveling dress—clothes the likes of Polly would not ever have seen. With a sigh of regret, she handed Polly the dress.

"Pay another woman to help you dress, and, this is important, you must leave the pouch behind. Hire a hack from the coaching station to the north. Tell the driver to take you to the Dowager Duchess of Wynchester in Mayfair, London. With luck, the man back there will follow you and I will gain a few hours."

Polly gave her a dubious look. "What happens if he finds me?"

Sophia went through the possibilities—would Randolph *hurt* Polly? Certainly not.

But, if she truly believed him to be a ruthless killer, why would she be certain of his benevolence toward Polly?

"You are innocent. He may try and frighten you, but he will not waste his time when he realizes you know nothing. He will let you go on your way while he continues to search for me."

Polly shifted her weight from foot to foot. "What will you do?"

"Do not worry about me." She never put all her eggs in one basket. "When you reach the home of the Dowager Duchess of Wynchester, tell her butler Lady Sophia sent you and she will lend you help."

Polly lifted a dubious brow. "Why would a Dowager Duchess care for the likes of me?"

"She will care." Sophia smiled kindly. "She will care because long ago, she arrived in London in the same condition as you. Do it for me. And do it for your babe."

Polly covered her only slightly rounded stomach and nodded.

Sophia patted her hand. "You won't be able to hide it much longer."

"I know," Polly said glumly.

Sophia touched Polly's cheek. "Be quick, be stealthy, be brave. Your fortune is about to change."

"Thank you, my lady."

As Sophia watched Polly weave her way back into the small town, she removed her mobcap and the padding around her waist. As Polly disappeared, she opened a jar of fine ash and talc, and doused her hair.

Skinny, elderly "Meg Cook" had a private coach to catch.

• • •

Earl Baneham's Rules for Winning
"MASTER THE ART OF INTERROGATION."

"I told you, Sir. A nice lady gave me money and then told me to go to the home of the Dowager Duchess of Wynchester."

Randolph kept his feet planted hip-width apart. He clasped his hands behind his back to keep from strangling the young woman. Which would be unfair, of course. Not just because he was larger, stronger, and male, but because his men had tied her hands.

Still, his sympathy had limits. The little chit had cost him hours. He would not allow her wide eyes and shaking limbs to deter him from gaining *something* from this exercise.

"You left behind a pouch embroidered with the initials of Lady Sophia Baneham. You hired a hack using her clothes and her coin. What do you think the magistrate is going to do with you when I tell him you stole from, and then impersonated, a peeress?"

The young girl took a shuddering inhale.

He leaned down and looked her in the eye. "Have you ever been to a gaol, my dear?"

She broke into tears. Tears laden with fear, and hunger, and weary confusion. She shook her head from side to side.

Damn. *Too far.* Clearly, he had scared the miss out of her wits.

"Pull yourself together, girl," he said, frowning.

He pulled a handkerchief from his pocket. With a sigh, he handed her the fine fabric. She eyed the cloth, then him, and then the cloth.

"*You*," she sniffed, "can keep your fancy things."

"You will take from my *wife*," he refolded the handkerchief and returned it to his coat, "but you will not take from me?"

Her eyes narrowed. "If you *are* her husband, you must be a very bad man to have scared her so."

"She is not scared," Randolph said, though she should have a healthier fear of Kasai. "She is angry."

The girl snorted. "I seen scared and I seen angry, and the color she turned when she saw you meant scared. Ye'll get nothin' more." She shook her head emphatically. "If I go to a gaol, I go to a gaol. I've been in worse. I'm not helpin' you kill the nice lady."

Randolph took a step back. "*Kill* her?"

"Why else would she be so scared?"

He scowled. Sophia could not possibly think *he* was after her life? *No.* She ran because she was angry. Ran because she wanted to watch him suffer. Ran because she had some dubious plan to confront Kasai on her own. Ran because… because…

…Because she thought *he* was out to harm her.

Shit-smeared spur.

A sharpened sense of fear sliced him through. Had he given her any reason not to believe such a thing?

She had spoken her father's name in hatred, and just an association with the man had made her furious. Baneham had been a brilliant strategist.

And suspicious. And conniving. And brutal. And ruthless.

All things that had won his admiration, but all things that would have been anathema to a gently bred young lady. A young lady who set surprisingly conventional moral standards for herself.

What if she had hated her father's work enough to dismiss its value to crown and Company—and had seen Baneham only as someone who would do anything to get what he wanted?

If so, she would believe the same of him.

He frowned. Yes, he intended to use her as bait, but very *protected* bait. He would never hurt Sophia. To his shock, it cut him to the core that she would believe such a thing. He used those rules to maintain a controlled response to a world of chaos—not to *create* chaos.

Then again—he looked down at the shivering young miss, who looked as if she was going to faint—he had not exactly been acting himself lately.

He pulled opened the door to the private parlor the innkeeper had allowed him to rent, called for a servant, and requested water. When the servant returned, he took the glass. He reentered the room. Behind him, he quietly closed the door.

"Tell me your name," he said to the young woman.

She looked up. "No."

"There has been a misunderstanding." He pulled over a second chair and sat opposite the young woman. "I would like to talk to you. And, to make our conversation more, shall we say, cordial, I am going to untie you. First, you must promise to remain in the chair."

"What will you promise me?" she asked.

He snorted. The chit had grit.

"I will promise one of my men will see you to the Dowager Duchess of Wynchester—just as your friend Lady Ran—" he stopped and cleared his throat. "Lady Sophia wished."

"Why should I believe you?"

And in her words he heard Sophia's voice. *Why indeed.* "I swear I would never do a thing to harm Lady Sophia."

"Why does she think you would?"

He doubted *because she has gone mad* would endear him to Polly. He looked more closely at the girl. "Because there have been many bad men in her life. There have been a few bad men in your life, too, no?"

Polly nodded slowly. "I will not run," she said, lifting her hands so he could untie her wrists. "My name is Polly. Miss Pollyanna Jakes."

"Well, Miss Jakes," he said as he worked the knot, "I suggest we begin again."

He freed her wrists. She rubbed them while her gaze remained pinned to his face. If she gave him any information at all, it would be a matter of pure luck. What had he been thinking? She was little more than a girl—not a Newgate-hardened criminal.

"For you," he said, handing her the water.

Polly drank, and then wiped her mouth with the back of her hand. "Obliged," she said.

He stood to pace.

"Let us go over what happened again." So far, each time she had told her story, she had added another small detail. She *was* hiding something, he could feel her resistance.

Polly took a deep breath. "After four days hungry, I earned meself a bit of coin helping out with the planting. I bought meself a bun. I was about to eat it when this fancy miss sat opposite my bench. She pulled out a right fine spoon to eat her meat pie and I told her it was the nicest I ever seen. She said women must stick together."

That sounded like Sophia.

"What else did she say?" Randolph prompted.

"She gave me the spoon and told me to eat her pie. In return, I gave her me bun. Then, you burst in like Lucifer's servant."

He almost smirked. Her characterization of him was the only thing in her story that had not undergone slight alteration.

Polly continued, "She looked terrible affright, so I took her back into the kitchens and out the side door. She said she needed time to escape. She gave me her pouch, told me to dress like she had been dressed and to use the coin in her bag to hire a hack to take me to London."

"Are you sure you have told me everything?" he asked.

Polly blinked and looked away. "Yes."

He placed his hands on his knees and crouched. "What aren't you telling me, Miss Jakes?"

Her blush deepened. "Please do not send me to the gaol. *Please*."

"Not if you tell me the truth."

Polly reached into her stocking and pulled out a spoon. The edge was carved with a beautiful scrolling letter—not B for Baneham but S for Sophia.

"I didn't mean to steal, Sir. I swear," Polly stammered. "I forgot to give her the spoon and she forgot to ask me for it."

A spoon.

He stared at the piece of silver feeling his hope disintegrate like paper in flame.

He had spent an hour questioning Miss Pollyanna Jakes only to recover Sophia's spoon. He ran his hand through his hair.

"You have no idea what happened to the lady?"

"No. She disappeared just like a ghost."

A ghost. Which was what she would become if he couldn't find her before Eustace and Helena. His only lead — wasted. Now he had to begin again — combing through all those who had entered and left the village. His only consolation was, if he could not find her, Kasai's agents could not find her, either.

After giving Polly a curt and uncomfortable farewell, he arranged to have one of his men take her to the dowager. Once she was on her way, he trudged up to the welcoming solace of his rented room. He settled into the bed and rested his head against the simple wood backing.

How had things so right gone so very wrong?

Behind his closed lids he saw Sophia as she had been the night they had made the wedding wager. She had been in her study, counting and recording the night's gain. Her hair had come loose and one lock had drifted perilously close to the inkwell as she'd scratched numbers into her ledger.

...*"You are a bit too cavalier with the blunt you collect,"* Randolph said.

"Are you offering me your brutish protection?" she asked without looking up.

Tenderly, he lifted a lock of her hair and tucked it behind her ear. "I know you find this hard to believe, but most men find me intimidating."

"If you say so," she replied.

Candlelight made shadows on her soft cheeks. She bit the side of her lip as she concentrated on her ledgers. Randolph wanted her with a lust impossible for him to deny.

"Why do you call everyone dearest—" he started.

She closed her ledger and scrutinized him. Her gaze made him harden.

"—but me?"

He did not know what she thought she read in his expression, but she smiled. A small, satisfied upturn of those plump and strawberry-red lips.

"That is all the answer I get?" he asked. "A smirk?"

Her expression remained unchanged. "Would you rather a grin?"

"Ladies do not grin," he replied.

"A shame, truly," she sighed, disappointed. "I have a winning grin."

The devil within him stirred. "I would rather a fuck."

She laughed out loud. "I have just come to a realization."

"That I make you wet between your legs?"

"That," her eyes sparkled, "and, apparently, I love to be shocked."

He raised his brow. "Is that a 'yes' to the fuck?"

She shook her head and the loose lock again fell against

her cheek. "I do not bed my guests."

Her answer altered—slightly. Interesting. "What if I stopped attending?"

"Tsk." She waved her finger back and forth with a governess's pinched lips. "You just promised to use your talent for intimidation for my protection."

"Scold me again and I will happily lay other talents at your feet."

She raised her brows. "I do not doubt your talent—especially after the imaginary tryst you described the other night. But"—Her gaze raked him, slow and with deliberate purpose. Temptation danced in her eyes for a brief but extraordinary moment. "I am not interested in a cicisbeo."

He sat on the edge of her desk, draping himself in front of her ledgers. "How about a wager?"

The little smirk returned. "I would be mad to agree to such a challenge."

"Ah, but you like to run mad, don't you?" He ran the errant lock of hair between his fingers. "You like to live life sliding as close as possible to the edge of a sharpened knife."

"In certain things," she replied. "What do you propose?"

He squinted, knowing a simple wager would never satisfy the infamous Lady Scandal. He inhaled and her scent, like wine, made him reckless.

"A series of ten games. The terms would be private, the games public." he forced himself to release her hair and look away from her hunger-laden, noonday-blue gaze. He examined his fingernails. "Imagine the crowd such a sensation would draw. Imagine the numbers you could scratch into your ledger."

She laughed low in her throat. Randolph glanced up,

knowing he had hit her mark.

"If you win," she stated, "you would expect a fuck."

"Something of that nature." The word on her lips nearly unmanned him.

"Randolph," she leaned forward, "I am going to tell you a secret."

Her breath fanned his lips. "Good thing, then, I am discretion's very soul."

"Well," she said, "when it comes to the body beneath this costly, low-cut gown, I am shockingly conventional. I have thoroughly enjoyed, as you would say, a good fuck, but within the marriage bond." She pulled back. "I am many things, Randolph, but I will not be your whore."

Her confession left him unable to breathe. She had turned the tables. If he wanted her, he would have to propose. He forced a coldly rational analysis.

The idea of marriage to Sophia had some merit beyond the slaking of his lust. As her husband, he could keep her close. He could search for Baneham's papers while continuing to earn her trust. And once married, her fortune would be beyond Kasai's direct reach.

He admired the way she charmed her guests. He respected the skillful way she managed London's most dangerous men. She was young enough to provide an heir but with enough experience to display a woman's polish and presence.

Despite her notoriety, she would make as good a countess as any...and certainly far more satisfying in the bedchamber than the chits his mother and sisters had suggested so far. He liked the idea of transforming Lady Sophia Baneham into Sophia, Lady Randolph—and not only for the reason visually obvious beneath his breeches.

"My wager stands in the light of your revelation." The feeling between them charged, becoming a living thing. *"If I win, I will humbly ask you to become my countess."*

She hit the back of her chair with a thunk. *"You have shocked me again, Randolph."*

"And since you love to be shocked, I will count that a point in my favor."

"And if I win?"

"What could I grant a woman who has everything?"

Her delightful button of a nose scrunched. *"I do, don't I?"*

"Although, I imagine a lady can never have enough silk."

"Mmmm," she murmured, *"silk."*

"I will buy out a whole shipment—enough silk for you to throw away if you wish. Imagine a bedroom awash in silk. Silk bed curtains. Silk bed coverings. Silk dressing gowns. Silk night rails. Perhaps a silk nightgown."

Her eyes widened. *"Silk nightgown? Unheard of...and quite possibly delightful."*

"I take it I have earned another point?"

"Perhaps. But then again," she said, *"I could lose."*

"Would being my countess truly be a loss?" he asked.

Her gaze dipped to his casual display. She bit her lip and a shrewd light entered her eyes.

"Before the games," she looked him in the eye, *"You will draw and execute a contract allowing my fortune to remain under my control. I have loyal trustees I would like to retain."*

"Of course," he said. *"I do not need your wealth."*

"I would want acknowledgment in writing that the soirees may continue, as long as Lavinia and Thea have need of funds."

"It will be done."

"And I would want enough pin money to set tongues wagging," she said, clearly believing her last demand would make him balk. "I have no need of your funds, either, of course, but what fun is being a wife if one cannot have her wardrobe billed to her husband?"

The thought of her dressed in clothing paid for by his coin increased the heaviness in his groin.

"You can have whatever you wish…" He leaned forward. "…so long as, anytime I wish, you let me set my tongue to your mound."

She pinked and her breath hitched. "A boon I could be persuaded to grant, provided we are alone."

He raised a brow. "I never share."

Her shoulders settled. "I will take on your wager. Our games will end the soiree—best of 21, I think."

"Best of 5, and a kiss to seal the deal."

"Best of 15," she countered.

"Best of 9, and you include the kiss."

She grinned and held out her hand. "Agreed."

Instead of shaking her hand, he lifted it to his lips. Her palm had been warm in his, and though her movements were slow and languid, her fingers quaked.

"You are aroused, sweetness."

"Anticipation of my silk, of course."

"Forget the silk."

He slid off the desk, cupped her cheeks, and took her lips. He kissed her until she rose to her toes and entwined her hands in his hair. Then, somehow, they were both atop her desk, with her beneath him, pinned and panting.

"How was that?" he asked.

"That will do for now." She looked at him from under her

lashes. "You can do better."

"You are infuriating."

"Do you really think so?" she asked as if he had called her stunning.

"Completely."

"How marvelous," she mused.

"Call me dearest," he demanded.

Her eyes twinkled. "Not yet."

Randolph groaned and turned on his side. He hoped he could somehow prevent *not yet* from transforming into *not ever*.

Chapter Five

Earl Baneham's Rules for Winning

"REGRET IS FOR THE LOSING SIDE."

Sophia scratched her chest through her high-collared dress. Her high-collared, *woolen* dress—not finely woven wool dyed with pleasing color, but coarse, grey wool. Worse still, the dress fit her with as much grace as a sheet fit a chair.

She groaned.

Ah, but she was safe from Randolph and Kasai's men, and for that, she must be grateful. A working farm run by a former Quaker was not among the places they would search for Lady Scandal.

She was fortunate she had remembered this farm. When the Earl had returned to England, he had told her he required a sojourn to help his recovery. She had accompanied him to a village not too far from this farm, but when they had arrived, he had disappeared for a whole morning.

While she nervously awaited his return, the innkeeper's

wife had happily filled Sophia in on local gossip. She had told Sophia all about the farm, its rather eccentric owner, and the slightly mad people who worked the lands.

The owner, Elizabeth, was a naturally white-haired woman with a heavy presence and an old-fashioned way of speaking. She had been raised a Quaker, or as she corrected, a member of the Society of Friends. She still observed the strictures, although she was, as she had put it, no longer *in unity* with her meeting.

Sophia had felt terrible about the lies she had told the older woman — one, her name was Jane Donald, and two, she was on the run from a lecherous employer — but they had worked. Elizabeth had been happy to take in Sophia, just as she did many "unquiet souls," provided Sophia respected her rules, including calling everyone by their first name and spending the days in quiet industry.

At the time, Sophia had thought Elizabeth meant for her to do something like read to the more troubled residents, teach the younger women embroidery or song. But the only books in Elizabeth's house were bibles, and residents indulged in nothing so frivolous as song or embroidery.

Quiet, she learned, meant *silent,* and *industry* meant *hard work.*

She stretched her arms over her head and rolled her neck from side to side. Every part of her was very much in use, despite being unattractively hidden.

She sighed. Just looking down at the pot she had been scrubbing made the ache in her arm muscles throb. If she had known how difficult extracting duck skin attached to the bottom of a pot could be, she would have paid her scullery maid higher wages.

She fended off an overwhelming sense of loss. How long

would she have to remain in hiding? Would she ever see her beautiful home on the Thames again? She missed it. She missed beauty. She missed song. She missed her late night gambling parties with Thea and Lavinia.

Heaven help her, she also missed *him*.

In her mind's eye, she saw him as he'd been the night of The Furies' most recent soiree—the soiree where she and Randolph had played the game they had agreed would be their last, the soiree during which Lavinia had discovered her husband had been murdered.

…the soiree, in short, when all hell had broken loose.

…Sophia turned up the collar of her cloak against the late spring's night air, crisp with hints of winter. The Furies thought it a lark to hold their gambling party out-of-doors, despite the questionable weather. But the upturned collar of her fur-lined cloak was not what caused the sudden warmth in her cheeks, any more than her blush was caused by the mischief of forcing the cream of London's deep-pocketed rakes, dandies, and libertines out into the cold spring air.

Randolph and she were evenly matched at four and four out of nine. Sophia swallowed through her tight-as-stays throat while sliding her fingers over her unturned card, wishing she could divine the numbers on which her future rested.

She raised her gaze and locked eyes with her opponent.

He leaned to the side and draped his elbow on the back of his chair, looking as if he hadn't a care. Tonight, in perfect form, he had powdered his dried-wheat hair. White made his penetrating grey eyes positively abyssal. Slight creases in his skin whispered of pleasures past and held the promise of pleasures future.

Most men had some measure of appeal, of course, but only one word captured her reaction to Lord Randolph—spellbound.

She settled her nerves. While she did not believe in love, and she believed even less in vulnerability, she did not need to deny herself the luxury of Randolph's fluid movement, nor the appreciation of his coat's expert fit.

Randolph was a rake through and through. A rogue and a libertine, just like the other men gathered around the table. Who but a rake would speak to a lady in such a shocking fashion? If she lost the bet and they had to marry, she knew exactly how to manage him, just as she had managed her first husband.

"Turn the card, turn the card!" The usual chant gained intensity, and her heart thudded along with the rhythm.

"Stalling, Lady Scandal?" Amusement danced behind Randolph's eyes and something else she could not read—a mystery that left a thrill in her blood.

"I am waiting for my Furies."

Where the devil were her fellow hostesses? Lavinia—Lady Vice—and Thea—Duchess Decadence—had flanked her every time she had turned the final card.

"Lady Vice was called away," one of the men said. "She ended her game with Bronward before a winner was declared."

That was odd. She frowned.

"Looks like you will have to face your fate on your own." Randolph leaned forward and spoke in whispered tones surprisingly clear beneath the racket. "Courage, sweetness. Surely you are not afraid of me."

"I have courage," she said indignantly.

She had lost a husband, survived the brutal murder of her father, and had taken in two ladies abandoned by society. She'd been siphoning men's coin through exclusive gambling parties for years.

Sophia was not afraid of him and she had more courage in her little finger then he had in the entirety of his lean-muscled, lascivious form. And should she lose, she had the benefit of the outrageously generous marriage contract he had already signed that awaited the scratch of her quill.

Sophia flipped the card, eyes never leaving his.

A cheer thundered, but for whom?

One of the men clamped Lord Randolph on the back. "Beat again, old boy."

She exhaled, but, strangely, without relief, as she mirrored Randolph's nonchalant pose. The fleeting pressure in her chest could not possibly be disappointment.

"Indigo silk, I think. The color will bring out my eyes," she said. "I will expect an obscenely large shipment within a fortnight."

A smile tugged his mouth's edge. If he was vexed by the outcome or concerned with her extravagant demand, he did not show either.

"As beautiful as you will be in a gown," the word sounded lewd on his lips, "of soft and rippling indigo silk, how would you like to extend the wager? I propose one more game."

A thrill shot through her heart, leaving her tingling. And the honeybee buzz in her body battled with her common sense.

She could make a higher demand—porcelain perhaps... or boatloads of the finest Portuguese port. And if she lost...

Well, the scales on which she had first weighed the bet still balanced. If she lost, she would be consoled by the protection of his position and—her gaze settled on his mouth—the advantages of his bed.

"I would expect higher stakes from you," she said. "And I want my silk, regardless."

He tilted his head in a slight nod.

The man who'd slapped Randolph's back swayed forward. "And what is it you have that Lord Randolph wants with such determination, Lady Scandal?"

Randolph's eyes shot to the impertinent man. "Stakes are between the lady and myself."

"But—" the man started.

Randolph's expression turned dark, silencing the man. A fluttering sensation passed through her belly.

Sophia thought to decline his offer. She had escaped.

Then again, the promise of another game with Randolph would draw spectators. Spectators would spend the evening making their own bets on who would win—a portion of which would be collected by the hostesses. Either way, so long as the entertainment continued, Sophia, Lavinia, and Thea, would pad their already over-plump coffers.

Certainly, it was a sound enough reason to extend the game—but not the real reason she acceded.

She wanted, God help her, to be his wife.

"If you seek another trouncing, my lord," she smiled as he turned back to her, "who am I to deny you?"

His eyes glowed. "Excellent decision."

Sophia felt heat rise into her face as if the exchange had just happened. Within a few days of that agreement, Randolph had testified on Lavinia's behalf, in order, she had thought, to save her friend from being charged with murder. That night, she and Randolph had commenced a private game, which she had lost.

On purpose.

She had been a foolish, foolish chit. A *weak* and foolish chit.

She stomped over to the well, drew a bucket of water, and doused her face.

Elizabeth looked up from laundering. "Art thou well?"

Why did Elizabeth's cheerful smile make her feel the combined guilt of every lie she had ever told? "Right as rain."

"Jane," Elizabeth said, "keep thy mind on thy work."

"Yes, Elizabeth."

She returned to the troth, imagined Randolph as the pot, and resumed her scrubbing with renewed vigor.

Although peace-within-industry was everywhere at Elizabeth's farm—workers and residents intermingled and moved about with a remarkable calm, especially since the residents all had troubled pasts—peace was something Sophia doubted she could ever achieve.

There was no peace for the child of *The Ruthless*. And certainly, no peace for a woman so thoroughly controlled by her needs, she'd fallen victim to a spy. Just as she always suspected, she had succumbed to her need for touch. Why had she not been satisfied with the home she had created? With the Furies, she'd been happy for the first time in her life.

She dropped both pot and scouring stone. Maddeningly, her eyes filled.

Elizabeth set down the potato she had been peeling and walked to Sophia's side.

"I observe," Elizabeth said, "the testimony of quietness. But, I sense thee wishes to speak."

Sophia sniffled, straightened her spine, and shook her head. "I do not need to speak."

She resumed scrubbing. But instead of going away, Elizabeth remained quietly watching. Something in the woman's serene, sympathetic gaze tapped at a door in Sophia's heart that she kept solidly locked. The wetness filling her eyes spilled out onto her cheeks.

Elizabeth took the pot from Sophia's hands and set it down. "Shall we walk?"

Sophia nodded, and then allowed Elizabeth to lead her from the house. They wandered toward a nearby wood on an ancient lane. Elizabeth said nothing, but her presence was like a balm. As Sophia walked, her breath became easier, her footsteps more sure.

At the edge of the wood, they stopped. Not far away, a scattered few of Elizabeth's sheep grazed. One lifted his head and bayed.

"Jane," Elizabeth began, "Thou art troubled by thy past."

And future. "I am no more troubled than your other guests."

Elizabeth looked off toward the farm. From here, the tidy group of buildings formed a picturesque aspect. A cheerful bit of smoke twirled up from the house's chimney.

"Art thou wed?" she asked.

Sophia paused, uneasiness heavy in her heart. If Elizabeth

had believed her story—that she was a maid, running from a lecherous employer, she would not have asked such a question.

"Yes," she replied.

"My husband hast gone to his rest." The faraway look in Elizabeth's eyes was laced with pain.

"I am a widow as well," Sophia could admit that much. It was her current husband of which she did not wish to speak. "Will you marry again?"

"The Light alone leadeth," Elizabeth answered. She settled her even gaze on Sophia. "Hast thee sought guidance through thy troubles?"

Elizabeth was not speaking of earthly assistance, she knew. She'd been told of Elizabeth's belief in a heavenly force outside of one's self, a light one could follow with proper discernment.

"No," she said. "I know nothing of your light."

Even the word *light* felt unfamiliar. The Earl had moved, quite literally, in shadow—sleeping through the morning and conducting his affairs within the cloak of night. Since his death, she had unwittingly adopted his habit. The Furies had entertained in darkness and, without reason to see or be seen by those who kept more refined society, had eschewed the day.

"Hast thou," Elizabeth hesitated, "a mother?"

Sophia shook her head no. "My mother died many years ago." Made frail by the constant threat of Baneham's volcanic rage as well as his rare bursts of possessive ardor. "As did the Ea—I mean my father."

"Surely you have friends."

The Furies. She swallowed. "I am," she said, "not able to return."

"I, too," Elizabeth said quietly, "am cast from my community."

She looked back into the Quaker's kindly eyes. "Why are you no longer with yours?"

Elizabeth's smiled with sadness. "I married out of unity. A break with tradition my family couldst neither understand nor accept. But, I sought my heart's truth." She looked back to the farmhouse. "The main house my husband and I built together. The cottage beyond is older."

Sophia frowned. When she had married Randolph, she had anticipated his bed but had no expectation of a true joining. She had *seen* marital unions produce homes and love, but such things were for other people—people whose fortunes were not soaked in blood, treachery, and deception.

Longing induced a singular ache, and that ache wound through Sophia like a fast-growing vine. Suddenly, her cavalier treatment of marriage seemed as shameful as Randolph's deception.

"I hope," Elizabeth said, "thee will find peace and guidance here," Elizabeth paused, looking troubled. "But I am led to say thee cannot run from thy trials."

Sophia frowned. She most certainly could. She *had* to leave, to preserve her life. She had to leave, to gain protection from a threat that could be coming from any quarter. She had no other choice.

Or did she?

"Shall we return?" Elizabeth asked.

"If you mean to my scrubbing," Sophia said, "then yes."

She wanted to scrub—no, she needed to scrub. Only work could alleviate her heavy heart.

As they drew closer to the house, Sophia recognized the form of a young woman weeding in the kitchen garden—Anna. Even in this place, gossip spread like fire through a hay-filled barn. The girl did not sleep in the long, dormered room with the rest of the women. She stayed with Elizabeth. Even so, her late night screams could be heard every night.

"Good morning, Anna," Elizabeth called.

The girl smiled and waved.

As they got to the kitchen, Elizabeth turned. "Thee hast heard, I am sure, Anna's nighttime terrors. The more she works in the day, the less she is troubled."

"Are you saying the work is meant to bring me peace?"

"Yes," Elizabeth replied.

She returned to her pot, pondering the equation. Could peace-in-industry provide her with a much-needed reprieve from her worries? She hefted the scrubbing stone.

If Anna could find peace-in-industry, the least Sophia could do was make a sincere attempt. Peace was a preferable alternative to warding off the past's insistent haunting.

She set to scrubbing. *Scrape. Scrape. Scrape.* She stopped worrying about the eventual cleanliness of the pot and instead found a rhythm. Progress, infinitesimally small, but reassuringly constant.

Late that night, when she slipped onto her simple cot, she did not lie awake as she had the last fortnight, staring at the ceiling and longing for her fine lawn nightrail. Nor did she listen with envy to the untroubled breaths of the other women who shared the room.

Instead, she noticed how the moon painted a silvery glow across the wood furniture and marveled at the beauty that cost not a penny. She savored the ache in her upper arms. The ache told her she had been useful. She inhaled with a sense of deep satisfaction and she promptly fell into slumber.

Not even Anna's midnight sobbing caused her to wake.

• • •

Earl Baneham's Rules for Winning
"ASK THE RIGHT QUESTIONS."

For a fortnight, the inn where Randolph had lost Sophia had become his makeshift headquarters…and his hell.

While receiving regular reports on the hunt for Helena and Eustace from a group headed by Sullivan, one of the men Kasai had imprisoned with Eustace and Harrison, Randolph had sent men in every direction in search of Sophia. The final man had just reported back, and the news had not been pleasant.

He shoved the chair he had been holding. "I will not accept this."

"You may accept," said the messenger, whose sincerity— and unlined face—revealed he was new to this game, "or you may not accept. Either choice will not change the truth: I have searched every town within twenty miles. There has been no sign of someone matching the description of your wife, nor of the missing agent, nor the translator. There have been no travelers out of the ordinary."

Randolph slammed his fist against the table. Two *full* weeks with nothing to show for his effort.

A knock sounded at the door.

"I said I was not to be disturbed," Randolph roared. The door squealed open. He turned and froze in startled surprise.

"Harrison!"

Harrison's gaze slid between Randolph and the young man who he'd been questioning. "Things are going well, I see."

"Wait in the taproom," Randolph instructed his man, this time with more control.

For all his bravado, the boy did not need to be told twice. He left, letting the door slam shut behind him.

"I am here to help," Harrison said.

"You," Randolph said, "told me you would not join my investigation."

"That was before you went and involved my lady."

Pfft. "*I* did not involve Lady Vaile."

"You told her Kasai's agent had been seen in England and Eustace is alive. She is half-mad with worry for Sophia, and the duchess is nearly out of her mind for information on Eustace. For some reason, neither of them trusts you." He smiled. "Lavinia sent me to set things right."

Meddling women. "You suggested I enlist the duchess to watch over the duke until we find Lord Eustace."

"And a fine idea, that," Harrison said. "Especially, since we do not yet know if he is an innocent pawn or working for Kasai. But I do not recall suggesting you involve Lavinia in the mess *at all*."

"What one Fury knows, they *all* know."

Harrison snorted. "True. The duchess believes the latter of Lord Eustace, by the way. She is convinced he will use his 'triumphant' return to manipulate the duke. She will not reveal why, but clearly enmity exists between her and Eustace Worthington."

He sat down into the chair Randolph had been holding, and propped his crossed ankles on the table.

"By all means," Randolph grumbled, "make yourself at home."

Harrison grinned. "Lavinia said you would be beside yourself with worry about Sophia."

Of course, she had. "What plans have the remaining Furies concocted?"

"The Wynchester estrangement runs deep, as everyone who has set foot in London for the past few years knows. The duchess cannot just pack up her belongings and reunite with the duke."

"But she is willing?"

Harrison pursed his lips. "Willing is not quite the word. If the duke dies, Lord Eustace is next in line. She fears for the duke's life. She does not intend a full reconciliation—just the assurance the duke is under no threat from his brother." He shrugged. "Call it loyalty to the title. Call it patriotism. Or call it hatred of Lord Eustace. No matter—she and Lavinia are devising a plan—a plan which requires Sophia."

Five years in service to the Company and, occasionally, the crown, and all of a sudden three women had upended his life and his career. He shook his head.

"In Parliament," Randolph said, "the duke is well protected."

"Even Wynchester cannot work all day," Harrison said. "Servants report the duke's every move to the duchess. If he ventures from his routine, she will intercede, but despite her protections, she is anxious to implement a plan. Any luck finding Sophia?"

"That boy," Randolph pointed to the closed door. "Was the bet most likely to yield fruit—and he gave me nothing."

Harrison dropped his feet to the floor. "She cannot have gone far, but before we discuss Sophia, I have other news of interest."

"Yes?" Randolph asked.

"I have combed my contacts at the Company. Turns out, Sullivan, Lord Eustace, and I were not the only ones in England who survived imprisonment by Kasai."

The skin on the back of Randolph's neck tingled. "Tell me everything."

"There is a survivor of the same raid Lord Eustace, Sullivan, and I survived—one of the men who pledged his loyalty to Kasai. Interestingly, he was confined to the madhouse by Baneham."

"Where?"

"Not ten miles from here."

"Interesting, indeed," Randolph said.

Harrison cocked his head. "I know Baneham worked for the Company, but I cannot discern the apparent connection between Sophia and Kasai. There is a connection, isn't there?"

Randolph exhaled. "You do not know the half of it."

"Well then," Harrison said, "if you want my help, you had better start talking."

Grimly, Randolph recounted the history between Baneham and Kasai through Baneham's final mission for the Company. How Baneham's accidental death may have been murder-in-disguise, and Baneham's cryptic warnings.

"So the woman I met at the brothel who called herself Helle was actually Helena, and is Sophia's half-sister?"

"Yes," Randolph said.

"She had seemed familiar—family resemblance, I suppose." Harrison grew contemplative. "Does Sophia know about Helena?"

Randolph ran his hand through his hair. "I have no idea. But one thing is certain: Helena certainly knows about Sophia—and no matter who she is working for, her intentions cannot be good."

"We've got to find out what Baneham knew about Kasai."

"I know," Randolph said. "But Harrison—I am not sure who can be trusted. What I have told you stays between you and me."

"Of course," Harrison said. "Garrett—the man in the madhouse—may provide additional answers." He smiled. "You are welcome, by the way."

Randolph cast him a dangerous look.

Harrison laughed. "We will have a round of boxing later. You need an antidote to that glower."

Randolph nodded. "I could use one, I think."

Harrison's smile faded. "Sophia is formidable. Wherever she is, you have to assume she is safe."

Did he? Right now, he had no other choice. As for the thought that she could protect herself as well as he could protect her, well, that was absurd. Keeping her safe was *his* charge. A charge he intended to keep. And his reason had nothing whatsoever to do with the way she moved.

"Now that you have calmed," Harrison said, "how about we call beardless back in and ask him some additional questions."

"Harrison, are you telling me I do not know how to interrogate?"

"Wouldn't dream of it, Randolph. But, just for argument's sake, when was the last time you slept for more than an hour?"

Just the question made him aware of the burn in eyes he knew were bloodshot. Who could sleep when Sophia was unprotected and a killer was on the loose?

"Very well," Randolph said reluctantly. "You have a go."

Harrison called in the messenger.

"Since I was not present for your conversation with Lord Randolph, would you review the interviews you conducted with me? Did anyone mention any unusual travelers?"

The lad looked insulted. "I said no people matched the descriptions I was given—"

"Yes, yes, I understand. No person fit the description of the people we are seeking, but was anything else out of the ordinary—a young male traveler, perhaps, with a feminine way of walking?"

Randolph frowned. Dwelling on the thought of Sophia in tight buckskin was a very bad idea.

"No one," the lad said, "reported anything out of the ordinary."

Randolph's eyes narrowed. "Your breath hitched."

"Well there was an old, bent-over governess who disappeared off a private coach a half-day's ride out. But the man at the posting house said odd people occasionally sought shelter at a local Quaker farm." The boy shifted nervously.

Randolph stood so fast the chair clattered to the ground. "Why didn't you tell me this earlier?"

The boy swallowed. "Like I said, the man told me the traveler was old and hunched with grey hair and spectacles; his description did not match any of the people we seek."

He exchanged a look with Harrison. All could be faked— and to think he'd almost let the information slip through his fingers.

Harrison stayed him with a look and dismissed the boy. "That will be all."

"I am going," Randolph said before the door shut. "Now."

Harrison blocked the egress. "What are you going to do—charge in and drag her off in the middle of the night?"

"Yes." Charge in there and drag her off was exactly his plan.

"What if this woman really was an old lady seeking shelter?"

He gave Harrison a look conveying just how little credit he gave the possibility.

"Just wait," Harrison said. "I have had dealings with Quakers. Obstinate bunch. Once they feel they are in the right, there is no moving them."

"What would you have me do? Twiddle my thumbs?"

Harrison considered. "Let me go."

"No." Using her desire, *he* might convince her to stop her madcap flight. Harrison, on the other hand, had no influence. "If my suspicions are correct, I need Sophia to entice Lord Eustace and Helena."

Harrison's blue gaze turned icy. "Is that all Sophia is to you? An enticement?"

Heat traveled up his cheeks. Confess the deeper connection he was starting to suspect? *Never.* He could not reveal the extent of his potential weakness—not even to Harrison.

"I made her my wife, Harrison. My *countess*," Randolph emphasized the word. "What do you think?"

Harrison rubbed his chin. "Then go, but I would advise you not to act on your intention to drag her off."

"Do you have a better suggestion?"

"Go as if on unofficial business—just a man in search of his lost wife. Form an alliance with Sophia. You are going to need her consent to keep her protected."

Randolph snorted. "Her consent will take longer than an afternoon."

Harrison rubbed his jaw. "Take the time you need."

"You jest."

"Not at all," Harrison said. "You have to admit *no one*

would think to look for the infamous Lady Scandal on a Quaker farm. You two should be safe enough, and while you are there, I will take over the search for Helle—I mean, Helena—and Lord Eustace, and make arrangements to see the other survivor. If he has any information or if I need your assistance, I will send word."

Randolph blinked, his mind blank.

Harrison clapped a hand on his back. "You are no use to this mission in your state. Resolve this. Get a good night's sleep. Tomorrow, go hat-in-hand to meet your lady. Fix things with Sophia and come back renewed."

It galled him to admit Harrison was right, but, Randolph considered, if he were to win Sophia to his side, he *would* be able to concentrate on the mission. And if anyone was as qualified to take over the hunt for Kasai as he, it was Harrison.

Then again, was seducing a woman on a Quaker farm even possible?

He hoped so.

"Thank you, Harrison."

"Don't muck it up this time." Harrison's expression darkened. "I am not talking about the mission, either. If you hurt Sophia, you will have to answer to me…and worse, the other Furies."

"I would never," he said, "harm my wife."

"I speak of more than just the physical," Harrison said. "The Furies will not give you an inch."

Randolph snorted. "I do not suppose they would."

"One more thing," Harrison's lip turned up in a wry smile, "clean up before you go. You stink."

Chapter Six
Earl Baneham's Rules for Winning
"BE PREPARED TO BRIBE."

Randolph cupped his hands and splashed cool water over his freshly-shaven skin. The resulting tingle invigorated. The day had dawned with a new, though tentative, hope.

He tied his hair back with a simple ribbon, and left off his hair powder — Harrison assured him the formality would be out of place at the Quaker farm. He peered into the small looking glass and frowned. The severe reflection was about as pleasant as a gin-bitten grimace from a rookery drunk. He lifted and sniffed the shirt he had removed the prior night, just before he had quite literally fallen into his first restful sleep since Sophia had run.

Harrison, damn him, had been right about at least one thing. He had *stunk*.

Understandable, really, since he had been without the services of a proper valet for two full weeks. And those two weeks had ravaged the perfectly turned out gentleman who had caught Sophia's eye.

What if his assurances and arguments failed? What if Sophia told him, once again, to go to Hades?

Worse still, what if the be-spectacled woman hadn't been Sophia at all, but was some unfortunate woman seeking refuge after having been tossed to the streets without a reference? A strange weight sank like a tossed stone through his chest. He frowned, unable to identify the heavy feeling.

He brushed aside the questions and the feeling. No use wasting time arguing against one's plan. But, he could use something more enticing than his sorry self to win Lady Sophia's compliance.

Lady *Randolph*, he corrected silently. For a moment, he surged with the sense of power inexorably connected to the Randolph name and title. By *law*, she must obey.

Right.

A woman who had braved the wrath of the Duke of Wynchester by taking in his estranged wife, the woman who had survived by ensuring her illegal gambling parties were among the most sought after events in London, was simply going to follow him home because the law compelled her to do so.

A rotten mess had become of a portentous start. He had gotten himself into her soirees without an invitation and had slowly earned her trust. Convincing her to have him had been no easy feat, which, if he were honest, had earned her his respect.

She had been such a puzzle. Competence and vulnerability. A consummate flirt who made herself entirely unavailable. He had thought her nearly his. She had thought him a licentious rake. He had thought time was on his side. She had thought him easy to manage.

They had both been wrong on all accounts.

He threw his bag on the bed, opened the flap, and pulled out a paper-wrapped garment. Carefully, he pulled back the edges. The blue silk glowed within. The seamstress had argued with him when he described the commission. *Argued* was a light word—the poor woman had been utterly scandalized.

He had insisted on the creation nonetheless. Although Sophia had lost the final game—a game he had goaded her into playing after she had won their original wager terms specifying the best of nine games—he had thought he owed her a gesture of good will. Not to mention the thought of her in such a garment had kept him sleepless since she had first said the words *indigo* and *silk*.

He drew out the night rail and ran his hands over the thin fabric. So soft, so fine. Delicate looking yet surprisingly strong.

To get her to return, he was not above a bribe. He pressed his face into the fabric and inhaled.

Come on, sweetness. You must give me a chance.

• • •

Earl Baneham's Rules for Winning
"ALWAYS, *ALWAYS* USE THE FULL WEIGHT OF YOUR STATION."

Sophia curled her newly calloused fingers around a wooden pole and heaved in a carefully calculated push. The soapwort root-infused water sloshed through the aprons with a softly bubbling gurgle. Steam curled upward from the wooden bucket. This time, she had not spilled a drop.

She was getting better at laundry.

She did not mind the heat, did not mind the way water made the aprons heavy, and did not even mind the constant churning.

She stifled an inward chuckle. Thea would be horrified to know she actually appreciated manual labor. To her surprise, Elizabeth had been right: dull repetition was a reliable friend—as soothing as a friend's hand to the shoulder.

The slow drumming of fear had begun a few years past, after she had found the Earl's body, and had intensified with time until it had reached a near frenzy when she'd discovered Randolph had been one of Baneham's men. Now, for the first time in three years, she had silenced her fear.

While she worked, Baneham's sins and any impending retribution were distant smoke on the horizon. Of course, at night, things were not so simple. A disquieting shiver spidered up her spine.

Randolph came to her dreams, most of the time as a heartless executioner—deliverer of a fate she feared she deserved. Last night, however, he had haunted her dream in an entirely different form.

She had awoken on the cusp of a sigh with his phantom kiss teasing her lips. As she had blinked into the morning sun, she had felt a hollow around her heart. The dream was proof she missed the pleasure she had found in his kisses. A pleasure she would never know again.

She wiped her arm across her brow and banished thoughts of the rogue. They melted into the hot grey water below.

With a deep-breath heave, she forced the water to churn—a churn resembling the sensation in her stomach. Much like memories of Randolph, water was formless and yet almost unbearably heavy.

"Jane!" Anna hurried down the kitchen garden path,

waving her arms excitedly. "Elizabeth," she took in a gulp of air as she reached Sophia's side, "would like to see you right away."

Sophia frowned. "I cannot leave the washing."

"She sent me to take over," Anna said, not without pride.

Anna's broad smile and excited, little hop forced Sophia to relinquish the washing stick. After all, whatever her story, Anna clearly had as great a need for peace as she.

Sophia wiped her damp hands off on her apron and wandered toward the house. Urgency was uncommon here at Elizabeth's farm. An urgent summons *could* mean she had been found.

Sophia stopped walking. Remembering her father's rule — *always use the full weight of your station*. She listened for the sound of a peer's arrogant bombardment.

In the distance, she heard birds. The occasional mournful *mmm — baaa* of a sheep. The sounds of pots clanging. But no neighing of horses. No hooves stomping as horses driven hard stretched their legs. No angry male voices raised in outrage.

She resumed walking, heart lighter. If Randolph were here, he would have arrived as the earl would have arrived — with all the weight of his office making as intimidating an official presence as he could make.

She swung open the oak door, finding Elizabeth at rest on the table bench. The top of her quill darted to and fro as her words flew across the page. In her former life, Lady Sophia would have announced herself, or rather, a servant would have announced her. Then, all present would have risen.

Those small details had once seemed important to the preservation of civility. Now? Well, the silent respect of waiting to be acknowledged better suited. There were times Quaker simplicity was very beneficial, say when you had no idea why you'd been summoned and no intention of giving your fear away with idle chatter.

Elizabeth's brow was furrowed, uncharacteristically, as she wrote. When she glanced up, the frown was gone.

"Jane, I did not hear thee enter." She patted the seat. "Come share the bench."

"Thank you." Sophia sat down beside the matron.

Every line on Elizabeth's face told a story. The lines from her eyes, the dimples now faded to soft wrinkles in her cheeks. There was cheer in her weariness, but great hardship had been written into her skin just as surely as she had written words on the parchment. Her gaze pushed aside all Sophia's defenses and reached into the pulsing center of Sophia's soul.

Elizabeth covered Sophia's hand with hers—plump, warm, and calloused. "I have asked thee few questions."

"And I have been grateful for your discretion," Sophia interjected.

"I know the distress of finding thyself without home or family," Elizabeth began. "I know sometimes we are called to make choices others cannot understand."

Sophia swallowed over the rough dust in her throat. "Yes, we are."

"None," Elizabeth continued, "who shelter with me canst afford revelation."

Sophia drew back. "I would never put the home you have created at risk."

"I believe thee."

Elizabeth pursed her lips and closed her eyes, as if seeking her words through some other medium than just her own thought. When she opened them again, Sophia saw greater peace…and a greater resolve.

"Art thou, in the world's words, a Lady?" she asked.

Sophia did not answer.

Elizabeth's grip tightened. "Art thou running from thy rightful husband?"

From the tone in the matron's voice, Sophia understood Elizabeth already knew. Sophia's heart hit the bottom of her well-worn half boots.

"I am." She turned her face to the sunlight streaming through the window and let its warmth fall over her cheeks. Her heart pushed upward into the dusty dryness of her throat. "Has he come?"

Elizabeth's voice was soft, "A Lord Randolph hath requested our direction at the inn."

"He is my husband."

Elizabeth sighed. "Thy husband has been sent the long way around the village—his journey here will take a quarter hour, at least."

Sophia exhaled. She still had a chance. "I will leave you and your borders in peace. I will not tell you which direction I take, so you may answer truthfully that you do not know."

She would gather her things together…she would find another place to hide. In her mind, a map of England unfolded. Roads spread like veins through hamlets and towns and stretches of wood and countryside.

If he could find her *here*, was there *anywhere* she could hide from Randolph? And what of Kasai and his men? Was there anywhere she could be safe from her father's enemies?

Elizabeth touched her arm. "Thee hast no other choice? Cannot the rent between thee and thy husband be mended?"

"No. It cannot." Sophia's answer was immediate. Her resolve, she realized with a growing distress, was not.

"*Canst*," Elizabeth offered, "is far from *wishith*."

The words were said without judgment. And for reasons she did not understand, tears stung behind Sophia's eyelids.

Elizabeth hesitated. "Is thy life in danger from thy husband?"

Was it? If Randolph had intended to cause her harm, she had given him plenty of chances—a fact which had escaped her angry, frightened heart the night she had left London. She hated, *hated* having been so easily deceived. But was shame reason enough to set out into the woods with only the clothes on her back?

Who was the real Randolph? The executioner of her nightmares or the lover of her dreams? Though to stay and find out was unwise, to run without destination could be worse. Despite the pride Sophia took in being strong, despite the renewed strength of peaceful sleep, she could not stop the wetness seeping between her lashes.

"Did the message give the number in Randolph's party?" she asked.

Elizabeth frowned. "I expect only thy husband."

Well, that was something. He had come alone. *Alone*, when he could have easily had her forcibly removed by the weight of his station backed by his right as her husband. When trapped in place with an opponent who may or may not be his enemy baring down, what would Baneham have done?

She had no answer. Baneham had been a ruthless, soulless bastard and Baneham was dead. He was dead because he had trusted the wrong man or men.

The question Sophia needed to answer was, could she live by trusting the right one?

• • •

Earl Baneham's Rules for Winning
"KEEP THE LARGER OBJECTIVE IN SIGHT."

To reach his wife, Randolph need only triumph over a petite woman whose snowy white hair was capped with an equally white bonnet. Unfortunately, the task was not as simple as he had first assumed.

"Randolph is thy title, not thy name." As she repeated herself, the old woman's melodic voice soothed, though her soft hazel eyes remained obstinate.

"*Lord* Randolph," he clarified.

"All men are equal in God's sight," she said. "Here, however imperfectly, we live according to His law."

"What of the laws of England, Madam?" he asked.

"I have told thee," she replied, "to call me Elizabeth. And, I will call thee…?" She paused with a pleasant smile gracing her face.

In the light of her smile, understanding dawned. She meant to somehow enforce their equal status in God's sight by using his Christian name. He blinked. Not even his mother called him by his Christian name—although, come to think of it, Harrison may have mentioned the first-name custom in his litany of Quaker peculiarities.

Randolph had only ever been called Randolph since the day his father had died. A day he could not remember that marked the loss of a father he could not remember.

The woman's gaze softened, as if she had felt the unexpected stab his lack of memory released.

"Friend," she said gently as she gestured to the bench by the table, "Wilt thou rest from thy journey? Perhaps thee will then be more at ease."

"Rest?" he snorted. "Madam—" he checked himself, "*Elizabeth*, I do not have the time or inclination to rest. What I have is—"

"Thou needest rest," she said firmly. "Friend...?"

Mad. He was going to go stark raving mad.

"Hugh," he said to the infuriating woman, taking a seat at her table.

"Hugh," she repeated. "Welcome."

The woman reached for a pitcher and poured a measure of water into a cup. Reluctantly, he took the glass and sipped. As if *rest* would help him. If Elizabeth had poured him a finger of strong Scottish whiskey, now *that* may have helped.

"I have come," he tried again, "for my wife."

A slightly worried light entered the woman's eyes. "Only the Light possesses the power to compel."

"You speak in riddle, Elizabeth."

The woman folded her hands in front of her chest, closed her eyes, and shut him out. When she opened her eyes, the troubled look had vanished.

"Thee may not use force. Thy wife may remain here, if so guided."

May remain here? As if this woman had the ability to force him out.

"Men and women," she said, "come to me in need of reprieve."

He looked away from the accusation behind the old woman's gaze and glanced out through the wavy glass to the courtyard beyond. Two weeks had taken their toll on his patience, but they'd also taken a toll on his certainty. Night after long night, he had imagined Sophia in the worst of situations...dead in the ditch, or worse, taken by Kasai—shackled and whisked off to a ship he would never be able to track.

He sucked in a country-scented breath.

All the while, she had been here. *Here*. And, safe.

He was *far* more comfortable in the bustling activity of a London street than in this place of peace. Which was to say, he was far more comfortable among thieves than those of virtue.

The thought nagged at his conscience. Virtue or no, he had but one objective.

Sophia may be his by right, but she was not yet his by volition. And by her choice was the only way she would return.

If he thought differently, he need only talk to the duke of Wynchester about his estranged wife, Thea.

He stared at the little woman—the only person remaining between he and Sophia. Certainly, she must be some sort of witch. For he was about to make a devil's bargain.

…Or was he, perhaps, making an angel's bargain?

"I understand, Elizabeth."

She cocked her head. "And thou will not use force to compel thy wife?"

"I swear," he said.

"Thou hast no need for an oath. A simple 'I will not' will suffice."

Was the woman in earnest? He sighed. "I will not use force to compel my wife."

She smiled, *finally* satisfied. "Then, I will happily retrieve her."

Retrieve her.

Happily, no less.

As if he had misplaced Sophia. He had clearly misplaced something. Several things, in truth. For instance, his pride, his purpose, and his mind.

Lady Scandal

He glanced around the now empty chamber. The door through which he had entered opened directly into a dining area like an old medieval hall, but without the tapestries and torches. In fact—he looked around—the room had no ornamentation.

He thought of Sophia's stuffed sofas and the decorative inlay in her opulently carved desk. He thought of the Belgian lace that spilled from her cuffs and the diamonds that dangled from impossibly perfect little ears.

Begrudgingly, he had to admit this farm had been an excellent choice for a place to hide.

The floorboard creaked without a discernible footstep, and he looked up. The woman standing at Elizabeth's side possessed Sophia's face—but the rest of her body caused him to question his recognition.

Gone were her silks. Gone were her jewels, her artfully piled hair and, most disconcertingly, her secure superiority. This apron-clad, bonneted servant could not possibly be Sophia. Out of habit, he stood, but could move no further. Surely, some iron-jawed trap had burst through the floorboards and snapped closed around his legs.

She raised her eyes to his, and the woman he knew came alive in their blue depths. Awareness grabbed his lower gut and twisted its fist.

"Hugh." Her voice quivered as the unfamiliar name rolled off her tongue.

"My lady," he managed.

His hostess—Elizabeth—cleared her throat. "I have explained to thee our ways, Hugh. Here, she is Jane."

He raised a brow. "*Jane?*"

"Sophia Jane." She glanced nervously at their host and

then back. "You have had a long journey, Hugh. Would you like — ?"

"Sophia!"

She jerked back.

He hadn't meant to growl—but it was all too much, the meek voice, the servant clothes, and the Quaker talk.

Elizabeth placed her hand on Sophia's shoulder. "Perhaps Hugh would appreciate a turn in our lane. The view from the hill is very soothing."

Sophia's eyes clouded and the skin around her strawberry lips pinched. Randolph read distrust in her expression—and was ashamed at the consequent surge of power that flooded his veins.

He was well within his rights to have her forcibly removed, but he had sworn—no, *given his word*—he would not use force to compel Sophia. Even if he did possess the legal power to drag her if he wished to do so…and *if* he were the amoral animal she evidently believed him to be.

"I would enjoy," he said, with as much gentility as he could muster, "a turn in Elizabeth's lane. I have told Elizabeth I will not use force to compel you to leave."

Elizabeth looked him right in the eye. "Remember."

He shifted his gaze, taking in the soft curve of Sophia's cheek and the small glimmer of hope within her cornflower blue eyes. The shock of her presence raced through him like a living thing, stronger than the fury in his pursuit, stronger than his fear.

"I have given my word," he said.

In fact, he would have given a great deal more for a few moments by Sophia's side.

Chapter Seven
Earl Baneham's Rules for Winning
"TRUST NO ONE, LEAST OF ALL A FRIEND."

Sophia headed toward the lane, matching strides with Randolph, or—she eyed him askance—Hugh. She had dutifully echoed the Bishop's words as they wed, but she would not have thought to call Randolph by his Christian name. Somehow calling him *Hugh* made him less threatening.

...slightly less threatening.

As they headed in silence toward the hill, invisible tension grew heavy in the air as if a storm approached—a storm whose ravages she could not fathom. Internal, scattered lightning coursed through her body, leaving her with heightened awareness. Her emotion lurched from a prisoner's grim impatience awaiting a verdict, to a pilgrim's daunted anticipation of untamed land she must forge into a home.

She was stirred. She was wary. She was—she checked her heart—decidedly *not* in fear for her life.

Would a ruthless killer have arrived hat-in-hand, *alone*? Would a callous villain have promised Elizabeth he would not use force to compel his wife, when the law allowed him force and so much more? Would a peer intent on vengeance reveal his Christian name to a common Quaker?

Perhaps he would have done those things...if the killer-villain-peer were lying to win her confidence. But *if* her demise was Randolph's aim, he had easier means than elaborate deception. And only a heart seeped in generations of corruption would expect so many layers of malfeasance. She did not want to be so distrusting, so certain of widespread villainy. Although she would never be as kind as Elizabeth, she wanted to live differently than she'd lived under Baneham, differently even than she'd lived with the Furies.

But she did not know how to create a life of candid simplicity while maintaining some protection from the hazardous residue of her Baneham heritage.

Randolph stopped at the edge of the wood. She kept moving, unable to be still in her confusion and in her apprehension of the torrent yet to come.

"Sophia."

She halted. Randolph's voice might have been a line in the darkness, or a band clicked closed around her arm.

A breeze sang through the leafy branches and wafted over her skin like a lover's soft caress. In contrast, he approached from behind, each footfall a crack of thunder. Through wool, his heat overwhelmed the gentle heat of the sun. As always, he radiated strength.

"Look at me," he said.

Why did she feel that if she turned, she would lose what little she had left? He was a man—*just* a man. Every London rogue had clamored for her favor. Could she not handle Randolph?

"You promised," she reminded, "not to compel me by force."

"You promised to obey me."

Something in her crumpled—discarded pride, perhaps. She had been deceived. Such fundamental deception was hard to accept and harder still to forgive. So he was furious, was he? She could meet such rage.

She turned, ready for battle, only Randolph did not appear as she expected. His arms hung loose at his side. His grey eyes held hers, not damning but inquisitive and expectant.

"When I married you," she said, "I married you under false pretense."

"I challenged you before, and will challenge you again. Are you *certain* I deceived you, sweetness?"

A swollen river of feeling roared between them.

"Yes."

"Whom did you think you were marrying, then?"

A frivolous man. A man she could manage. Her gazed dropped from his broad shoulders to his leather-wrapped thighs. A man who had made her hot with longing.

"Not you," she answered. *But for the last reason.*

With the gentle promise of agility and skill, he rested his hands on her shoulders. His scent infused her senses and her skin sighed in anticipation. A shiver of pure longing skittered down her arms, stopping where she held her stomach before settling deep within. She closed her eyes against urges beyond her ability to master.

"Why then," he asked in the same smooth voice, "*did* you marry this false version of me?"

She bristled, pushing back against an unseen, ever-tightening web. "I lost a wager."

"You did," he agreed, "but *you* first suggested marriage, not I."

"I did not," she said firmly, "I merely told you my charms were not for sale."

"If you had not wanted to marry me," he continued smoothly, "you could have had your solicitor draw up an addendum to the marriage contract with additional terms I never would have signed."

"You signed the most outrageous terms I could imagine."

"True. Still, no one beyond you and I knew the terms of our wager, let alone the outcome of the additional game. You could have offered me an alternate prize—or you could have extended the wager."

She opened her eyes. "There are no higher stakes to play than my freedom. I had given you my word."

His eyes softened. "If you had broken your word, you would not have been to blame."

"Oh?" She swallowed. "Why is that?"

"Because," he replied, "I unfairly used our mutual desire to force the wager."

Mutual desire. The words hardly captured the frenzied nature of her starvation-laden need. She had wanted Randolph enough to fix the outcome of their final game.

Denial was of no use. Randolph was right. If she'd had her wits fully engaged, she would have recognized his nature. Looking at him now, she could hardly credit the assurances she'd used to quiet her sense. *No one* looking at Randolph would believe him lazy. Licentious, perhaps. But driven by ennui? Never.

Again, she'd been a servant to her weakness.

What a foolish chit she had been. She had wanted to marry the lie…a widow's flimsy creation, constructed from the ache of too many a nights alone. Watching her good friend Lavinia fall heedlessly in love had not helped. She had grown jealous of the ease and closeness between Lavinia and Maximilian Harrison. Love was not for the likes of her, but she had believed she and Randolph could share laughter, and banter, and lust.

"Did you," Randolph asked, "truly marry me believing me to be weak and frivolous?"

"Frivolous is not weak, Randolph."

"No," he released her shoulders, "but admit…" He lifted her hand. "…You thought you could meld me," he drew his thumb down her palm, "like putty."

Maddening, he was. And oh-so-attractive, blast her penchant for mysterious eyes.

…and muscular thighs.

…and squared shoulders.

…and a scent so enticing she wanted to take a bite out of his shoulder.

"Instead," she said, while his heavy hands baked her shoulders, "you intend to meld me."

"No." He looked surprised. "I wish you to be nothing less than you are."

If he had swept in demanding her return, she would have known how to fight him. This manifestation of Randolph, however, was a squirming snake she could not grasp. Her perception was near legendary, but she could not accurately read Randolph in any manifestation. The loss of her most vital skill left her cold. Which, in turn, made her more susceptible to the power radiating from his body.

"More lies." She swallowed. "You are a deceiver. A sheep-clad wolf." *With wolf-hungry eyes.*

"Ah, sweetness. *You* abandoned *me.* You put yourself in danger. You jeopardized my mission. And yet, I *almost* understand."

She narrowed her eyes and damned him through her gaze. Damned him for successfully using soft words as tenderizing weapons.

"If I had told you," he continued, "that I worked in your father's organization, would you have welcomed me to your soiree? Would you have invited me into your study and into your arms?"

She blinked, and then took a step back—away from the temptation of his warmth. "Of course not. And I would not have married you. I cannot live in the same corruption, lies, and blood as Baneham did."

He frowned. "Do you give your father any credit for the good he did?"

A blow too low. "Do not *ever* speak to me about the earl."

"I do not presume to know your father as you do, but again and again you have insinuated I share Baneham's limitations. I am *not* Baneham. I have been called stubborn, daring, and determined, I have never been called ruthless."

"You share Baneham's arrogance."

"I do not rage as he raged."

Blood crept up her neck and flushed her cheeks. "You kicked the poker."

"So you would not *maim* me." His voice rose with exasperation. "What would you have me do, Sophia?"

"Let me go." Lonely darkness followed her words, leaving her stomach hollow.

"Let you go, so Kasai's men can come for you?"

She ignored the specter of her present danger. "Kasai will not find me."

"You are my wife. It is my office to protect you."

"I am not your wife." She pressed her palms against her eyes, pushing back against the pain. "I mean—I am your wife, but I do not wish to be." Shame, anger, and fear danced a mad reel within her mind. "Leave me, Randolph. Just leave me. Sue me for Criminal Conversation. Request a Parliamentary divorce. I do not *care*, do you understand?"

"Do you find me heinous enough," his voice had become strangely detached, "that you would blacken both our names just to be rid of me?"

She dropped her palms. "I told you Baneham was murdered. You told me some things were better left unquestioned. You asked me to reveal what I know and relinquish to you anything he may have left behind. Why else would you do so, unless you had a hand in his death? Unless you were charged to make certain his secrets died with him."

"So," he sighed, "you *do* think me a killer."

"The man who wielded the knife in Baneham's back must have come from within his circle."

"Is that what you believe?" he asked, gaze speculative and intent.

"Baneham should have listened to his own rules. *Trust no one*," she repeated rule thirteen, *"least of all a friend."*

"Sophia,"—he reached out and cupped her face with a gentleness at odds with the urgency in his tone—"you may be right, but look me in the eye and tell me you believe *I* had a hand in Baneham's death. Look me in the eye and tell me I mean you harm."

She could do neither. "I do not know what to believe."

"I have never killed for personal gain and I have *never* betrayed a friend. Baneham was a friend. *You* are a friend."

His words and their meaning settled slowly into her mind. A *friend*. He had come to think of her as a friend. Somehow, *friend* was more disconcerting than *husband* or *lover*.

Mind-numbing questions nagged her conscience. She had already come to the conclusion he did not mean her harm—not intentionally. But, could she believe he, too, was struggling to transcend the sticky mess Baneham had left behind?

"I do not think I would survive," she altered her earlier words, "a return to Baneham's world of corruption, lies, and blood."

"I wish I could give you a choice," he said. "Kasai wants you. Do you have any idea of what his emissaries will do if they get to you?"

Again, Randolph had done a subtle pivot. The brutal reality of Kasai, she realized, could not be separated from the course of their marriage—not yet.

When she spoke, she spoke with a softer tone. "I am safe, as you can see."

"Because," he replied, "you are *unharmed* does not mean you are *safe* and it certainly does not mean you are protected."

"I am," she said, "as far from where anyone would look for me as I could be—although your presence compromises my hiding."

"You prefer Quakers and lunatics to me?"

She looked out over the pasture. "I will not again live a lie—and lies carve out the very heart of every spy's life. I can promise you I will not be reckless, however. I have no wish to die by Kasai's agent's hands."

He frowned. "Do you think Kasai's men are here to kill you?"

"Kill me, yes. Just as they killed Baneham."

"Then why would you think I also wished to kill…" his voice faded. "You thought I was working for Kasai."

She bit her lip. "I was scared."

He cocked his head. "When I said you have something of Baneham's Kasai wants, I was not only referring to clues Baneham may have left behind, I was referring to your fortune"

"My fortune?" she echoed.

"Kasai does not want to kill you. He seeks to force you into marriage. He wants Baneham's fortune."

• • •

Earl Baneham's Rules for Winning
"No matter what your true motive, suggest to others the best."

Sophia's color drained, a mirror of the sinking sensation in Randolph's stomach when she revealed she thought him capable of taking orders from Kasai.

He hadn't time to complain of offense. The truth had taken the wind from her lungs.

Though pale, she did not shirk. Her courage filled him with a surge of something very close to affection. The desire to protect her made his arms ache—and, he had to admit, his desire had nothing to do with his long-ago promise to Baneham.

But he could not protect her while she remained elusive. Rulers need the acquiescence of the conquered—something Baneham had never thought to include in his rules.

He frowned.

While Baneham's rules had been effective in Randolph's line of work, *ruler, conquered,* and *enemy* were not words belonging next to *wife.*

He had acted the worst sort of cad—a bully. She was a bundle of nerves, anger, and distrust. Knots woven so tight, he had almost no hope of reaching her core.

"I thought," he said, "you understood Kasai's ambition. Baneham had been adamant that you, your fortune, and England were a part of Kasai's ultimate plan, though I did not believe him at first." *Not until he had rescued Helena and she had confirmed Kasai's aspirations.*

She placed her hand over her stomach. "Kasai wants to marry me…" He watched the implications tumble through her mind, each one clear upon her features. "But now, because of you, he cannot."

"Not without killing me first." He had married her for his own purposes, but by marrying her, he had placed his own life between Kasai and his aim.

She balled her hands into fists and placed them on either side of her head. "You have stolen what he set out to take."

"I have, to my risk, put myself between you."

She looked away—down past the rise toward the horizon.

When clear she would not speak, he continued, "I want you safe with me, but I have told Elizabeth I would not force you to leave. I will keep my word."

Oh, he wanted to break his word. He wanted to capture her in his arms, fit them both onto his saddle and urge

Charlemagne toward home. But this was a *war*, not a battle. He could not win by gaining the advantage in the first skirmish.

Damnation.

Was he absolutely incapable of dealing with his wife without thinking in military terms? All he knew was she must be firmly ensconced at his side while this game of cat and mouse played to its final conclusion. But seduction had not worked. Reason had not worked. What more did he have?

His gaze traveled over her face, her clothes. Who would have imagined Lady Scandal had been dressing in coarse wool and spending her days working harder than a servant?

She was proud, as she should be, of her choice for a hiding place. He thought of the silk night rail in his bag. The Sophia he knew would not truly wish to remain indefinitely in a place like this.

…Not if given a viable alternative.

His idea could rebound, and he would be worse after than he was now. But Sophia was worth a gamble.

"I intend to honor my promise to Elizabeth. You may stay here."

Her eyes widened. "Pardon?"

"*You* ran from *me*, sweetness."

"I ran *after* I was deceived," she said. "I believed you capable of any deception. You could have been working for Kasai. You could have been the man who killed my father."

Believ*ed*. *Past*. Not believe. *Current*. He still had a chance. *Please do not question this ruse.*

He placed his hands behind his back and aimed for a very innocent, yet grave, expression. "Naturally, I was concerned. I am much relieved, now I see you are safe." He furrowed his brow as if he were formulating a plan instead of inventing a desperate pretense. "I would insist on a guard, of course. A better one than I placed outside the dowager's."

She blinked. "You are planning to leave?"

"Clearly, you wish to be left."

She narrowed her eyes. "And if I decide to become a Quaker?"

He laughed out loud. "You, who purred at the thought of fine silk?"

She flashed a furious scowl. "You make me sound frivolous."

"Sauce for the duck is not sauce for the gander?" He squinted, trying to recall… "'Just a rake' you called me. Nothing more than a libertine controlled by his appetites."

"I never intended to insult you."

"No. You *intended* to use me as you pleased."

She swallowed. "I have been disabused of that notion."

"Have you?" He fixed his gaze on her hunted-fox eyes, acutely conscious they had lost their former sparkle, their former mischief. "The Sophia I know would not give up with such ease."

He closed the distance between them. Again, he cupped her face. He savored the feel of her tiny oval jaw in his over-large hands. Her barely there, involuntary pout invited him to dine.

Ah, her taste. *Sweet*. So sweet.

He had not planned the kiss, but how could he resist a mouth so delicately pink, so tempting, and so terribly close? His lips touched hers, dewy soft and achingly ambrosial.

She was better than strawberries, freshly picked and still warm from the heat of the sun. Her lips moved against his, creamy and fluid. Just before the blood rushed downward, he had the short-lived sense he was complete.

He seized his final thread of fraying strength and broke free from the mysterious force compelling him to keep her close.

"Goodbye, Sophia Jane."

• • •

Earl Baneham's Rules for Winning
"PREPARE FOR THE UNEXPECTED."

Sophia remained frozen with shock as her husband broke his affectingly poignant kiss, turned on his heel, and walked away.

She blinked to be certain her eyes had not deceived her — but the reality remained. The utterly infuriating, consummately arrogant, cunningly seductive bastard she had married was going to strand her with the Quaker and her mad eccentrics.

She had never understood why one *must prepare for the unexpected* until now.

She was whirling — afloat on a churning melee of emotion. Randolph had tempted her with trust. He had taunted her with fear. He had knowingly placed himself in mortal danger when they married.

And now, he was going to leave.

No. No. *No.* She was going to decide when this ended, not him.

Immediately her cheeks heated. How had he turned this on her? She had had very real concerns which, with one seemingly magnanimous swoop, he had made nothing more than flimsy protestations. But, this was no coquettish game. So much more was at stake.

Her life, for instance. *And his.*

"Wait!" she commanded.

As he turned, the sun caught the angle of his face, making him look harsher than usual, and more devastating. The emotion rushing through her veins felt suspiciously like relief.

This was a dangerous man. A man not to be trusted. A man who would try and crush every hard-won attribute she possessed.

A man who made her soul come alive like none other.

She assessed him, but to no avail. He was a book in a foreign language with mysterious, dark slashes of script forming words for some but, for her, they remained swirls of incomprehensible artistry.

"You have said," she asked, "all you mean to say?"

"Did you expect something more?"

She bristled. "Yes."

"I came to see for myself you are safe. I came to tell you I believe your father was murdered and will do my best to see his killer brought to justice. I came to convince you I mean you no harm." He looked as if something more was on his lips, then he changed course. "I will send word when it is safe for you to return to London."

"To London, not to you?" Immediately, she wished her words back.

"You have made your opinion of me clear," he replied.

Again her cheeks heated. "I was angry."

"Was?"

She cleared her throat. "Am."

Randolph slowly nodded. "I am angry, too."

"Will you seek a divorce?" She waited, heart thumping in her throat's restricted column.

"We will leave such decisions until after the threat to us

both is past."

"I do not," Sophia shook her head, "understand you."

"I know." His eyes, cold and cryptic, suddenly warmed. "But I am beginning to understand you."

Beginning. Unfair promise lived within the word. Just as unfair inducement beckoned both times he had used the word *understand.* Instinct she was afraid to trust pushed her heart back down into her chest and directed its new tempo—a light, quick thrumming calling her to hope.

As if enticed by her heartbeat, Randolph trudged back up the rise. He took her by the hand and drew them both beyond the thicket. His body concealed the afternoon sun. She stood in his shadow.

"You asked me what I wanted of you. But what do you want of me, Randolph?"

"A chance," he said.

Yes. *Please.* "The price is high."

"Is it, sweetness?"

She sorted through the easiest and most obvious responses, searching the deeper abyss.

"Baneham's corruption was like an ink stain. Living alone in darkness has been better than living day-to-day in the sick world of his mind."

He wrapped her in his arms and held her cheek against his chest. Through his shirt, his flesh was solid and warm. His breath rocked like a cradle.

"You believe I will drag you back into the muck," he said.

She lifted her face, looking up into his eyes. "I am scared."

"I know," he replied.

He brushed her lips with his, more a suggestion of a kiss

than a kiss.

"I have no answer," he said finally. "Baneham lives in me as much as he lives in you."

"Therein lies the danger," she replied.

"A gamble I hope you are willing to take," he replied. "Like your father, I provide services to Company and crown. But I am not Baneham. And, you and I are not joined solely because of your danger."

"We aren't?"

His eyes gleamed with intent. "I have wanted to make you mine ever since you uttered the words 'Cousin Charles has brought me a gift.'"

A pleased shiver rippled down her spine. "My exact words. You remember?"

"Of course. Your voice sang in my blood. Everything changed. I am in unchartered waters, sweetness."

Suddenly, under the layers of worsted wool blandness, the heady power of being Lady Scandal, a woman who devastated men with a single glance, surged in Sophia's blood.

Randolph was making himself the conquest. Oh, the temptation was irresistible.

As if he could sense her vacillation, he gently removed and discarded her bonnet. Threading his fingers into her hair, he kissed her as if his thirst was insatiable and she was a draught of whisky to be drained.

She was caught, suspended, knowing she had finally been rent by lightning and the distant thunder would soon rumble into her bones. This need for him, this draw, came like a shock, blotting out all sense and reason. This was a call she must answer.

Challenge.

Panic rolled toward her like approaching rain. As if he sensed the impending clatter, Randolph broke the kiss. He held her tight and silent, sheltering her with his body and his strength. In his arms she felt something she should not feel—safe.

And unbearable longing blossomed. But hope and deception made deadly bedfellows. He did not work for Kasai. He did not kill her father. He did not mean her harm.

But he *was* a spy. A spy's work was never done, and a spy's world was never safe.

But even as her mind protested, she had already given her answer. She accepted his challenge. What other choice did she have? After all, she had used a cursed set of weighted dice to throw the game that had made her his wife.

• • •

"FUCK THE RULES... YOURS TRULY, RANDOLPH."

Randolph held Sophia tightly; pouring into the fierceness of his embrace everything he could not put into words...his protection, his hope, and his fear.

There was good reason to fear.

Helena and Lord Eustace were out there. One or both were likely working for Kasai. If the duchess's suspicions were correct, Lord Eustace was the tool Kasai would use to bring down the English government.

He pressed his nostrils to Sophia's hair and inhaled. Her scent was roses on a hot summer day, a presence setting right something he had not even known was wrong. If he could capture everything enveloped in her scent, he would.

But she would disintegrate under an autocratic hold—or, less metaphorically, run again.

He knew how to manipulate. He knew how to fight. He had no idea how one nurtured a shrewd but vulnerable woman. He was going to have to learn before they returned to Kasai's arena.

Harrison had bought him time by taking charge of the search for Helena and Eustace. He thought of the sharp-eyed glint in Harrison's eyes as he questioned the young man. In some ways, Harrison was the more qualified man for this mission.

Randolph's muscles unwound. Harrison would be fine and he had promised to send word of any development. For now, Randolph could think of no better way to ensure Sophia's safety than to remain by her side.

Here, in the peaceful environs of Elizabeth's farm, only the two of them existed. Baneham's ghost still cast a pall—but Sophia had opened, just enough to give him confidence he would prevail. But, when they returned to the trappings of Baneham's wealth, the constant reminders of Baneham's misdeeds—would he lose the small advance he had gained?

He released Sophia. The slightly dazed look in her eyes sank into his groin.

He replaced her frumpy little bonnet—she must have been truly frightened to hide with people who prized simplicity as much as she valued lush grandeur. But what better place to woo the infamous Lady Scandal than a place where she was, essentially, stripped of all her defenses?

"Maximilian Harrison," he told Sophia, "has taken over my post." *For now*.

"He has?" She frowned. "Poor Lavinia."

He gave her a dubious expression. "*Poor* Lavinia was the one who sent him to meddle. I will stay here until some progress in the mission forces us back to London."

Her gaze traveled over his face—part wonder, part concern. "You would remain with me—*here*?"

"For a time." They would *all* call him *Hugh*. Another blasted internal shudder. As much as he found he liked the name on Sophia's lips—being called by his first name by the mess of farm workers was going to sting. "You are unharmed and unlikely to be found. Harrison, and Harrison alone, knows I am here."

"I am not ready to live as your wife." She blushed. "Yet."

Yet. His whole world turned on a three-letter word. "I expect nothing you are not ready to give."

"Elizabeth does not abide idleness."

Wonderful. He forced a smile. "Do you think the prospect of a little labor will make me flee?"

An infinitesimal grin flashed on her lips. "I think you have no idea what you are getting yourself into."

"My lady wounds me again," he said. "Does she not yet realize I would perform any feat to ensure her good regard?"

She sighed. "Now I think *I* do not know what I am getting myself into."

He laced her fingers with his. "Whatever 'it' is, we will be mired together."

He would win her over this time.

He must.

Chapter Eight
Earl Baneham's Rules for Winning
"WATCH THE ENEMY WITH HAWK EYES."

Watch the enemy with hawk eyes. Sophia mulled Baneham's rule and decided this one of his rules, at least, had merit. At the moment—*a-hem*—she did not object to *very* close vigilance.

Muscles under Randolph's shirt bunched and then rippled as he swung the ax up high and then brought it down. The wood made a *squeaking crack* as the cleft pieces toppled to each side.

Sophia inhaled. Who was she kidding? She was not watching Randolph because of Baneham's blasted rules; she was watching him because he moved with a hunting cat's grace. And *his* grace made *her* want to brush up against his side and nestle her head under his chin.

He raised the ax again, and brought it down with another satisfying *crack*.

Squeal. Clatter. The wood split and fell away.

Having brought the ax down too hard, he struggled to

retrieve the metal head from the block.

Far be it from her to criticize, however. His forearm counted among one of the most fascinating things Sophia had ever observed. *Ah*, what things she had missed while gracing the sitting rooms of London! The pleasures of the country had not been adequately explained.

He released the handle, lifted his arm, and wiped the sweat from his brow.

Sophia sighed. He looked up in surprise. His smile deepened the creases fanning out from his eyes. Her stomach flipped. She craved his smiles. When he smiled, every sense she possessed danced.

"Jane," Elizabeth's voice broke Sophia's reverie, "art thou weary?"

She flashed Elizabeth a sheepish grin, but kept her eyes on her husband. "No, I just…"

Sophia fell silent as Randolph touched his hat and then lifted his ax again.

"Such hard work," Elizabeth observed, "draws thirst."

"Yes…" Sophia said distractedly.

"If thou wishes to fill Hugh's cup, I will take over washing."

Sophia's lips formed an *Oh* as she realized what Elizabeth suggested.

Such an odd thing. Such a little thing…to bring Randolph— *Hugh*—a drink. Had she ever done so? Of course, she had prepared tea for them both. She had performed any number of the mindless pleasantries society demands, which had become so second nature they'd lost their power.

But as Elizabeth suggested, he likely had a need. A need she could aid.

"Go," Elizabeth said with uncharacteristic exasperation.

"I will take thy burden. Assist thy husband."

Sophia released the washing stick but remained motionless. Her anticipation slightly appalled. Since when were gestures of a domestic nature appealing?

"Is going to him so difficult?" Elizabeth asked.

Yes. No. He-is-a-wolf-can't-you-see?

"I will do as you ask," Sophia replied.

"I would rather thee do as thy heart commands," Elizabeth said in a tone so low only Sophia could hear.

What did her heart command? Apprehensive and shy, she hauled a bucket to the water line, lowered it down into the well, and then retrieved the filled bucket by turning the crank. She filled a simple wooden cup and headed toward Randolph.

A vision of those opulent parties given in her garden materialized in her mind's eye. The be-laced gentlemen who smelled of wig powder, spirits, and expensive German cologne. The games, the raucous laughter. Why did the simple act of taking Randolph water take more effort than scandalizing London?

She reached his side. Work and wind had flushed his cheeks and his dark blond hair lay in damp disarray to his angled cheeks. She handed him the cup, her fingers brushed his.

"Elizabeth suggested thou may need refreshment—."

"Thou?" His lip turned up, bemused.

"*You.*" She shook her head. "Elizabeth suggested *you* may need refreshment."

"I appreciate refreshment." He raised a brow. "My needs are of a somewhat different nature."

She laughed. She hadn't laughed in a long time.

He took the cup and drank deep, Adam's apple bobbing

as he swallowed.

She inhaled. Truly, these good people must think her depraved if she did not take her eyes off her husband.

"Would you like a drink as well?" he asked.

She took his offer and sipped the cool, renewing water. As she drank, his intent stare coaxed a second blush to her cheeks. What had happened to her? Lady Scandal did not blush in response to a simple glance. She was scarred and tainted and a serious shock was required to make her blush. But here in her little white bonnet and scratchy grey dress she felt like a different person. Demure. Almost innocent. The world yawned anew in the shining whiteness of possibility.

"Hugh," she whispered.

"Sophia," he said her name like a plea.

If he had asked her then—*come to me tonight*—she would have been tempted. Her gaze followed a bead of sweat down his neck and past the V at the base of his throat until the droplet disappeared behind the laces of his partially open shirt.

So tempted. So desperately, terribly tempted.

His muscles would ache tonight. She could ease the ache with her fingers. She could follow the trail the bead had taken with a soothing caress.

Ask me! She gave him a silent and furious command.

He asked nothing. He just held her with his eyes. Then, he smiled, slow and wide.

"Thank thee," he said softly, "for the drink."

She felt the warmth in his gaze. He knew she had been won. But outside of these walls, back in their world…how would she feel then?

"Good day…Hugh," she said.

• • •

~~Earl Baneham's~~ *Randolph's Rules for* ~~Winning~~ *Wooing*
"IF GIVEN AN OPPORTUNITY, ~~TAKE FULL ADVANTAGE.~~ ...
ADMIT YOUR MISTAKES."

The moment Sophia's gaze had fallen to his chest, Randolph perceived her imminent surrender. Damnably welcome relief, because each time he heard *Hugh* on her lips, her voice ran like a warm cloth down his chest and across the sensitive flesh of his stomach. He could not endure much more. The slight curve of her lips—so gentle, so feminine—left him feeling as if she had brought liquid gold instead of water. She turned and sauntered back across the courtyard, hips swaying. He studied her retreat. By God, he *had* to have her in his arms, and soon. Where could he plan a tryst? He slept in the upper floors with the men, she, with the women. He wasn't above a tumble in the hay—

He closed his eyes and shook his head. Was he—*the Earl of bloody Randolph*—actually considering seducing his lady wife while surrounded by animal stench?

Absurd.

Sophia needed—and deserved—so much more than a simple satiation of desire. But what did he need? And what did he want, even?

Her little, secret smile.

In bed.

Every day.

He shook off the notion, took aim at another log, and attacked. A gratifying sting burned his shoulder.

Who was he to be thinking of Sophia's smile? He was

at war with Kasai, and this sojourn's purpose was to secure Sophia to his side. Mooning about smiles was for poets and fools. Poets and fools *in love*.

He shuddered.

Love was a softening agent. And love, he suspected, was not for people like Sophia and him—people who had seen more than they wished to admit and darkness they could never forget. The equation here was simpler than love: he and Sophia were stronger together than they were apart. He needed her in this fight. He wanted her in his bed. That he rather *liked* her was irrelevant.

…As was the thought that when they won this war, he looked forward to bringing his countess home.

"Woolgathering, Hugh?" Elizabeth asked.

"I apologize," he said.

"There is no need…"

Elizabeth turned toward the house and held her hand to her forehead to shield her eyes. At the threshold of the kitchen door, Sophia paused, turned back to them and flashed one of her infamous smiles. Randolph groaned aloud. A groan which he attempted to cover by clearing his throat.

"Walk with me?" Elizabeth asked.

"If you wish." He fell in step with the Quaker in silence… and not because he observed her strictures, but because, as much as possible, he avoided speaking to his unsettling hostess.

"I have appreciated thy work," she said.

"My thanks."

"Thou taketh much care with thy wife," she continued.

Now he was truly uneasy. There was no one anywhere with whom he would feel less comfortable discussing his marriage.

"I come to thee with a concern," she continued. "Anna is much on my mind."

"Anna?" He asked, startled.

Elizabeth nodded. "When Anna arrived, she suffered night terrors. She hath been my bedfellow, but she is recovered enough to sleep among the other women, which is her wish."

Randolph frowned. "Do you need assistance assembling a bed?"

"Oh no," she smiled brightly.

He cocked his head, "Are you requesting Sophia and I leave?"

She gave him an admonishing look. "Thou wilt have shelter here as long as thou hast need." Elizabeth stopped by a small building, just beyond the barn. She looked up into the tiny, resident-less cottage with a wistful fondness in her gaze. "This is the original farm cottage—bed chamber above and kitchen below—all that was here when my husband and I purchased the property." She smiled in fond remembrance. "We built the main house and dormitories as funds allowed."

He stepped into the shadow of the house and looked up at the thatched-roof.

"Thou wilt be comfortable here…thou and thy wife."

"Pardon?" He looked at her in surprise.

"Anna requires Jane's bed." Elizabeth pinked and quickly turned toward the house. "I will send Jane."

Randolph rested his hand on the wall, stunned. A simple cottage of timber and whitewashed mud may be a far cry from his estate, but it was certainly a cozy step up from a barn-loft tryst. At the moment, the modest dwelling was worth far more to him than the intricately carved buttresses and impressive columns where he had begun his life.

Elizabeth had answered his prayers—if he could call his deepest desires, prayers.

Baneham's rules and Randolph's experience told him to seize the advantage. On the other hand, Sophia's shy smile had been a gift he would never have received had he been following those rules. One did not coax a spark to flame by tossing the largest log on new embers.

For years, he had referenced Baneham's damned book more from habit than for guidance. He had not been blind to his mentor's faults, of course. Just certain that the preservation of the state and the state's interests won out over morality's lesser strictures. And grateful something had finally given him the means to subdue an internal spirit whose excesses he had too often indulged.

But, useful as those rules had been, they did not apply to wooing. And his wife required plenty of wooing.

Wooing. Randolph snorted. Baneham would be mortified.

"Randolph?" Sophia had approached with nary a sound. "Elizabeth has sent me to you," she said, part-amused and part-exasperated. "If she were not so pious, I would think she was playing matchmaker."

"The pious cannot match-make?"

Sophia reflected and then shook her head no. "For Elizabeth to intercede, she would have to believe the couple had been, as she might put it, drawn together by the light and were suffering due to their willful refusal to unite."

Drawn together by the light. Her words echoed in his mind, bouncing from thought to thought, searching for a place to settle.

"Well," he grinned, "neither you nor I could be called

willful."

She laughed. "Of course not."

"Shall we explore the cottage?" he asked.

Her smile faded. "I have to attend to my work."

"As do I, but Elizabeth specifically requested we go inside."

"She *must* be matchmaking."

"Matchmaking?" he asked, "When we are already wed?"

The ground floor tour was brief: a small hearth and table made up the contents. Randolph took his time climbing the steep and narrow stair behind Sophia, enjoying his favorable view.

The single upstairs chamber contained a chair, a dressing table and basin, a privacy screen and a bed. Sophia glanced at the bed, and then spun around, nearly knocking him back down the stairs.

"We are finished."

"Surely you wish to step inside?"

She frowned. "Why?"

"My lady, I present your temporary sleeping quarters."

She blinked. And then blinked again. "Tell me I did not hear you correctly."

"Anna wishes to move into the women's dormitory, but there are no extra beds," he explained.

"Elizabeth wants me to relinquish my bed to Anna?"

He nodded. She folded her arms. The panic in her eyes simmered down to a low-roiling anger.

"You," she accused, "had something to do with this."

"On my word, I did not." Steadily, he held her gaze. "In full truth, however, I find the change in living arrangements providential."

"Providence," she narrowed her lids, "has nothing to do

with the look in your eye."

"Doesn't it?" He stepped past her, caught her by the waist, and swung her into the room. "Without the look in my eye, humans would cease to propagate."

She snorted. "I am angry. You cannot make me smile."

"I just did." He drew his finger down her dimple. "You've a lovely smile, you know."

"My smile tends to transform men into the most accommodating creatures."

"Smile again, then." He lowered his voice. "Allow me to demonstrate how accommodating I can become."

Her eyes widened. "Oh dear. I am not ready for this," she waved her hand behind her in the bed's general direction, "or that."

The honest little crack in her voice unraveled him.

He cupped her cheek. "Do you still believe I mean you harm?"

She swallowed. "No."

"You do not fear me, but you are not ready to trust me."

"An impasse," she whispered.

"Perhaps. Perhaps not." He reached down and grasped her hand. Cradling her fingers in his open palm, he ran his thumb across her knuckles. He placed a lingering kiss on the spot he had warmed. "There is something between us, is there not?"

"There is," she sighed long and full of suppressed longing, "*something*. There has always been *something*."

"*Something*," he ruminated. "Sweetness, no garment in England could be less alluring than what you are wearing."

"Just what a lady wishes to hear," she derided.

"But even clothed in this version of a sack, you drive me

mad. I always know when you are near. You can cover up all your feminine attributes," he ran his hand up her back until his palm cradled her neck, "and I would continue to find you the most desirable woman in the world."

He pressed her against his body—knowing she'd feel the proof of his words.

"Desire," her voice came out treble-high, "is not grounds enough on which to build a marriage."

"And yet, desire was ground enough for you to accept my wager." He brought his lips ever closer to hers. "Test your earlier supposition: smile and see if I transform into the most accommodating of creatures."

The corners of her lips turned up a fraction.

"Of course," he continued, "you *could* employ more drastic methods."

He pulled off her cap.

"You claimed," she accused, "to desire me without the display of my feminine attributes."

"I desire you the same." He stroked his cheek against her tresses. "Nonetheless, I miss your hair."

Her muscles drained of tension and she willingly rested against his chest.

"What else do you miss?" she asked.

"You, leaning across a table to stroke my arm." He worked his fingers over her shoulders. "I miss your touch."

Hesitantly, she swept her hand across his arm. He groaned and gathered her more dearly.

She tilted up her face. "What else, Hugh?"

"I miss," he whispered, "your lips against mine."

He lingered there, her body lending him courage to confess again.

"I *am* truly sorry I deceived you, sweetness."

Her gaze searched his, troubled and intense. "I may not fear you any longer, but I fear *this*."

He understood. *Completely.* "Make a command. Anything."

Her soft release of breath caressed his cheeks. "I am not in charge."

"Aren't you?"

"Damnation, Randolph. Kiss me."

"Scandalous little mouth."

He touched his lips to hers with the care he'd take sipping costly cognac. Her light but lingering taste had the same luscious complexity.

She locked her arms around his neck and lifted herself to her toes, demanding he go deeper. Triumph flooded his veins and handed passion all control. Thought disengaged—ravenous hunger remained. She was fire, he the heat...no longer large and small, male and female, now one, single beast.

She pulled back, panting. The sting of her nails lingered on his back.

"Here," she said, eyes wild as if making a devil's deal. "I will be with you, as your wife. *Here*. I will not speak for London."

"Yes, here." *Here* was enough...for now.

She pushed him back. "I must go and collect my things."

She stepped out of his arms and he allowed her to pass. At the top of the stair, she paused.

"This time," she said, "you win."

If he told her he no longer saw this as a war, would she believe?

"How is it I have won," he asked, "when I vow only to act on your command?"

She rolled her eyes. "I will believe *that* on a hot day in

January."

She turned and descended the stairs. He was in no condition to follow.

"You know what else I miss?" he yelled. "My valet, my cook, my groom, and my library!"

From the entry hall, she leaned over the railing and peered up. "A small price to pay for an enthralling wife."

With her parting shot volleyed, she left.

Randolph pulled back his shoulders and stretched his neck trying to think of anything but the kiss they had just shared...and the bed lounging against the wall.

Sophia was wrong. He'd paid dearly in trouble and sense to have her as his wife.

...Which was only one of the reasons why he did not intend to give her up.

Chapter Nine

Earl Baneham's Rules for Winning

"...Pardon, of what rules were we speaking?"

Sophia peered into the small reflecting glass placed beside the bedchamber basin, pondering how to proceed. The rare times she had called on Baneham's rules to help her survive in a world hostile to a woman alone, she had won her goal but had been left jaded. Tonight, she was determined to indulge in one of the few things she had ever truly allowed herself to want—Randolph.

Those rules had no place in this indulgence.

This short time may be all she and Randolph would have. She would allow nothing to intrude...not the Earl, not Kasai, not the past, and most certainly not the future.

She dipped her hands into the water Anna had delivered. She closed her eyes and held her face over the rising steam. Like everything at present, the steam was a contradiction—at once invigorating and soothing. She had come to Elizabeth's farm to get away from a husband she could not trust, and yet here she was, anticipating the sharing of his bed. She was a widow of experience, yet her body hummed with the uncertain excitement of a virgin bride.

She remembered her first husband as a generous lover, but, even so, he had never sparked the kind of fire that smoldered within when Randolph's hungry gaze met hers.

What if she did not please Randolph?

What if, heaven forbid, Randolph did not please *her*?

She opened her eyes. Her mirror reflected back a distinct whom-do-you-think-you-are-kidding expression. She and Randolph had danced around passion's fire long enough for her to be certain they would complement one another.

What she truly feared was something far worse.

…Despite her belief that what she felt was merely lust, she feared their joining would mark a point-of-no-return. Once she had Randolph, she feared some part of her would claim him as hers and hers alone. What would become of her if she started to want—no need—more from him than his touch?

Where would she be then? Such desires would come to no good end.

He had put himself between her and Kasai. But he was who he was. A spy who took orders from the man who had lied about Baneham's death.

At this game's crux, where would Randolph's loyalties lie?

Beyond the screen, the door clicked open. She listened to his footsteps as he crossed the floor. The bed squealed, adjusting to his weight. Her body warmed as if she had stepped into a steam-filled room—steam which came from more than the water in the small basin.

The time for caution had passed. What would happen after they returned to London was a problem for another day.

She dabbed away the excess and straightened the neckline of her simple cotton shift. What she would give to have just one of her wide selection of beautiful, embroidered fine-lawn nightgowns—all with lovely, matching rails. Donning something beautiful would be just the thing to smooth her fraying confidence.

"Sophia?" Randolph's voice was low…a simmering brew of hunger and anticipation.

"A moment, please," she called.

"Take as long as you like."

He threaded his words with irony. She could almost hear his unspoken thoughts: *What are a few more moments? We have waited long already.*

"I have a wedding present."

"A present?" she asked, foolishly pleased.

He rose, approached the screen, and laid a shimmering froth of deep indigo blue silk over the top. She touched the exquisite fabric with reverence.

"Randolph," she said in the way she might have said *oh my—mounds of glimmering diamonds!* Her heart leapt to the roof of her mouth and remained fixed, preventing further comment.

"An offering of peace." He lingered for a moment, and then returned to the bed.

She lifted the—what should she call it?—the *creation* off the screen. It was unlike any nightgown she had ever seen. Sleeping in such a splendor would be neither practical nor, necessarily, comfortable. But, as she ran the fabric through her fingers, the silk whispered seductively against her skin—a perfect metaphor for her attraction to the man beyond the screen.

Pleasurable, costly, utterly irresponsible to indulge… and, so, so marvelous.

She pulled her shift over her head and banished the cotton garment to a hook on the wall. She slipped the silk down her body. The fabric tickled her arms as she fit them in the short, ruffled sleeves. She tightened the drawstring of the loose-fitted neckline. As she tied a bow, she remembered the fantasy he had described—he said he would tie her hands and free her breasts and—

Her breath caught on her inhale.

Scandalous.

She actually felt she could own the name *Lady Scandal* wearing this gown while the details of Randolph's fantasy danced on the fringe of her memory. The beauty, the expense, and the sensation of being wrapped in luxury were more than enough to inspire the feeling. Randolph had created this gown for her, carried it from London, and had kept it secret until just the right time—perhaps he was wrapped around her finger, after all.

She wished she had a larger mirror.

"You were right," she said.

"Of course," he replied. "But on what point?"

She peeked beyond the screen. "I am a vain and frivolous woman."

Clad only in a nightshirt, Randolph curled his lips into a knowing smile. "Now *there* is the lady who stole my fancy." He leaned back on one elbow, and the linen edged up, exposing his thighs. "Come out. Let me drink you in."

She blushed. "I am not sure I should be seen."

His gaze gleamed wolfish and dark. "Come out. This has been one hellish carnal fast and I intend to feast."

A thrill made her grin. "Close your eyes."

He groaned, glanced heavenward, and shook his head, but he did as she bid. As she tiptoed across the floor, silk rippled against her skin in delicious caresses. She stood, her knees touching his, with only a film of fabric between.

"May I open my eyes?" he asked.

"Not," she breathed, "yet."

She took her fill of him, letting her gaze roam over his chiseled face. She had wanted to bury both her hands in his hair for as long as she could remember. He had such thick, lovely waves.

He held his weight on his elbow. Her gaze fell to the untied collar of his linen nightshirt where his chest muscle peeked out. Everything about Randolph was strong. Strong neck. Strong shoulders. Strong chest. Strong...*oh dear heavens*. A sharp stab of heat sank into her belly. Quickly, she brought her gaze back to his closed eyes. She parted her lips to tell him to open his eyes but her words died on her tongue.

Fuck cards and gaming. Fuck Kasai and his nefarious games.

This was risk. *This* was complete vulnerability.

Involuntarily, she shivered. "What if...?" She began.

"*Shh*," he said, peeking out from one eye. "Neither of us can predict the future."

Of course, he did not know the answer to *what if*. He did not know anything more than she knew. And all she knew was she wanted him. *Now*.

Well, that, *and* she was resolved to have him.

"May I look at you now?" he asked.

"You may," she said.

He opened his eyes, and his gaze traveled leisurely over her brazenly clad body.

"Do you approve?" she asked.

He chuckled low.

"Don't laugh!" she cried, stepping back.

"*Shh*." He wrapped his hands around each of her thighs. "I am not laughing *at* you. You are delectable. The perfect sustenance," he parted his knees and yanked her between his legs, "for a starving man."

Looking down into his eyes was novel. Something churned in those grey depths...something she wished he would share.

"Perhaps we cannot predict the future," she echoed, "but tell me what you know right now."

"I know," he said, "this night rail brings out the color of your eyes in just the way I had hoped." His low tone held stretched-to-breaking patience. "And I know," one hand traveled to touch her cheek, "I love the sight of your faint dimple—"

Her favorite feature. She was preposterously pleased.

"—and I know," he dropped his finger to her neck, "when you swallow, the little valley here at the base of your throat cries out to be kissed."

Her heart dropped, thick and liquid inside her belly. "Does it?"

"Yes."

She swallowed.

He leaned forward and placed his lips on the spot he described. Heat traveled to her cheeks as her nipples peaked against the gown. He dropped his hand to match the other's grip on the back of her thigh. His fingers crept upward, dangerously close to her feminine place.

"Anything else?" she whispered.

He stroked her lightly through the fabric—a touch designed to tantalize more than to please. She gasped.

"I know," he said, rumbling and dark, "my lady so fiercely needs a fuck her wetness is seeping through the silk and onto my fingers."

His hair tickled the skin beneath her chin. His breath warmed the space between her breasts. She wrapped her arms around him, threaded her fingers into his hair, and pressed her lips to his part.

This breathless feeling was more than just lust. The feeling was two dissonant notes played by a single bow swipe. Vulnerability and strength. Need and fulfillment. And something else— something that sounded beyond the jarring notes. The hopeful start of a melody she had never heard before.

Dampness bled between her lashes.

"You can loosen your grip, Sophia Jane. I am not going anywhere."

With a second gasp she realized her hands had fisted in his hair. She let them fall away, filtering his satiny, warm strands through her fingers.

He leaned back to look up into her eyes. "Nothing could tear me from your side."

Not long ago, such a vow on his lips would have been a threat. Tonight, his words touched her, flowing inside and brimming in her broken places.

"What do *you* know, sweetness?" he asked.

"I know I want you more than I have ever wanted

anyone or anything in my life."

"More than silk?"

"Yes." She parted her lips. "More, even, than the fear burning," she touched her breastbone, "in here."

"You need never fear me, my love."

My love was nothing more than an expression, but her heart swelled as if he had spoken words of true love.

"Kiss me," she demanded, for the second time.

"My wife's wish," his hands spanned her neck and he rested his fingertips inside her hair, "is my pleasure." Gently, he guided her lips down to meet his own.

She remembered every kiss they'd shared. Each had left her reeling. This kiss was like none other. This kiss was softer than the silk against her body, hotter than the growing fire under her skin. She sagged against his chest, careful not to crush him. This kiss threatened to buckle her legs.

He answered her unspoken need and brought her to rest on his knee. His rough stubble pricked against the calluses on her hands, and she loved the rough caress. Their mouths melded—a swaying dance of taste and dominance.

"We have," he said breathlessly, "no cause to rush."

"So *you* say. While *I* am hot, and wet, and mad for your touch."

She delighted in his deep-throated laugh. He pressed his lips to her hairline, as she had done to him.

"If my lady wants pleasure, then pleasure she will have."

She squealed as he lifted her and stood, cradling her like something precious in his arms.

"You will hurt yourself!"

"Please," he snorted, "you are a bag of feathers."

"I am a *bag*?" she asked.

He settled her on the bed. He rested his weight on one knee and hovered above.

"I amend my description." He kissed her dimple, then her chin, then her ear, then her neck. "You are lighter than a fanciful array of ostrich plumes."

She closed her eyes and moaned.

"What I am is on fire," she said, "everywhere."

"*Le pauvre bébé*," he murmured. "Allow me to make amends." He settled himself by her side and propped up his head with his elbow. "Air, I think, may help." He pulled loose the bow gathering the neck of her gown and pulled down the fabric. "There," he said with deep satisfaction. "Better now?"

"Not in the least."

He lowered his head and took a nipple into his mouth. Languidly, he taught himself her preference, just as he had promised he would in the fantasy he'd shared on that long-ago night. Blood moved beneath her skin, pink heat spreading like unfurled ribbons down her body, her color giving him every answer he sought. He nipped hard and she cried out in pleasure-pain.

"Not helping," she whimpered.

"It is helping *me*."

"Rogue." She forced his mouth back to her breast.

His finger traced a light line from her ribs to her thigh and then—fully aware of the sensations the fabric would cause, he slid her gown up her thigh—higher and higher until she was fully exposed. He left his hand resting on her hip.

"Touch me." She shocked herself with her bold command.

"Touch, yes. But how?"

He disappeared, leaving one hand resting on the valley between her breasts, directly over her heart. With his other hand, he parted her thighs.

He stretched her intimate folds and then acceded to her command—not with his finger, but with his burning-liquid tongue. He teased her where she felt her greatest sensation and commenced an intricate game of advance and retreat, carefully measured against her sighs and her moans.

Could one die of delight? Her frenzy was too decadent. Yet, she craved more. She gave herself over to the passion, over to the desire flowing from her core. Pleasure which couldn't exist, and yet it did—pleasure infusing vitality she had never experienced.

All her simmering emotion, burst forth, erupting in an explosion that lifted her to her elbows and forced her to cry out hard enough to wet the corners of her eyes.

He lifted his face. Holding her gaze, he licked his lips. So carnal, so intimate—of Eros, but pure. This man who had so easily commanded her passion was not the man she had imagined him to be when he had lounged on her sofa. Nor was he the man she had feared when she learned of his past. This man was so much more than either.

Together, they were locked within life's seed—a messy, sacred, human passion.

"Hugh," she breathed.

· · ·

She whispered his name—the name he had never been called until he had found her here. The consonants shivered across his skin, an incantation marking him as hers.

"Say it again, sweetness." He tasted her musky flavor anew.

She wrapped her tiny fingers in his hair and whispered, "Hugh."

His name became a living thing, a chain stretching from his primitive center to hers. He would claim her as she had claimed him, else the chain would tighten until it strangled.

He brought his lips to hers and she opened her mouth to him without shying away. She kissed with a passion he would have doubted a gently bred lady could possess.

"I am," he said between kisses, "a very lucky man."

Sophia laughed from her belly; the sound drove him wild. "…about to be blessed with greater luck, I hope?"

"Impertinent hussy," he said with affection.

"Yes." She hummed against his lips. "Now would you please take off your blasted shirt?"

He pulled the shirt up over his head and cast it to the floor.

"Ah, Hugh." She made a soft and sensual sound of approval; his cock jumped. "You are magnificent."

Yet again, he grew in appreciation of his given name. He stopped her from shimming out of her nightgown and he forced her back against the pillows.

"Keep it on," he said roughly.

The costly bit of fancy he had commissioned had been reduced to little more than a rumpled band round her waist. But it was a band of his making and he preferred it to remain. He came to his knees at her feet.

"I want my fuck, sweetness."

Her wet lips parted. "Yes."

He pushed apart her ankles until she was exposed, knees bent. He wanted to slam into her with despotic possession until they both reached oblivion. He conquered his urge with greater needs. The need to savor. The need to remember. The need to cherish.

She extended her hand toward his neck. He grabbed her wrist and held her palm against his heart as he tucked his knees under her thighs.

Kneeling above her prone body, he placed his cock against her opening and, with an aching slowness, he slid within. She took him hot and deep—tight and sublime—like they had been formed by the same hand, two pieces long lost to one another and finally united.

Consummate satisfaction sent a subtle shudder from his neck to his toes.

He stopped there, though restraint cost him his breath, and he burned the moment into his memory—her eyes, wide, fixed, and intent, her body slick with sweat, one arm flung up over her head and the other arm stretching toward his body; her hand trapped beneath his palm and against his heart; her nails digging into his skin.

Sophia. His sweetness. His lady. His wife.

At long last, they were one.

. . .

Sophia latched onto her beautiful, panting man as if she could grab this moment. She was stretched and yet whole, still and yet adrift in a spring of hot, ambient water.

He released her hand, gripped her hips, and moved.

She matched his thrusts while running her nails over his taut skin. He carried them to a place where sensation reigned supreme. His tempo increased; he ground swift, full, and fierce, forcing staggering pressure to build within her womb. She hung on—listening, feeling—as the sensation increased in an unfamiliar way. Her legs quivered beyond control.

Too much. Too much…

Caught between the urge to pull him closer and the urge to push him away her *petite mort* shattered yet again, this one not from the sensitive place he'd stroked with his mouth but from some unfathomable place within.

White light sparkled behind her closed lids. For a second lasting into infinity—she experienced nothing but peace. Oneness. Her arms around his neck, his cock in her body formed an infinite loop she had no wish to escape.

A light shudder through his thighs signaled the beginning of his release. From afar, she recognized his roar of completion.

He collapsed atop her body; she welcomed his weight. She bit into his shoulder and his taste was salty and real.

Chapter Ten

Sophia tightened her arms as Randolph eased away. If he untangled their bodies, the magic would end.

"I will crush you, sweetness."

"I do not care," she replied against his shoulder. "Just stay."

"I told you before," he lifted his head to look into her eyes, "I am not going anywhere."

Her sweat-dampened hair stuck to her cheeks and neck. From his aspect, she must look a disheveled, wanton fright.

"Perhaps you had better unpin me after all."

He rolled onto his back. She propped her head on her elbow. She loosened her hair from her cheeks and swept her curls over her shoulder.

He smirked. "I liked you fine before."

She blushed. "A lady well-pleasured?"

"*My* lady well-pleasured."

He was a beautiful man. He had given her an incredible experience. She could not possibly tell him how deeply she had been moved. But was she *his*?

"Strange thoughts," he said, "are playing across your face."

"No thoughts of significance."

"Oh I doubt that." He smirked. "You have the look of a woman plotting."

"Honestly, Randolph, I haven't the energy to plot."

"Neither do I." He sunk into his pillow, and fixed his gaze on the ceiling. "That was…"

Her heart leapt up—

"…exhausting."

—and plummeted.

Of course, he had not felt the same connective sense of mystery. He was a man, after all.

Her first husband had enjoyed her body—but never once had her charms inspired him to proclaim a deeper affection. His detachment had never caused her heart to twist as her heart was twisting now, because he had not enthralled her the same way as Randolph.

Oh damn.

She was more than enthralled with Randolph, wasn't she?

Bad. Bad. Very, very bad.

"Soon," she stated the obvious, "we will have to return to London."

"Eventually."

"Aren't you worried about Kasai?"

He turned, his shadowed gaze hollow. "He never leaves my thoughts."

She never thought she could be jealous of a killer, but there jealousy was—hot and oozy beneath her ribs.

He leaned over and kissed her forehead. "Nor do you."

She sent him a dubious glance. "You say what you think

I want to hear."

He searched her eyes for a long, silent moment, then sighed. "Perhaps your untrusting nature will one day work to our advantage."

Oh, this was worse than *very bad*. She wanted him to talk. Then, she wanted him to stop talking. She wanted him to keep his promise to stay by her side. Then, she wanted to be as far away from him as possible.

What the devil? She could not parse her conflicting feelings alone. She needed the Furies—if Lavinia could not help, Thea would have thoughts on the subject.

…Thea had thoughts on *every* subject. She smiled, somehow comforted by the thought of her female friends. "I miss my Furies."

"You are thinking of the Furies." His voice was wry with self-depreciation. "And here I believed you dazzled by my erotic skill or, at least, my sartorial ingenuity."

The dancing flame on the cruise lamp cast Randolph's features in a softening glow. Sophia let her gaze run along the faint laugh-lines at the corners of his eyes. She had no idea when he was teasing and when he was speaking the truth.

"Ah, well," she said, hiding the deep effects of their union. "Both *are* impressive."

"To impress you was my aim."

"Have all your lovers been as easily dazzled?"

He elbowed her ribs. "Jealous?"

Like a growling lioness. "More like curious about the source of your skill."

He snuggled in the space between her pillow and neck. "My talents did not come from bedding curious and maddening wenches like you. However, I foresee a honing of my talents to one, particular end."

He kissed just below her ear and the bells of St. Paul's rang beneath her skin.

"I warn you," he continued, "my study will be long, detailed and" —he rolled her onto her side and tucked her against his body so her back nestled against his chest— "painstakingly thorough."

His chest-hair tickled her back while his stiff-and-ready erection fit against her bottom.

"You are," she said not unhappily, "a ravenous devil."

"So I have told you from the beginning."

He kissed her neck, nibbling with slow intent from her nape to her shoulder. His free hand roamed over her breasts, wicked and teasing.

"You think." She moaned. "You are terribly clever, don't you?"

He stopped kissing. "…so do you."

She was going to ask if he meant that she thought he was clever, or that she thought herself clever. But he rolled her nipple between his fingers and her question was lost to his very clever hands.

Everything between them may be uncertain, but if she had coaxed him into touching her there again, well she must be very clever indeed.

…Which was her last thought as he tucked her top leg into the crook of his arm and thrust into her wetness from behind.

She pressed her cheek into her pillow and her breath made a small indentation in the fabric as she panted with captive content.

. . .

Randolph awoke with a start. He shifted onto to his side. Sophia lay sleeping—peacefully—outlined in silvery moonglow.

He drew in a shuddering breath. He brushed her hair away from her face, careful not to wake her from her rest. Gently, he kissed her brow. Strong feeling coiled around his heart, one combining the triumph of an Ascot win, the pride he took in running his estate, and the single-minded determination produced by life-threatening danger.

How had Sophia done this? How had she clawed her way into his chest and nested?

He never expected her—a whirlwind of a woman who was as strong as she was smart. He never expected someone who would challenge him at every turn and yet meld with him in perfect symmetry. And he certainly never expected to feel the way he was feeling.

He had wanted her, of course. By St. George, he had wanted her. But he had also grown to anticipate and enjoy their exchanges. He admired her pluck. He had even admitted to a general sense of *like*. But this was more. Could it be love?

Shit.

It was love, wasn't it? Though beyond his experience, he'd seen the effects before, most recently in Harrison: Distraction. A poorly-planned and unavoidable reordering of one's concerns. A blithe lack of knowledge that one was now joined to a woman and could be led like a bloody dog.

Well, perhaps not *lack-of-knowledge*—for some time

he'd been well aware that he'd grant Sophia any request. He had dismissed such impulses as part of his seduction. Only now that he'd won her body, he would *still* give her anything in his power she wished.

What concerned him more was his lack of proper indignation.

Now he knew the reason love matches were frowned upon. Nothing would get done, if every man faced this kind of feeling—this sense of mad frustration, this sudden inability to see anything but the lover by your side.

Yes, he'd seen the effects before. What he hadn't understood was the buoyancy, the explosive energy, the heady sense of power and privilege. Her yielding had laid him low with profound gratitude.

These feelings for Sophia were more than just inconvenient, they were potentially disastrous. He would require absolute command of his faculties if he meant to untangle the mystery of Kasai and then defeat the bastard. And, if his concentration failed him with only Sophia to protect, what on earth was he going to do when they had a child?

A child.

And since he had spilled himself inside her in the heat of his first release, the creation of a blood legacy was no longer an abstraction.

Baneham had been ashamed of his own attachment to his legitimate daughter. He had drilled into the men he commanded that family was nothing more than a liability.

Back then, Randolph had found no reason to see differently. He had more than one cousin who would make a competent earl, so—young and brash and certain such things as wives and heirs were the concerns of older men— he had been happy enough to steer clear of entanglements.

But now?

In this, Baneham had been right.

He could not continue to put his life at risk when he was responsible for a family.

Family. He'd never known his father. He'd be damned before he'd willingly pass on such an affliction to his son. Something sentimental stirred within. He thought of his mother and sisters—and the fussing attention he'd always scoffed. His mother would adore Sophia. As would his sisters. And their husbands. And their children.

He sank back against his pillow and stared at the moon-shadows on the ceiling.

After successfully dealing with Kasai, Helena, and the missing records, he would have to limit the services he was willing to provide to the Company and the crown.

Sophia sighed and shifted.

Limit? She would have none of that, he was sure. If he was going to continue to play the game that had given his life shape, he would need to lie to Sophia.

Problem: he *could not* lie to Sophia. Not after a mere omission had nearly driven her away. He blew out his breath as if he just finished a round of fisticuffs. At the sound, her eyes fluttered open.

"My," she made a sleepy noise, "your expression is quite fierce." Her voice was heavy with satisfaction—low and throaty in a way that redirected the flow of his blood.

"Fierce," he said, "is an apt word."

She frowned. "Are you thinking of Kasai?"

"In part." He could not have her examining his thoughts—not until he mastered his feelings. "Ax-wielding left me with an ache." He rubbed his shoulder to cover his change of subject. "How many logs do you think are left in that pile?"

"A morning's work—if you continue at yesterday's pace." She yawned and stretched. "Speaking of axe-wielding, I have discovered unexpected pleasure in country pursuits."

"What do you mean?"

"You wield an ax," she said in a feminine purr, "with attractive ease."

"As much as I appreciate your regard," he eyed her askance, "wielding an axe is a pastime I will happily relinquish."

She wet her bottom lip. "What if I asked you to chop wood so I could watch?"

"Scandalous request," he said with feigned shock. Her request would have finished the readying of his member, *if* his thoughts had not been so weighted.

"Scandal," she murmured, "is what I do best."

"What you do best is take care of those around you."

He was as surprised he said the words as she looked to be upon hearing them. He could have bit his fist for revealing more than he had intended. He cleared his throat.

"What a nice thing to say." She hesitated. "Hugh."

For some reason, he had thought she was about to call him *dearest*—an endearment she freely distributed to everyone else but him. Months ago he had teased her—believing her reticence connected to her vulnerability to his seduction.

He'd asked her outright to call him dearest, and she had answered, *not yet.*

Perhaps he had realized the depth of his feeling for her, but she was still in the region of *not yet.* Even if he bested Kasai and ended the current threat, would she welcome a life with him? They had shared lust, but, over and over, she had insisted she did not wish to share a future with a man who held her father and his methods in esteem.

The possibility was a splash of icy water.

If his attachment to her was unequal to hers for him, *all* he had built would be thrust into perdition—not just any future missions.

"We have," he said, "spoken little of our future."

"Let us continue in that vein for a while longer," she said lightly, "You told me this evening the future was something neither of us could know."

He had, hadn't he? At the time, it had seemed a rational response to her fear. Then again, he'd been concentrating on getting beneath her nightgown, which was no time for complex philosophizing.

But, since being inside her had been so indescribably good he had failed to take other precautions, the future was no longer something they could deny.

He lay back against the pillows and took her hand. He closed his eyes and brought her fingers to his lips to brush a light kiss on her knuckles.

"Sophia," he said gently, "you do realize our joining could result in a child?"

. . .

An alarm sounded from somewhere deep within—a cacophony warning of life-altering danger. A child. Hugh's child. Her child.

A Baneham…if not in name, then in blood.

While the earl still lived, she had been terrified of bringing a child into his world. Her first husband had allayed her fears by never coming to completion while still inside her body—something he said would decrease the likelihood.

She had become so lost in Hugh she had forgotten.

Before she had learned that Randolph had trained with Baneham, she had been warming to the idea—one did not wed a childless earl with only sisters and fail to do their duty, but she had shuttered the possibility, believing Randolph composed of all the Earl's bad qualities.

He was not, though, was he?

Baneham had never admitted mistakes. Hugh had asked forgiveness when he wronged. Baneham had believed he had every answer. Hugh changed beliefs proven false. Baneham had sacrificed everything—including her mother—to his work. Hugh had set himself to watch over her here, where he could not have been more out-of-place. Baneham had raged like a hell-bound demon. Hugh remained in control of his anger, no matter how challenged.

Baneham had not allowed those in his service to have families. If Hugh wanted a child, then perhaps he was considering a different life.

"Does the," she swallowed, "prospect of a child please you?"

He dropped his lids. "I do not *need* an heir. The Randolph line of inheritance is awash with capable cousins."

She propped her head up. "That was not an answer."

He pursed his lips, apparently fascinated by a spot high up within the rafters.

"Hugh?"

He sighed. "I would not be *opposed…*"

He would not be—she blinked—*opposed*.

Clearly, he regretted not having taken precautions. *Family is a liability* was printed in bold black letters in Baneham's book.

"Baneham," she spat.

He sighed and rubbed his forehead but did not look her

way. "Sophia, your father has nothing to do with—"

"Do *not* call him my father. To me, he is Baneham or the earl. And I know his rules about families and split loyalty. He had a weakness for me—but he had hated his weakness."

"Again," he said to the ceiling, "you are confusing my values with his."

She flipped onto her back and searched for the point fascinating Randolph. "I thought I was done with the Earl. I had wanted—no, I had *sworn* to live my life without the influence of his damn rules and his twisted way of thinking. Do you know what it was like to be his daughter?"

She wrapped her arms across her chest and held on as if her physical strength could keep internal fissures from snaking through her heart. He moved against her side, but she refused to turn.

"You described it once as hell."

"The sick world of Baneham's mind *was* a level of hell. Not melting flesh hell, but bad."

"Make me understand."

She inhaled. "I created a world for Lavinia, Thea, and I. Elizabeth created a world of solace for troubled souls. Baneham, too, created a world. Only his world was built on harshness and cruelty. He formed his world so he could play absolute monarch. He held the power of life and death over those he fought, those he commanded, and those unlucky enough to be called his own."

"Do you believe I would have blindly followed Baneham to death?"

"No." She pressed the back of her hand to her lips and staunched her tears. "My mother," she waited for the wobble in her voice to pass, "withered under his constant rage and criticism. Yet when he'd leave for India, she would pine for him as if he were her breath." She hiccupped. "She longed for something that would destroy her."

…and the apple had not fallen far from the tree. All this time she'd been afraid of becoming Baneham while forgetting to guard against her mother's much lonelier fate.

"She died and left me alone. For all of Baneham's professed love—he did not return for months. But," she snorted, "he sent me a copy of Baneham's rules for comfort."

"Ah, Sophia."

She resisted the urge to snuggle against his side and ask him to hold her tight. Why would he hold her out of comfort? His care for her had been confined to mutual desire.

"I knew then that I needed to get away from him before he could shape me into his creature," she said. "I proposed an elopement to my first husband."

"Of course," he said wryly, "you were the one who proposed."

Yes, of course. "I do not expect you to understand."

"How can I understand when you have not helped me to understand? How am I in any way like Baneham?"

Randolph was his own man. But still a dangerous one. "Yours is a world of lies and intrigue. A world as threatening to me as a vat of gin is to a slobbering drunk." She lifted an arm into his line of sight and ran her finger down her wrist. "Through these veins runs ruthless blood."

"Sophia," he said with a sharp intake of breath, "Are you afraid *you* share Baneham's character?"

"My proposal to my first husband came *after* the loss of my virtue. I transitioned from innocence and obedience to complete rebellion with horrifying ease, at first rejecting every stricture—even the sound ones."

He placed a comforting hand over her stomach. "The scoundrel compromised you?"

"Compromised? No. He had my enthusiastic participation. I realized I lacked whatever part of a soul Baneham lacked. I never sank to Baneham's amorality, but I was on a direct descent into hedonistic wantonness."

"Is that why you insisted on marriage to me?"

"Yes," she admitted.

She had never told anyone—*anyone* about her deepest fear. Not even the Furies. She rolled over, seeking judgment in Randolph's eyes. She saw none. He drew her into his arms and cast his leg over hers—a gesture of either possession or protection. She was not sure which.

He studied her thoughtfully, his breath deep and even. "Who was he?"

"My husband?"

"Your *first* husband."

"He was my cousin's friend. The same cousin who introduced you to me."

He did not respond to that pearl. "…And your first husband had no idea the power your father wielded."

"No," she said. "Not at first."

"Baneham wanted to have him killed."

She drew her brows together. "You speak with an authoritative tone."

"He expressed such a desire."

She should have been surprised the earl had gone so far as to speak his murderous intentions aloud, but the knowledge only served to remind her how mired in Baneham's world Randolph had once been.

"In a way, Baneham *was* responsible, for his death."

Randolph made a sound of disbelief. "Your husband died, if memory serves, in a duel. Someone accused him of cheating at cards."

"Something of that nature." *Dice. Hazard, to be specific.*

"Sophia, your father was ruthless and arrogant. Hell-bent on protecting the interests of the Company, and through the Company, the crown. But no one ever questioned his honor. He would not have influenced your husband to cheat."

She considered telling him about Baneham's weighted dice—the dice Baneham had passed to her unwitting husband the night of his death. Maybe then, Randolph would understand his mentor's nature.

But, if she told him about the dice, eventually he'd realize she'd used those dice to ensure she lost their last game. She rubbed her temples hard—as if she could massage away her conflicted feeling.

He rubbed small comforting circles on the small of her back.

"May I ask if you loved him?"

"Baneham?" she asked.

"No."

She pressed her fingers against her eyes. "Why ask?"

"I would like to know."

"No," she answered. "I was happy enough during our short time together, but I did not love him."

He untangled their bodies, retrieved the cruise lamp from the hook on the wall and, very carefully, he held it aloft beside the bed. He stared deeply into her eyes. Her heartbeat slowed and she fancied she could hear the insistent pounding in her chest.

"Hugh…is there something you wish to say?"

His mouth formed a grim line. "Just trust," he said, "that I will see you safely through this nightmare."

He returned the lamp to its hook. He lay back on the bed and pulled her back into his arms, but his embrace offered no relief from her disappointment.

Randolph believed the earl had been a man of strength and honor. And though Randolph treated her with tenderness and care, he did not have the kind of feeling for her that would inspire him to question those beliefs, let alone alter them.

She hoped she had not conceived.

She may have been able to create a safe haven for Lavinia and Thea, but with much more jaded hearts, she and Randolph had no hope of creating a life suited to raise an innocent child.

• • •

Baneham's Rules for Winning
"NEVER LOSE SIGHT OF THE LARGER GOAL."
Randolph's notes.
"NEVER."

Not long after dawn, Harrison's messenger stopped Randolph on his journey from the cottage to the main house. The news was not good. Randolph was needed. Today. Randolph decided Baneham's rules may not apply to wooing, but they applied to everything else of importance.

The farm's main kitchen was alive with the cookery clinks and, to Randolph's consternation, Sophia remained busy amid the noise and discord.

…Busy, silent, and seemingly oblivious to his presence.

He had seen his lady in triumph, he had seen his lady in anger, and, last night, he had seen his lady in the throes of an all-consuming passion *and* in the grip of encompassing grief. This coolly indifferent Sophia was a version of his lady he had never met.

He tilted his head to try and catch her eye. "Are you certain you understand why I must leave?"

"I told you I understood, did I not?"

He was no expert of the behavior of women, but he knew he was missing something. Sophia's voice was falsely gay, and she had not looked up from her scrubbing.

"Perhaps thou should take thy wife at her word," Elizabeth said from the hearth.

For a former-but-still-observant Quaker, the woman was certainly an interfering wench.

"Will you walk with me to my horse?" he asked.

Sophia glanced up from under her lashes with a distinctly unwelcoming look. "Thy eyes should answer for thee."

"Jane," Elizabeth said with the loss of her usual patience, "plain speech is not something to be mocked." She stopped stirring the large pot of stew and sighed. "Walk thy husband to his horse. The pots will not wash themselves in thy absence."

"Very well." Sophia's tone suggested Elizabeth had just asked her to muck out the stable stalls. She lifted her hands from the water and wiped them on her apron.

He held out his arm, but she pretended not to notice. She walked brusquely across the room and let the door slam behind her.

"I do not," he said under his breath as he turned, "understand."

"It is not my place to comment on thy trials." Elizabeth pursed her lips in self-chastisement

"*Please* comment." He needed any help he could get.

"I can," she said with a faint smile, "tell thee of my own

experience. My heart did not rest easy when uncertain of my husband's affections."

"No," he said immediately. "Sophia is not concerned about the nature of my affections."

Last night, Sophia had admitted she married twice out of fear of her wanton nature. She showed no deep jealousy and revealed a distinct preference to remain childless. Looking into her eyes after she had said she'd been *happy enough* with her late husband, he had finally given up hope she would ever form a deeper attachment to him.

"Perhaps thou should not assume." She returned to her stirring. "May the Light guide thee on thy journey, Hugh," she finished, firmly ending the conversation.

He thanked the crazy bat, bid her farewell, and then wandered toward the stable.

Could Elizabeth be right? Was Sophia angry because he had not spoken of his regard? If so, what did that mean... especially in light of his discomfiting devotion and the danger his devotion invited?

Last night had been magic—magic that had transformed into hell. Not only had his control failed at a crucial moment and, consequently, he and Sophia could have created a child, but he had finally understood how little she had ever expected of marriage.

She twisted her vision of life and marriage to protect herself from Baneham's end. She hated Baneham so much, she had created the fiction that Baneham had influenced her husband's death. Such hatred was enough for destruction—not only of the enemy but of the self.

He embodied everything she hated. She truly did not want to live if she must live in the world of a spy.

If he loved her—and he did—he would free her. ...*if it were not a legal impossibility*.

A chill shivered through his spine.

Never lose sight of the larger goal. Baneham's rule pulled him back from the abyss. *Right*—the larger goal. He shook his head. *Kasai.*

Harrison had written to say the man at the madhouse had refused to speak to anyone but Baneham. Harrison had not told the man Baneham was dead. He thought it best that Randolph, with his greater knowledge of Baneham and his dealings, should handle the man.

...which Randolph intended to do.

Baneham's rules may not apply to wooing, but Harrison's note was a stark reminder how far Randolph had strayed from the mission—*again*—and how much he had put at risk.

When Baneham had first given him a copy of the rules, he had felt like someone had given him the illusive key to the *Answers of Life*.

His father's early death had left Randolph at the mercy of swindling stewards and solicitors with interests other than his own. With the help of those rules, Randolph had learned a different way. The way of power. When following those rules, everything had lined up for his benefit.

Until her.

There was nothing in those rules about what to do with a woman who opened freely in your arms and then retreated into a shell of suspicion. Nothing to guide his response—if the Quaker was to be believed—such a woman told you she had married without feeling and yet secretly longed for you to shower her with assurance.

What would Earl Baneham have done?

Uneasily, he had some idea. Baneham would have ignored the woman. Chalked her anger up to the female nature. Moved on to the next quest. But in this case, quest and woman were intertwined.

Last night, he had resolved to disregard his uncomfortable feelings for Sophia until he completed his larger goal—Kasai's defeat. If the Quaker was right, however, and Sophia was in want of reassurance, reassurance she must have. He could not distance himself from Sophia to the extent he would sabotage his true aims: her protection and the mission. If she ran from him again, all would be lost. He had to provide reassurance without frightening her by revealing just how deeply he'd been smitten.

Inside the stable, Sophia held her forehead against Charlemagne's strong jaw. She spoke in low tones of affection. His horse nuzzled back. *Traitor.*

"May I approach?" he asked.

Sophia wrinkled her nose. "Have I been awful?"

"You have been angry."

She sighed, giving Charlemagne one last pat. "I have."

"I explained why I must leave. Harrison wants me to question a man who could help us identify Kasai."

"I know." She glanced at him out of the corner of her eye. "Last night, did you know you would have to leave today?"

"No," he said firmly. "Harrison's letter came this morning."

Her shoulders settled. "Oh."

Damn me, the Quaker was right. A tiny hope blossomed anew.

"I will return by evening, I promise."

She sucked in. "What if Kasai has reached this man? What if this is a trap?"

She was *worried*? "Though private, the madhouse is regulated by the College of Physicians. The county magistrate is to introduce me to the steward. Even Kasai-trained mercenaries could not have manipulated *all* the above."

She exhaled.

"Do you feel better?" he asked.

She gave him a warning look of which he was actually becoming fond.

"If I am not back by the setting of the sun," he offered, "you may send out riders."

"From Elizabeth's vast network of servants?" she asked with sarcasm that befitted her friend the duchess.

"Send for Harrison via the innkeeper. Lord knows I have given the innkeeper funds enough to do your bidding, as well as mine."

"You are asking me," she said—more statement than question, "to act as Lady Randolph."

He kissed her forehead—which was safer than taking her lips. "You *are* Lady Randolph. Looking out for me is your right and responsibility. Just as looking out for you is mine."

She closed her searching eyes and then rested her head on his shoulder.

Surprising sensation, though not an unwelcome one. In her gesture was nascent trust. A trust he needed in order to save them both.

…How to temporarily stall the deepening of his affection while encouraging her trust was one hell of a conundrum. But, at least while they were safe at Elizabeth's farm, there was one thing he need not deny.

"I will return," he said. "Because no one is going to keep me from the pleasure of my wife's bed."

"Truly?" she asked.

Astonishment swept through him. Did she really not know he had been pleased—in fact, *too* pleased?

"Truly." He set her back and placed his fingers beneath her chin. Such a tiny thing she was. So tiny, and yet with a power he could feel from his height. He bent his head and placed a light but lingering kiss of her lips.

"Go then." The line of worry still marred her forehead. "But take care, Hugh."

She held her skirts up from the gravel with a strangling grip and started back toward the house.

He doubted anyone—even his mother and sisters—had ever *truly* worried for him. The sensation was odd, like the first time he had donned his dead father's oversized court robes.

Sophia worried for him. She wanted reassurance he enjoyed her bed.

….Which meant she cared for him.

How extraordinarily terrifying.

Chapter Eleven
Earl Baneham's Rules for Winning
"BEFORE YOU ENGAGE, BE SURE YOU HAVE CHOSEN TO FIGHT
THE RIGHT ENEMY."

Randolph followed an asylum keeper down an unornamented, whitewashed corridor. He had been welcomed with utmost civility and had yet to witness mistreatment of patients, but an air of hopelessness thickened his every breath. For those confined within this pile of stone, the future was as bare as the corridor walls.

The steward stopped in front of a door painted with the number "23."

"The man you want—Mr. Garrett—is in there," he pointed with a sideways thrust of his head. "If you know what's good for you, you won't interact with the other one."

"What would happen if I did?" Randolph asked.

"At best, he will not respond." The keeper held up his arm and displayed a series of teeth-shaped bruises. "*At worst*, this is a sample of what you should expect."

Randolph responded less with fear than with commiseration. If confined in a place like this, he would do more than just bite.

"Does Mr. Garrett, too, become agitated?"

"Not of late." The keeper unlatched a small observational panel and peered within before unlocking the door.

"If you'd rather," Randolph said, "this interview could take place below stairs."

"Those in 23 are not to interact with the others." The keeper's keys jingled as he dropped the length of chain. "That's Mr. Garrett, by the window. The biter is in the corner. Any trouble, give a shout. Mind you, I cannot promise quick help. There are too few of us and too many of them."

Randolph nodded. The biter huddled in the corner by the door, eyes closed and lips moving as if in silent prayer. Garrett sat in a wooden chair, staring out the window, gaze still. Neither marked his entrance. The keeper's key clicked ominously as he turned the lock.

Randolph observed the man who was his best hope of shedding light on the hidden links between Baneham, Eustace, and Kasai. Harrison and Sullivan had failed to force a response from him—and they had shared with Garrett the horrible bond of imprisonment after ambush by Kasai—the imprisonment that had led to Garrett's pledge of loyalty to the mercenary.

Someone in the Company must have known the men from that ambush had voluntarily joined Kasai's army, but had led everyone to believe that they had been killed. How many other ambushes and subsequent "recruits" had there been? And why did Garrett insist he would speak only to Baneham?

How had Garrett known Baneham and why did he not

know of Baneham's death?

Randolph would do whatever necessary to get answers. He eyed Garrett carefully. Shaking knowledge out of the man was out of the question. He could not yell, and intimidate, and make demands—Sullivan had tried all three to no avail. Randolph walked to the window and leaned against the frame. Outside all was grey. Constant lines of rain blurred the inner courtyard bricks.

He turned back to Garrett.

"Mr. Garrett," Randolph began, "you requested Earl Baneham. I have come in his stead."

Garrett did not move—his eyes, the color of lichen, haunted his gaunt face. "Harrison and Sullivan shared a cell with you when you were imprisoned by Kasai."

Nothing. Randolph eyed the scar on the lobe of Garrett's ear marking the place it had been pierced.

"I suppose he told you, how surprised he was to find you alive and in England after you had—what do the pamphlet writers call it?—*gone native*?"

The flesh beneath Garrett's eye quivered, but he made no voluntary response. Randolph sucked in a frustrated breath. At least he was certain Garrett heard.

"Kasai offered freedom to those of you who pledged their loyalty—didn't he? Harrison and Sullivan witnessed Kasai's brute shave your head and pierce your ear. Submitting to a killer must have galled, even if you had thought you had seen them kill a duke's heir."

Still nothing.

Randolph dragged a chair from the praying fellow's side of the room. He intended to face Garrett, but something in him made him change course. He placed the chair by

Garrett's side and faced the window. He copied Garrett's posture and gaze.

The empty courtyard beyond remained unchanged but for the streaks of rain. The drops rat-a-tat-tapped the glass. He inhaled as Garrett inhaled, exhaled as Garrett exhaled, trying to understand, trying to see what others had missed.

Garrett had loved life so much he had chosen to save himself by doing the unthinkable—committing treason by renouncing his country. And yet, what did he do with his life now but waste it in the impenetrable silence of these walls. Why?

Randolph's eyes hurt, but he continued to stare, fixedly. As he stared, he let the feelings of hopelessness rise like mud from a swollen river. Powerful. Rushing. Heavy with the scent of death. Hopelessness worse than what he had felt when walking down the hall to this cell. Hopelessness possibly rooted in the choice Garrett had made. A choice that, since he was here, had not turned out as Garrett had expected or intended.

How did he come to be here?

How had he slipped past the customs agents? He must have had falsified records, and come back into the country under an assumed name. Why return with the proof of his change of allegiance obvious in his ear? Had service to "the butcher" been too much for him? What had he seen?

Randolph turned to look at Garrett's profile. Only, now that he was able to look closer he noticed—there wasn't just the dot of a scar. The ring had been pulled from his ear.

Kasai? Most likely not. If Garrett had been suspected of reneging on his pledge of fealty, he would have been killed in an instant.

"Did you do it?" he asked. "Did you pull the sign of your subservience from your ear?"

Again, Garrett's cheek twitched, but he said nothing.

"I understand a weary conscience. Treason weighs heavy on a man." He rubbed the bottom of his chin as he thought. "And for you, sedition twice over—once when you denied England, once when you denied Kasai."

Nothing. Not even a twitch.

Randolph clenched his teeth. Anger born of his failure tightened the tendons in his neck. He must have bloody *answers,* and soon. Sophia—who he loved, God curse his weakness—could be with his child. The fight had become intimate.

He narrowed his eyes at Garrett. Perhaps family *was* the answer. Garrett could remain aloof here. But what if Randolph dangled something that mattered to Garrett before his eyes? His former home, perhaps? His family. Then, they'd see how long he would remain impervious.

He would ask Harrison to make arrangements to transfer Garrett. He stood, walked to the door, and called for the keeper. The keeper replied, distant and unintelligible.

"A trip, I think, is in order, Mr. Garrett."

Garrett's eye twitched. He jerked his head to the side. His lichen gaze glowed with murderous rage.

Ah. A response.

"What do you know of Baneham?" Garrett's voice was gravel and pitch—heavy and low and nearly indecipherable.

"He is dead."

Garrett nostrils flared as he inhaled—sharp and deep. "When?"

"Murdered. Three years ago."

Garrett looked back out into the courtyard. "Then Kasai will win." The look in his eyes grew bleaker. "No one but Baneham had any hope of defeating him."

"What do you know of Kasai?" Randolph asked. "Of Baneham?"

"The question is—what do *you* know? The answer: less than you think."

Randolph felt a tingling in his neck—the awareness that a missing piece was vitally close. But what could Garrett know? He'd been here in this cell for four years and four years in such a place could do terrible things to a man's mind.

"I trained," Randolph said, "with Baneham."

Garrett's Adam's apple bobbed as he swallowed. "If Baneham trained you, what is rule 23?"

Randolph answered instantly. "So long as you have breath, the fight is not over."

Garrett exhaled. "You have your answer, don't you? Baneham is dead. The fight is over."

"The fight," Randolph said, "is *not* over. Baneham said Kasai would come for his daughter. His daughter still lives."

"Kasai and Baneham's daughter." Garrett laughed. "A brilliant end to a complex tale."

"He wants her fortune—"

"Of course he does. With her hand and her fortune his *entre* back into society would be complete. A viper right in the heart of the *ton*."

Randolph frowned. "He has set his sights on England, yes. But why would society welcome a Mughal mercenary?"

Garrett turned to Randolph with a chilling smile. "You think you know a great deal."

"What am I missing?"

"Kasai was a fiction Baneham created—a fiction someone chose to make real. And that someone is just as English as you or I."

The words were low and barely whispered, but they stilled everything within Randolph. Even the man in the corner stopped his murmur.

He lurched forward and grabbed Garrett's shoulders. "Who?! Who has been playing Kasai?"

"Do you think I'd be alive if I saw his face?" Garrett's voice was layered with disgust. "That abduction was meant to be a fiction—a scare to use as leverage. Someone turned."

Randolph let him go. "If you never saw Kasai's face, how do you know he is English?"

"Baneham knew—when he *temporarily* sent me here for my protection. Eustace knew. Men in the government know." He smiled another terrible smile. "The plot ran far above even someone with Baneham's power. He was gathering proof—of which I was to be a part. His proof—I suppose—that is now as lost as he is. As is any hope of stopping Kasai."

Sophia said she'd found nothing in Baneham's papers—but it had to be there.

"If you looked through Baneham's papers," Randolph asked, "would you understand what you saw?"

Garrett cocked his head. "I could try. But you'll find getting me out of here to be difficult."

"Nonsense," Randolph said. "The Under Secretary will secure the means—"

"The Under Secretary?" Garrett inhaled. "The Under Secretary owns the madhouse." He shook his head. "If the Under Secretary is your only ally, it is already too late—for me, for you, for Baneham's daughter, and for England."

"I swear I will get you out." Randolph set his jaw. "I will return."

· · ·

Earl Baneham's Rules for Winning
"DEMAND A COMPLETE AND HONEST REPORT."

The residents of Elizabeth's farm had gathered around the table with their heads bowed in silent prayer. Every resident but the one who had not yet returned. Sophia's prayer was simple, direct and urgent.

Keep him safe.

She opened her left eye and squinted out into the courtyard. The door remained firmly closed, and the lane beyond devoid of the thump and clatter of hooves. *Nothing.*

Worry squat in her gut, wet-rag heavy. Randolph would be back. She must believe. She must trust. She closed her eyes, willing herself toward a deeper presence with what Elizabeth called the *Light.*

She let the silence of the others' prayers seep into her presence. Wordless. Amorphous. More feeling than thought. But worry's weight still clung like a bell-clap to the base of her exhale. Beneath her closed lids, her eyes stung with unshed tears. She had not cried since she was a child, but she'd become a fountain these past few weeks.

Worry wasn't even the right word for the restless need pervading her being.

Last night, she had been sure Randolph was too mired in a dark world. But this morning, he'd been patient with her fears. When he had asked her to act as Lady Randolph, the feeling had been right, like a satisfying end to a life-long wait.

Two futures unfurled in her mind. In one, she remained solitary. In the other, there was Randolph. Neither felt quite right. She needed the Furies and she needed them fast.

But first, Randolph must return.

What could she use to counter-balance her worry? She attempted to conjure a sense of peace, as Elizabeth described — perhaps not divine, but peace nonetheless. Sophia's peace was in part, a half remembered dream from the time before she had learned the truth about Baneham and in part, the feeling that enveloped her when she placed her head on Randolph's shoulder.

Wrapped in peace, she uttered another prayer. *Bring him home.*

Which did not seem enough. She added, *please.*

Better, but still not enough. *Bring him home, please, and I will...*

She would what?

She thought of the hardest thing she could do—harder than giving up her silks, even. The answer came easily enough: tell Randolph the truth. Tell him she threw the final game because she had wanted to be his wife.

She bit her bottom lip hard—admitting her foolish deception would be difficult, but something else scared her more: mending the mockery she had made of marriage. She should tell Randolph she had not intended to care for him—she felt a cold shiver through her heart—but she had come to care and now wanted...

More.

Her heart galloped. To admit such a vulnerability aloud, and then to wait in silence for his answer...*impossible.*

But the tug in her heart said that was what she must do.

Frustratingly, her heart failed to assure her of Randolph's response. On the other hand, she had the sense that, if she risked telling Randolph those things, peace—real peace—could be hers, even if he did not wish to give her *more.*

She took a deep breath and silently spoke the vow into her heart: *Bring him home please, and—*

She stopped, suddenly imagining what Elizabeth would say...*do not bargain with the Light, Jane.*

She amended her prayer yet again: *Bring him home* so *I may tell him the truth about our wager. I will show him I care.* She had the same sensation she experienced when she finished the day's washing—sweaty but accomplished, like something she had done mattered.

The silent time ended. She hoped her tenuous peace would be enough to allow her to swallow.

As she stood, she heard a sound. Faraway. *Hooves.* She strained, parsing the noise—no carriage rattle, just hooves.

"Go," Elizabeth said.

Taking the lamp she had lit in preparation for Randolph's return, she went out into the yard. She fisted her apron in her hands. In moonlight's haunted glow, he and Charlemagne together formed a silhouette she would never forget.

Thank God. She backed toward the stables, hooked the lamp in the doorway, and leaned against the stall.

Charlemagne slowed as they approached. Randolph's greatcoat was spattered with mud; he had ridden hard and the afternoon had been wet and windy. Only his eyes shown out from the scarf he had wrapped over his face, and in the dark, she could not discern his expression.

"You came back," she said, blinking to stem the sudden rush of wetness.

He pulled down the scarf.

"I should have gone to Harrison first but I half-expected a militia on my heels."

"I did not call them," she said. "Elizabeth's farm is a place of peace."

"You were not concerned, after all?"

"I was terrified. Will you go to Harrison now?"

"I will go at first light." Randolph dismounted. "Half the road clings to my coat. Right now I would just like—*oomph*."

Sophia launched into his arms. He smelled of sweat, horse, and dust, but she did not care. All that mattered was he was safe in her arms. His life-heat soothed as she inelegantly wrapped him with both arms and legs.

His hands, warm from exertion, cupped her bottom. He kissed her deeply, thoroughly. A kiss leaving her without a doubt there was no place he would rather be than right there.

She broke the kiss, touched her forehead to his, and sighed.

"I have to attend to Charlemagne, sweet." He let her slide to her feet. "He was under strict orders to deliver me into your keeping before nightfall."

"And so he has." She *knew* Charlemagne was a good horse.

Sophia watched Randolph work by the glow of the stable lamp. He took great care with his animal—the bond between them was touching and real. But, she noticed he looked different than he had this morning. *Weary.*

When finished, he took her hand and headed toward the cottage.

She asked, "Did you see the man?"

"Yes." His pace quickened and she had to skip to catch up.

"Well?" she asked.

Randolph stopped walking.

"Did he reveal anything of importance?"

His greatcoat shifted as his shoulders tightened. Heart in her throat, she waited. Would he trust her with his knowledge or leave her, literally, in the dark?

"Must we speak of this now?" His gruff answer spoke of fatigue and something more.

The dark and menacing presence of her father loomed at her shoulder. *Demand a complete and honest report.* The call of her heart was stronger. There would be time for them to talk, she reasoned. Randolph was weary. Doubtless hungry, too.

"They are eating within," she offered. "We can go—"

"After that welcome, I am no longer hungry, at least not for food." His smile, though plainly carnal, was neither as deep nor as wolfish as usual. Something was weighing on his mind.

"I—I…" She what? She wanted him to trust her with his news. And, she had things she needed to tell him, too. *Important things.* Things she'd used to bargain for his life.

"Ah, sweetness," he wrapped an arm around her waist and yanked her close. "I've thought of nothing but you the whole way back."

…Things that could wait.

"Let us go clean you up."

He grinned. "I need a very thorough cleaning."

Her knees grew weak—but her stomach commanded she think of the future.

"I will get some bread and hard cheese from Elizabeth's larder—for later."

"Do not tarry," he said.

She nodded.

She retrieved food, vowing she would tell him all she had promised to tell him once she'd brought him comfort. She placed the food on the table in the cottage kitchen, and returned to the door, where his greatcoat hung on a hook. She pressed her face into the coat's still-warm folds and inhaled.

"Sophia," he called. "Is that you?"

…she would definitely tell him by tomorrow, just after she asked him what had transpired at the madhouse.

She climbed the stairs and entered the bedchamber, joining him by the side of the bed. He had stripped to shirt, breeches, and hose. Gently she ran a finger beneath his braces following the line from shoulder to waist.

She caught his eye with a shy smile. "Shall I help?"

"Please," he answered.

As she pulled each brace down from his muscled shoulders she continued, "I miss your court dress. But simple clothing has its pleasures."

"Oh?" He asked.

"No need for a valet," she whispered. "Nor a lady's maid."

"Turn around, sweetness. We'll share the burden of service."

He went to work on her clothing—a bundle of ties and buttons his hands removed with speed—although not without fumble. When left in just her shift, she pivoted. She gathered his shirt in her hands and lifted it over his head. She cast the shirt aside and left her hands resting against the smattering of hair on his chest.

I care. I care. I care. Once was not enough.

"Do you have something you wish to say?" he asked.

Hell. Not yet.

"I am happy you are safely home." She lifted herself to

her toes and kissed his neck. "Hugh."

She had said his name just for the sake of hearing the sound. She loved his name. Loved the way it sighed on her breath. Loved the look in his eyes when she said it.

"Does my lady have a command this evening?"

She nodded. "Ravishment. Complete and total."

"My lady is demanding."

"Indeed she is."

"Well, then." He sat on the mattress in an echo of their positions last night. "Where shall I begin?"

She pointed to the sensitive valley between her jaw and her ear. He obliged with soft kisses that hardened her nipples.

"I have not seen you yet," he murmured.

"You *have* seen me."

He shook his head no and his lips tickled her ear. "I have not seen *all* of you." He drew back, eyes dark and arresting. "Take off your shift."

She lifted the shift over her head and cast it aside, feeling no compulsion at all to cover herself. There was something terribly intimate about being naked in the presence of a man. She had been so before, of course. But she hadn't had such a deep longing for her first husband's regard. Her flesh cried out for Hugh, cried out from every inch.

She rested a foot on his knee, loosened the tie holding her stockings, and slowly rolled them down. They were simple wool stockings, not like the silk ones with the pretty ribbon closures she had at home, but the failing did not seem to dampen his fascination.

When she was without a stitch of covering, he drew her down onto the bed, took her foot into his hands, and began rubbing his thumb along the ball of her foot. She moaned.

"You like that?"

"Yes." Why could her body communicate with his with such ease, when she was unable to capture her stronger feeling for him in words? "Keep doing that, and I will do anything you ask."

"Be careful what you offer. I have," he watched her with care, "a truly depraved mind."

His rough thumbs touched only her inner foot and her whole body drained of tension. His hands were utterly brilliant.

"You already told me you would not share." She bit her bottom lip. "I fear nothing else you can imagine."

"Perhaps you *should*."

"You would not hurt me."

"No," he agreed. "But anything you find exciting, I would explore."

Little pinpricks rushed down her spine, making her wetter than she already was.

"Even things…" he paused. "No. *Especially* things that make you blush."

She only partially understood his meaning—she supposed it had something to do with his fantasized use of her fichu— but she felt indescribably naughty nonetheless.

She lifted her other foot and placed it on his chest.

"This one, please." Her prim request at odds with the blood-thrill in her veins.

He chuckled. "So quickly you've gone from promising anything I ask to demanding more."

"You should have stopped with what you had."

"As you should have, when you won the ninth game."

Her color drained. She could not tell him she had thrown the game. Not now. *Not naked*. How could she offer herself with no shame, and yet, not be able to say the words filling her heart?

"You assured me," she said lightly, "marriage to you would have certain benefits." She lifted herself on her elbows, lowered her eyelashes, and cast him a smoldering look. "I find I quite agree."

He ran his hands up her legs and rested his thumbs in the crook of her thighs.

"I told you," he said, "I preferred you in silk."

"Humm."

"I have changed my mind. I *much* prefer you without clothes."

"And yet," she said accusingly, *"you* retain your breeches."

He lifted his brows. "I thought ladies found the male form brutish and distasteful."

She made a sound of derision. "To whom have you been speaking?"

"Perhaps I have been misled," he said, "but my sharp angles and rough edges cannot compare to the loveliness of your form."

"Stop stalling and take off your breeches."

"A command?"

"A plea."

"Very well, then." He got up off the bed, and turned his back. He unbuttoned his breeches and slid them off along with his hose giving her an excellent view of the muscles in his nether regions. Fine muscles they were, too.

He returned to the bed on his knees, hovering above her body in all his male majesty. She should not compare, she knew, but his body bore little resemblance to her first husband. Where her first had been wiry—her second was thick. Where her first's chest had been bare, her second's had a smattering of silky hair. Where her first had been adequate—her eyes dropped to his cock—Randolph was…

She had a sudden hot and heavy feeling between her legs. Randolph was hers—*all of him*—hers to do with what she pleased. She licked her lips and came to her knees, matching his kneel.

"I have changed my mind," she said. "I would much rather ravish, than be ravished."

She placed her lips against his neck, in the same spot that had driven her wild. There, he tasted savory. She touched her palm to his heart, and, with her smallest finger, flicked his nipple.

"Sweetness," he said hoarsely, "I am not sure I can survive ravishment."

"You are strong," she quipped. "Be brave."

Steadying herself with hands on his hips, she explored his neck with tender kisses—delighting how the texture of his skin grew soft as she approached his ear.

"I love," she hesitated, "the way you look."

"You," he rejoined with a groan, "are not looking."

"Then, I love the way you taste, too."

"Much more of this and I will have to tie your hands."

She froze. The tightening in her stomach, the heat in her cheeks gave her answer. Traveling up his chest with both her hands, and then pushing them over his shoulders, down his arms to his fingertips. She leaned back, eyes fixed on his cock.

"I do not need them for what I intend to do."

She glanced up to find his eyes fixed intently on her face. He took her wrists into his hands, pinned them behind her back with one hand and yanked downward. Her breasts arched.

He cupped himself with his free hand. "Is this what you want?"

She was not having any trouble being bold with Randolph. And, somehow, she knew he would not think less of her for matching the boldness he had shown. Safe in their little world, she could be as wanton as she pleased—so long as he remained her pleasure's source.

She sucked her lower lip into her mouth and nodded, not at all ashamed.

"Take me in your mouth, Sweet."

She bent forward, closed her eyes, and savored the soft feel of his hard manhood sliding against her cheek. He was warm, smooth, and already moistening at the tip. A few weeks ago, she had seen drawings of this particular act—an act she had only performed once, and then only in the dark.

This was *so* much better.

She closed her lips around his manhood. His deep-gut groan reverberated against her tongue. He placed his hand against the back of her head, encouraging.

With increasing speed, she moved her lips up and down the veined skin. Lost in the rhythm, she wanted to take him farther. Intentionally, she relaxed her throat. With the next thrust she took him back far as she could.

He jerked involuntarily. A surge of heady power swept through her body. She curled the tip of her tongue.

"Stop." His command was gruff and final. He pulled out, breathing deep and heavy.

She looked up, licking her lips.

His scent was powerful and the look he was giving her—

like the rest of the room had gone black—made her breasts heavy. He kissed her with his taste still lingering on her tongue as he unpinned her hands and guided her onto her back. The shock of his full weight unleashed an overwhelming flood of tenderness. The edges of her eyes blurred.

Then, his hand was on her breasts with the other between her legs—too many sensations to parse. Pleasure, overwhelming, soul-renting pleasure. She hadn't the time to resist, hadn't the time to keep him at arm's length or stay in control. He teased through her weakened defenses, forcing her into an ever-tighter point of pleasure until every muscle contracted and then she burst in unfurling waves of heat.

She shook as he entered her, and felt every inch of the exquisite, primal stretch. He held himself aloft, hands by each of her shoulders as he pumped. She held onto his rippling forearms and dropped her face to her side. She licked his inner wrist.

He built up to a shuddering climax. This time, however, he did not lose himself. At the crucial moment, he pulled out and held himself against her body. He hissed through clenched teeth before he crumpled, fully spent, into her arms.

Something inside her cracked and pained.

"Sophia, sweetness," he said hoarsely, "what am I going to do with you?"

"That is the question," she forced her voice to false lightness, "isn't it, Hugh?"

"*Ummm*," he responded sinking into the pillow and burying his head in her hair.

Chapter Twelve

Earl Baneham's Rules for Winning

"DRAW AWAY THE ENEMY'S RESOURCES BEFORE ATTACK.
THEN, ACT DECISIVE AND ACT FIRST."

The first scream cut through Sophia's sleep before her limbs had shed their pleasure-drunk weight. Randolph propped himself up on his elbows.

She turned toward him, tucked her arm beneath her head, and yawned. "There is no need for concern. It's just Anna."

"Just Anna," he repeated.

"*Mmmm*," Sophia murmured in assent. "Anna has nightmares. Elizabeth will wake her and she will quiet."

Another blood-curdling scream rent the air, this one followed by the shattering of glass. Sophia's eyes flew all the way open and she sat straight. Randolph shot his arm across her chest, preventing her from rising.

"Do *not* move," he said.

A door slammed, followed by unintelligible shouting.

"We must help," Sophia whispered through her teeth.

"I will go. Stay here," Randolph ordered. "Do you under-stand?"

Silhouetted by the faint light of the moon, he grabbed his breeches from the chair. He slipped his legs into leather with the ease of a man who often rushed to dress.

Sophia threw back the sheets. Randolph's hand clamped her leg as she attempted to swing her feet onto the floor.

"You will stay, even if I have to lock you in."

She searched his face. The stark crease in his forehead told her volumes.

"What do you know?" *Damnation.* She should have followed the rules, damn her heart. She should have demanded he relay what he had learned today.

"There is no time," he answered. "Please just trust me. *For once.*"

Unfair. She opened her mouth. His fingers tightened on her leg.

"*Please.*" He was truly concerned.

"I will stay in the room," she conceded, "but I must dress."

"Yes. Good thought."

He released her, grabbed her shift, and tossed her the garment. Their fingers touched—hot and urgent.

"Go," she said.

Something passed between them, unspoken and indistinct.

"Lock the door behind me," he said.

She donned her shift as she followed him down the stairs. He slammed the door in his wake without a glance back. She slipped a metal bar into place and then checked to ensure the windows were shuttered and barred. Outside, the shouts and the neighing of horses grew louder.

Clothes. She needed clothes. She took the stairs two at a time.

She fastened the ties of her woolen dress and then cautiously approached the window.

What could have happened? Clearly, this disturbance was not borne of Anna's nightmares. She'd seen the truth in Randolph's eyes. *They* were the reason violence and mayhem had come to this place of peace.

Out in the night, she spotted a dark figure against the trees—a lone rider heading into the forest. Her gaze flew to the stables. Randolph, his white shirt glowing in the moon, emerged on Charlemagne. The horse neighed, stomped once, and then headed toward the wood.

Sophia frowned. Something was not right. She scanned the courtyard, the house, and then the fields. Movement below caught her eye. A person cloaked in black rushed through the darkness heading directly for her door. Someone was coming. Someone who intended deadly harm.

The attackers had divided to conquer—another rule, not Baneham's but one he used nonetheless.

She flung open the window.

"Randolph," she screamed. Hoping to God he had heard, she turned back into the room and grabbed a fire poker. The Earl's image reared in her mind. *Harden your heart, Sophia. When it is you or them, your loyalties reside in one place.*

She swallowed a surge of bile and melted into the shadow of the corner. Over the mad beat of her heart, she listened.

The intruder abandoned the front door. A flutter of panic quivered through her throat. She was trapped like an animal awaiting slaughter.

Each shutter rattled as the intruder checked for weaknesses in a thatched roof house hardly capable of serving as fortress. Sophia closed her eyes and counted from memory—one window in the front, two on the side. Two in the rear. He worked clockwise and would soon be below.

Her uncertainty melted away in the cold sweat of terror. She became the daughter of *The Ruthless*. The poker she would save for a face-to-face fight. With cool calculation, she eyed the room, searching for the heaviest thing. She spotted an iron cruise lamp hanging on the wall beside the bed. She would light the twisted cloth wick, drop the contents, and rain liquid pig fat fire on the intruder.

But first, to make him still, she needed to get his attention…

Her eyes settled on Randolph's shining boots—the pair he had worn the first day he arrived. If only he had screwed spurs into the holes in the heels, but of course he had not. She tucked a heavy boot under her arm, lifted the cruise lamp, and then hastily lit the wick.

She waited by the window, boot aloft in one hand and burning lamp in the other. When the shutters below rattled, she aimed for his head and tossed the boot.

"Be gone or burn," Sophia yelled.

The dark form reared back, cursing. He looked up. A horrible, sickening recognition stung Sophia. *He* was a *she*.

…a *she* enough like Sophia to be staring into a portrait of her older self.

"Helena?" she breathed.

She'd never seen the half-sister Baneham had mentioned in his will. Never known of her existence until the solicitor had informed her that the earl, of his vast fortune, had granted Helena Baneham a mere two hundred pounds.

The solicitor had sought, but never found, the missing woman.

"Sophia Baneham," the woman raised her arm, "this ends tonight."

The spark of flint hitting gunpowder was the last thing Sophia saw before she hit the floor.

• • •

Earl Baneham's Rules for Winning
"STUDY YOUR ERRORS. DO NOT MAKE THEM TWICE."

A shot rent the air behind Randolph.

"Sophia!" A hoarse, strained call sprung to his lips before his mind could form a thought.

Rider and horse disappeared into the trees. His choice was simple: catch the bastard who had attacked Anna or save his wife. He looked over his shoulder. The moonlight painted the distant grouping of houses in shades of blue. She could be hurt back there. Bleeding.

God forbid—*dying*.

A musket held one ball. Unless the assailant had two guns, he'd have a minute, maybe more, to prevent another shot.

With a sharp expletive, he turned back.

Charlemagne sensed his urgency. Despite the darkness, the horse raced through the brush and then back across the field with impressive speed. Randolph called Sophia's name amid the thunder of his horse's hooves. *Sophia. Sophia. Sophia.* His repetition matched his heartbeat.

A dark shadow fled past the house toward the opposite wood. He let him go. Only one thing mattered.

He reached the farmhouse and dismounted in a leap.

He plowed toward the door, shoving his shoulder into wood with his weight's full force. A sharp pain ricocheted through his arm.

A howl echoed through the window.

"Sophia!" he yelled.

He fit his foot against the door handle and hoisted himself against the wall using every ounce of power in his strap-stretched cords of muscle. His fingers found the smallest of holds on the wood frame's edge. He propelled himself upward. His wrist strained—but he swung an arm over the window ledge just in time. With power fueled by fear and will, he lifted himself into the window.

"I have a pistol." His wife's voice was ground into his fear—low, deadly, and nearly unrecognizable.

"No you do not." Relief was a full-body dip into a warm-water spring.

"Randolph?" Her grating voice sounded confused. "Be careful. There is glass."

He swung his second foot onto the floor, grabbed his bedside candle and lit it in what remained of the fire. He turned.

"Sophia!"

In a heap on the floor, she held her foot. Blood seeped through her fingers. Her grey wool dress black with soot and wet with something smelling like lard. The look in her eye chilled him to his soul.

"Did you get her?" she asked.

"Get *her*?"

"My attacker."

He blinked. "No."

"Then why," she said through clenched teeth, "are you here?"

Gingerly, he wiped away the shards of glass and knelt by her side. "What happened?"

"Go," she seethed. "Get her! If she is not already beyond your reach."

The disgust in her voice wrung his already pained muscles. He'd chosen to give up Eustace. She would have had him choose differently. This was not his Sophia...

"The attackers," he said, "have gone in different directions."

Her head fell back. "Damn."

He searched her face for the woman who'd surrendered to him in wild abandon and could find no trace of his love. Yet, somehow, she was familiar.

"This attack was well-planned," he said. "By now, I have little hope of catching either one."

"Yes," she reluctantly agreed, "If they chose the path of their retreat in advance, an ambush could await."

Her voice was wrong. Flat. Her low, gritty tones kicked the strings of his memory.

She set her jaw; her cheeks were sallow. She opened her eyes and her glare's full force hit him like a gut-punch. Her eyes—unique, ethereal, and blue—had always dominated her face. However, the weak lamplight diluted the effect.

His memory slid troublingly into place. She looked like Helena. Moreover, she looked like her father. She'd warned him she feared a descent into Baneham's world—and he'd ensured her fears were realized. He'd done this. He'd done this because he had failed.

"You are bleeding," his eyes fell to her sooty, stained dress, "and filthy."

"Pig-fat." She fanned her bodice. "*Hot* pig fat from the lamp." She dragged herself up and leaned against the back of the bed. "I planned to drop the cruise lamp and set my would-be attacker alight."

Oh God. His Sophia, the woman who took others into her home, the woman who learned to scrub and wash just to keep her soul free of Baneham's corrupting influence had dispassionately planned to set someone *on fire.*

"What happened?" he asked gently.

She frowned. "She fired first. The ball shattered the window. I dropped the lamp and had to smother the fire—that's when I cut my foot."

His heart seized. "The house could have burned to the ground." *And I wouldn't have been able to save you.*

"I am well-aware what *could* have happened." Her breath slowed. "Baneham rule number fifteen: *Study your errors.* I will not lock myself away again."

Now she was *quoting* Baneham's book?

"The error," he said, "*if* there was one, was mine."

Her glance was hard and judging. "*We* should have attacked first. Instead we were—" She stopped abruptly and groaned. "I knew. I *knew* passion would be my downfall."

Her words hit him like a swift slap.

"We believed ourselves well-hidden."

"I *had* been well-hidden," she accused.

"Hugh!" Elizabeth's voice sang through the open window. "Jane!"

"We are here," Sophia called.

He cast Sophia a look communicating their conversation was not at an end and started down the stairs. He'd not been *vigilant,* damn his distracted mind. His mistake had led the enemy directly to Sophia.

How could he repair this damage?

What could he do to shield her? Where could he send her to keep her from those who intended her harm? If Garrett was to be believed, Kasai himself could be in England. He could be anywhere—even working for the Under Secretary.

Kasai could *be* the Under Secretary.

He must find Helena and Eustace. Find them, before they had time to execute another attack. Although, if Helena were working for Kasai, why had she fired on Sophia? Killing her would not give Kasai access to Baneham's records...or his fortune.

He opened the door. Elizabeth stood on the stone step, her unbound hair streaming like a thick white sheet past her hips.

"Jane?" she inquired.

"Upstairs," he answered.

She pushed past.

Randolph lit the candles in the kitchen and then returned to the bedchamber. He entered as Elizabeth slowly took in the scene. The shattered glass, Sophia's dress, the overturned oil lamp, the poker and the blood.

"Thy foot is badly cut," Elizabeth said.

Randolph entered the chamber and knelt by Sophia's side.

"The cut is not deep," Sophia said. "I just need to bandage the wound. Is Anna...?"

Elizabeth exhaled. "Anna hath suffered bruising...and something harder to heal."

"Could she describe the man who attacked her?" Randolph asked.

Two sets of bewildered eyes met his.

"You'll not," Sophia said, "question Anna."

"Not tonight," Elizabeth amended.

His request seemed reasonable enough. Elizabeth rested a steadying hand on his shoulder. Her calming presence, in this case, did the opposite. He needed to get Sophia out and away and he needed to turn to his mission with full diligence.

"How was she attacked?" he asked Elizabeth.

"The attacker came in through the window," she said. "He tried to drag her from her bed." Elizabeth shuddered. "He may have succeeded, but when the moonlight hit the window, Anna said he cursed, released her, and was gone."

"He was looking for me." Sophia spoke Randolph's thought aloud. "Elizabeth," Sophia's voice softened, "we have brought violence to your refuge, and I am sorry. We will leave at daybreak."

"Thou art in accord with thy wife?" Elizabeth looked back and forth between them.

Were he and Sophia ever in accord, outside of bed? "I agree we cannot remain here. And I am certain the attackers will not return once we leave."

Elizabeth turned to Sophia. "My concern lies with thee, not with those who would do thee harm."

Sophia's face lost tension and a measure of her warmth returned to her eyes. "You have done for us as much as you could."

Elizabeth sighed—too world-weary for a woman who knew so little of this world. "Thou will," she spoke to Sophia, "remember everything thou hast learned."

A subtle change came over Sophia. "I promise to try."

Elizabeth collected the lamp from the floor and set it to rights. "There is always," she said, carefully placing the lamp into Sophia's hands, "a way to light the darkness."

Sophia's lip trembled, cracking what was left of Randolph's

heart.

Elizabeth rose and took Randolph's hands in hers. "Take care of thy wife."

"I intend to," he said.

In the knowing weightiness of Elizabeth's steady gaze, he silently vowed to release Sophia from his darkness. No matter what it cost him. No matter how broken he'd be left.

Elizabeth nodded and then she left.

As careful as he would have been with a babe, he lifted both lady and lamp and carried them down into the kitchen. He set Sophia in the chair by the fire.

The flames he'd lit flashed across her face in a warm orange hue. He tucked her hair behind her ear. "Comfortable?"

She nodded.

"I will be right back."

He locked the door and then returned to the hearth. His was the fault, and hers was the wound. He was sick with the knowledge—sick and utterly unable to engage in the argument to come.

I will not lock myself away again, she had said.

But she must. She must be locked away so she could one day be free. She would not understand, of course. She may even hate him for awhile. But he prayed she would one day understand what his actions had cost him.

There was no way in hell he would allow Kasai, Eustace, or Helena to come that close again. And there was no way he was going to strip her kindness to serve his selfish need.

He added fuel to his fire and then swung the half-filled kettle hanging on an iron hook so that it would be warmed by the flame.

"Tea?" Sophia snorted. "Really Hugh?"

He closed his lids over his burning eyes and bowed his head, pretending to study the fire.

"Warm water," he said, "to wash away any remaining glass…and wheat tea, if enough water remains."

He located the vial he'd palmed from his bag and placed in the folds of his shirt between his hip and his breeches.

He turned. "Will you let me wash your wound?"

She nodded.

He poured a bit of the warm water into a bowl and set it on the floor. "Hand me your foot."

She held out her leg with a brave attempt to conceal her tremble. He forced a reassuring smile. He cradled her foot in his hands—a caustic visual echo of the way he had touched her hours before…shamefully unaware that Helena and Eustace, with murderous intent, had been making their way through a darkened wood.

Her foot was impossibly tiny for a woman who had such a sure step. The cut *was* small. It could have been much worse. Gently, he dipped the cloth into the warm water and then washed away any small remnants of glass. The washing must have hurt, but she remained silent.

A spine of iron and kiss like spring. She was a patchwork of opposites, his love.

His fingers tightened around her ankle.

His love. *His. Love.*

Perhaps he needn't send her away. He could keep her for his own—lock her away in one of his estate's medieval turrets. The mad and fleeting hope was useless. She would never come to her jailer with wanton and willing desire. Better to finish this and set her free where she had a chance to be happy.

He'd been wrong. Love was not buoyant. Love was anguish. Love did not make you weak. Love gave you the strength to do things you found unimaginable.

He had been close to catching the attacker. Then, he'd done what he had sworn to the spymaster he would never do: he had chosen Sophia.

…fail again, and I will assume your loyalty is not with the crown.

The Under Secretary's dichotomy had been false. His feelings for Sophia were rooted in the same honor driving his work for the crown. Life would always be the priority. Life. Liberty. Love.

He may have failed so far, but Sophia had made him a better man. A stronger man.

He wrapped her foot.

Because he was a better man, he must help her rest while he did the hardest thing he would ever have to do. *Leave.*

There would be sleep tonight, but not for him.

• • •

Earl Baneham's Rules for Winning
"GIVE NO GROUND TO THE SOFTER SENTIMENTS. VIGILANCE. ALWAYS VIGILANCE."

Sophia's heart had finally settled into a somewhat predictable beat, but like her hapless apron, the edges of her mind were fraying.

At least she was alive.

Alive, yes, but to what purpose? Only a few hours ago, she had sworn on her soul to tell Randolph the truth and confess she wanted more—a promise she now found naive.

She was being hunted by a killer. Vigilance should give no ground to softer sentiment—the most basic of all Baneham's rules.

But the rage screeching in her from the moment she'd laid eyes on her sister weakened when Elizabeth handed her the lamp. She had no call to promise Elizabeth she would try to remember all she had learned here.

Her older lessons—Baneham's lessons—would win out. They always did.

She searched her heart for the sense of peace she'd had when working—to no avail. In the last few weeks, she had thought to glimpse another way. And in the past few nights…

Randolph tended her on bended knee. He bandaged her foot with the gentlest of hands. Giving herself over to his care would be so easy…

Then again, his gentleness was costing him in spades. She could feel his heat, his frustration, and his anger.

He tied the bandage tightly around her wound. He held her ankle for a moment longer than necessary, and then he stood. He kissed her crown, running his hand down over her hair as if she were a child in need of comfort. His breath was deep and matched hers inhale to inhale, exhale to exhale.

Without warning, he broke away and moved back to the fire.

She watched his broad back, willing an answer to their future. None came. They had begun a journey together without a map or a specific direction. At night. Over mud-drenched, rutted roads. Without food. Or firearms.

…and their journey had somehow taken an even darker turn.

"Randolph," she said, "did you hear me say my attacker

was a woman?"

"Unlikely. Could it have been a boy?"

"No. She knew me by name and she said *this ends tonight."*

She had thought she had earned his trust. But withheld truths hung heavy in his posture. *Why would he try to make her doubt she'd seen her bastard sister?*

He rubbed his forehead. "The attacker fired first?"

"Yes."

Randolph's brow furrowed as if he were trying to order the nonsensical.

"Perhaps," she offered, "you could tell me what is going on?"

He returned to the hearth and stared down into the flames. "Like everyone else, I always assumed Kasai was Turk or Mughal."

"Something has caused you to question your assumption?"

"The man at the madhouse," he stoked the flame, "suggested Kasai is English."

A sheet of fear passed through her body like a driving rain, flushing away the thought of her sister. Kasai was *English*?

"If Kasai is English," she said, "he could be here even now. He could even have been a guest at my soiree."

Randolph turned. "Yes."

"Who is this man at the madhouse?" she asked. "Can he be trusted?"

"His name is Garrett. Harrison believed he had pledged fealty to Kasai after being imprisoned. The Company said he was dead. He, however, says he was working for your father." He hesitated. "Trying to fix a problem Baneham had created."

"Baneham." Sophia covered her mouth. "How could I

not have made the connection?"

"What connection?"

"I knew of Elizabeth's farm because I traveled with Baneham to the village just a few weeks before his murder."

Randolph exhaled hard. "Which lends credence to Garrett's story. Did Baneham tell you anything—leave you anything—that might have explained his work?"

"You accused me of hiding such before," she said. "The night he was murdered, his study—my study now—was ransacked. I suspected there may have been something, but I found nothing. Then again, Baneham was altered when he returned. Suspicious and frightened. I found nothing, but that does not mean something is not hidden."

Randolph paced. "Madness, the Company said. Baneham was not mad. He was uncovering a conspiracy."

"What will we do?"

His look was hard and unyielding. "You will rest. You must heal. Will you take something from Elizabeth's apothecary?"

She sniffed. "Of course not."

"Of course not." His half-smile was on his lips but not in his eyes. "Weak as it is, wheat tea will have to do, then."

He turned back to the hearth to pour water over the dried wheat he had placed in two copper cups. He handed her the tea with an odd, sad expression.

She wrapped fingers around the metal and leaned back. She took a long swallow of hot liquid. Wheat tea was always undrinkable but this cup was by far the worst. The nut-like bitter taste lingered on her tongue after she swallowed.

"When I get back to London," she said, "the first thing I am going to do is have cook serve us white soup with a proper cup of my most extravagant tea."

Had she imagined the pink tint to his ears?

He swirled the liquid inside his cup and watched the wheat settle. "Harrison is less than a day's ride. I will take you to the inn, meet with him, and we will make a plan."

"By *we*, you mean you and me."

Randolph took a sip from his cup. His Adam's apple bobbed as he swallowed.

By *we,* he had meant him and Harrison. "Randolph, I will accept nothing less than equal footing, since I already share equal burden."

"I know you are brave," he said without looking up.

His cheeks were wind-flushed from his time out-of-doors. If a master's chisel had carved him to her exact specifications, his perfection would have been no less. But, shadows had gathered beneath his eyes. Pinched skin marred the edge of his lips. This was draining him…as much as it drained her.

They were stuck. Without hope.

Then, in the dark and the muck and the pain and the mire, Elizabeth's light flickered. Why must she sink back to Baneham's level, when she and Hugh could rise—together?

Together they could fight.

Together they could win.

Together they could build something new.

The thought was so terribly marvelous, her head floated. What a pleasant feeling.

She conjured a vision of her home shimmering into the water of the Thames…the tall and stately windows, the gardens she had paid a fortune to tame and the gently sloping path to the edge of the river. But for the short sojourn with the dowager duchess, she had lived there all her life. Earl

Baneham had holdings in other places, of course, but she had been raised there—a child of London, a child of the river.

Their marriage contract had specified she could make her London home where she pleased.

"We can…" she hesitated. "What was I saying?"

Randolph frowned as if attempting to divine some message in the dried wheat. "*You* were about to agree to go somewhere you will be safe."

"No." No, that was not what she had been about to say. As a matter of fact, it almost sounded like he didn't intend… he didn't intend…

She blinked. "You want me, don't you?"

He sat down, placed his elbows on his parted knees and leaned forward, head bowed. "Tonight has changed things. Kasai has become bold. You will be better off with the Furies at the Dowager's."

The Furies…? She frowned. Was he sending her to the *Furies*? Why? When there were things they had to do. Both of them.

"You…you," she stuttered, "need my help." She forced the sentence—or, at least she tried.

She heard her voice as if through a closed oak door— slow and slurred. He looked up. His sparkling eyes were two, then four, then two. He set down his cup, came to his knees by her side, and took her hand, awfully interested in a close inspection of her face.

He sighed. "Let us not quarrel tonight."

Even from far away, her response to his echoed words was visceral. He was placating her. Her father had placated her as well. *There is nothing to fear, Sophia.* But after her mother had died, he had begun to drill her in his damnable…

His damnable…

Rules.

Yes, "rules" was the word she needed.

Her memory jumbled—one image tossed upon the other like dirtied clothes lying in a laundry basket. Thought grew impossible; images, indistinct. She grabbed the handles of the chair in an attempt to steady the swaying room and blinked down into her cup.

One word rose in the soup of her mind. *Laudanum.*

"Randolph." She spoke his title as an accusation but it did little to assuage the pain.

He kissed her forehead. "I am sorry, sweetness."

Sleep's pull grew stronger and her eyelids drooped. She could not fight when he lifted her from the chair. She could not push him away when he cradled her in his lap. She made no resistance when, with gentle force, he guided her head to rest against his shoulder.

Somewhere beyond the pull of sleep she formed will enough to vow. She would rejoin her Furies, and recover.

Her muscles lost form. She could not raise her head, but she found the strength to finish the vow: Randolph wasn't as sorry as she was going to make him when she woke up.

Chapter Thirteen

Earl Baneham's Rules for Winning

"THINK ONLY OF YOUR AIM."

The carriage Randolph had ordered arrived at first-light's haze, just as he packed the last of their things. He lifted the silk nightgown from her valise, carefully re-wrapped it in paper, and tucked it into his bag instead.

Maudlin fool.

He could not help himself. He loved Sophia.

Seeing her as she'd been last night and knowing he was the cause had brought him to understand what she had been trying to tell him all along: she could not survive a return to Baneham's world. Not intact. Not the way he loved her.

If Sophia was not with child and *if* he defeated Kasai, for the sake of Sophia's happiness he would attempt to make proof of their marriage disappear. Once he retrieved those missing brothel records and could use them for persuasion— he bet his task would not be difficult. They had married by special license with the minimum number of witnesses. She had run less than a day after the vows. Society and his family remained in the dark.

…However, he'd be damned before he would leave behind the gown and forever imagine her wearing it for whatever pink-skinned, light-and-laughter, lucky-bastard *ass* she would choose to take his place.

Randolph helped the coachman load the meager sum of their things as quick and quiet as he could. After tightening the last strap, he returned to gather Sophia into his arms. Her breath did not alter—not as he left the farmhouse, not as they traveled within the carriage and not even when he settled her into an upstairs chamber at the inn.

She'd be furious when she awoke, as he would have been. Adding his entire vial of laudanum to her tea was bad—a dirty trick worthy of Baneham—but looking down at her tiny body laid out on the inn's best bed while knowing this would be the last time he saw her hair spread across a pillow…

Well, the pain renting his soul had to be punishment enough for his trickery. Fate might as well have taken a rusty saw to his gut.

Now she will never call me "dearest."

He sighed over her pillowed head, the accusation in her voice ringing in his ears just as sure as his neck tingled with the whisper of her soft breath. He tucked the inn's quilt around her body, and placed a swift kiss between her brows.

"You are *my* dearest sweetness. Always."

He reached down into his draining reserve and pulled away. He trudged down the steps with a cannonball nesting in his chest.

Now, get to the heart of the mission. He owed it to himself and to Sophia to see this through.

He entered the familiar rooms below. Harrison looked up from conversing with a young man.

"Randolph!" Harrison greeted. "Got tired of playing Quaker, did you?"

He would stick to the basics. "There was an attack last night."

Harrison's forehead creased. "How did you know?"

"About the attack on the farm? I was there."

Harrison and the man at his side exchanged glances.

"I thought," Harrison said, "you were referring to the attack on the hospital. Garrett was found dead this morning."

The iron ball in his gut took a roll. "Let me guess, a knife to the back and choked?"

The man at Harrison's side answered. "Exactly."

Randolph pinched the bridge of his nose. "Did anyone see anything at all?"

"No," Harrison said. "The last thing out-of-the-ordinary was your visit."

Randolph frowned. "I left Garrett hale and whole."

Harrison's man cleared his throat. "Did you?"

"We will speak alone, Harrison. Randolph pressed both fists on the table and leaned forward. "Now."

"Bronward, go to the farm." Harrison placed a steadying hand on the young man's shoulder and spoke with clear authority. "See what you can learn."

Bronward. Randolph knew the name from Sophia's parties, but he'd never worked with the boy before. When had he joined the mission?

"Wait," Randolph called. "Be careful of the girl named Anna. Allow the owner to give answers."

Bronward stiffened. "That is not how we work."

"How we work," Harrison said, "is deferring to those with more experience."

The man glared before he left. Harrison watched through the window and waited until Bronward disappeared into the stables.

"The spymaster's nephew," Harrison explained. "More eager than skilled, in my opinion."

"Why bring him in?"

"Favor for a favor," Harrison grimaced. "And the only way I could obtain permission to see Garrett."

The young man emerged from the stables and set off in the direction of Elizabeth's farm.

"He's corrupt, you know."

"Bronward?" Harrison asked.

"The Under Secretary."

Harrison shrugged. "Every politician is corrupt."

Randolph shook his head. "Not like this. You had better ready a drink."

Telling Harrison he'd likely suffered at the hands of his countrymen was not going to be easy...but it would be easier than anything else he'd had to do today.

"Go on," Harrison said.

"Garrett believed Baneham used the specter of a blood-thirsty mercenary to intimidate and divide enemies of the Company. Kasai was a creation of Baneham."

Harrison's breath hissed between his teeth. "The killings, the ambush, the brute, and the prison—I can attest those were real enough. You saw the bloody results of his attack."

"I did," Randolph said. "The ambush that ended your imprisonment was supposed to have been fake. Only it was not. Someone brought the fiction to life. Garrett did not see the man, but he is certain the impostor is English."

Harrison rubbed his forefinger along his lower lip. "Do you think Garrett's accusations have merit?"

"Garrett was murdered. Baneham admitted him to a madhouse owned by the Under Secretary just before he, too, was murdered. We have to treat it as a possibility. Whoever took on the mantle of Kasai is killing off those who can identify him."

"The targets are down to Lord Eustace and Helena."

"Or the plot runs deeper than we have understood."

"I suggest we start piecing this together," Harrison said. "When did the attack on the farm take place?"

"Late," Randolph surmised, "three or four hours past midnight. And the hospital?"

Harrison's lips formed a grim line. "Just after midnight."

"*Shit*—I led them directly to Sophia." Randolph paced. "The attackers could not have gotten far—the moon was intermittent."

"Sullivan," Harrison said, "believes they are headed back to London. He lost them a few nights back."

"Sophia swore a woman fired on her—it had to be Helena."

"Someone shot Sophia?" Harrison sucked in sharp. "Not Kasai's style."

"I have been thinking the same thing. Before Helena attacked, a man tried to abduct a woman he thought was Sophia."

"Lord Eustace?" Harrison asked.

"Maybe."

Harrison rubbed his chin. "If Helena is working for Kasai, why would she shoot Sophia?"

"Unless she had planned from the start to cross us both." He snorted. "*Helena* is Baneham's daughter."

"So," Harrison said. "Helena could be working toward her own end while Lord Eustace works to Kasai's." Harrison tilted his head to one side.

Randolph narrowed his eyes. "What are you thinking? I can hear your wheels turning."

"They are headed to London because they expect you and Sophia to head to London." Harrison shrugged. "Dangle Sophia and see who emerges."

"Absolutely not," Randolph said.

"You *already* planned to use Sophia as an enticement."

"That was," Randolph hesitated, "*before*."

"Lower your hackles, Randolph. I am not suggesting we put her directly in harm's way."

"Sophia stays *entirely* out of harm's way." He paused to think. "We can use the duke to draw out Eustace."

Harrison shook his head no. "You'll not dissuade Thea from her plan to protect the duke. Lavinia and Thea are planning a Fury soiree. And Lady Vice and Duchess Decadence will need Lady Scandal."

Randolph reconsidered the merit of locking Sophia in one of his turrets. He looked up to the rafters, following a crack in the wood of an ancient-hewn tree. He could fit his soul into the crack—that was how fast he was shrinking.

Think only of your aim.

Sophia must be protected—but Harrison was capable of that. Especially, if Sophia was with Harrison's lady. *Think only of your aim.* His *aim* was Sophia's happiness.

"You will make sure the Furies are protected." He fixed his gaze on Harrison. "*I* will draw out Helena."

"Can you do that?"

Randolph nodded. "I can and I *will* do that. *Anything* that will help end the threat to Sophia."

Harrison's gaze gleamed. "Wynchester owes me a cask of his finest brandy."

"Why is that?"

"You have fallen for your bride, my friend." Harrison chuckled. "I never knew farm labor could — what's the phrase — further the course of true love?"

Randolph flashed Harrison his darkest look. "I am not in the mood. Just promise me you'll make sure the Furies don't put themselves at any unnecessary risk. And take as much care with Sophia as you would with Lady Vaile."

Harrison stood. "I will take care of Sophia during the Furies soiree."

Randolph looked away. "See Sophia safely to London. I will finish here."

"You want *me* to see Sophia to London?" The chair scratched against the floor as Harrison pushed it aside. "Randolph…what have you done?"

"I made sure I am free to do whatever is required to put down a madman." Randolph rubbed his forehead. "She will be the devil to manage when she wakes. I suspect she will be more amenable to you than to me."

Harrison groaned. "What did you use? Laudanum?"

Randolph nodded.

"I am not yet married," Harrison continued, "But using opium to settle an argument strikes me as damn foolish."

"This is no lover's quarrel." Randolph faced Harrison. "I almost had Eustace. Then, I heard the shot…"

Understanding dawned in Harrison's eyes. "….and you

rushed back to Sophia."

Randolph clasped his useless hands behind his back. "I have to finish this. For her."

"Unfortunately, I understand." Harrison sighed. "And I also understand my cask will have to wait."

"You and your cask can go to hell. I will plan her route to London," he said. "Then, I will arrange a meeting with Helena."

When he left the inn tonight, he would carry her nightgown like a talisman and pray one day she would forgive him.

• • •

Earl Baneham's Rules for Winning
"IF YOU MUST TAKE COUNSEL, TAKE COUNSEL WITH THE BEST."

The carriage carrying Sophia back to London jostled along the cobblestone streets. Heavy curtains blocked her view. Her return had been cloaked in almost as much secrecy as her flight. And, since the moment in the cottage when she'd fallen asleep in his arms, Randolph had not dared to show his face.

Which was fine. She preferred his absence, actually.

The first day, she'd traveled with Harrison—in silence. Brick by brick she'd constructed a wall of anger, sealing each layer with visions of the spectacular verbal gutting she intended to give Randolph. Anticipation of his humbling had satisfactorily passed the hours.

…until that night.

The horses had needed rest. To avoid curious eyes, Harrison had arranged for them to spend the night with a female cousin of Lavinia's. When Sophia unpacked her bags, her gold and her jewels had been where she'd placed them — but not her indigo silk nightgown.

Right then, as if drained by the mysterious sucking draw of a bog, her anger vanished into something larger — foreboding. Why had Randolph taken her gown? If he'd expected forgiveness and reconciliation, he would have aimed to keep their physical affinity foremost in her mind.

In the morning, she sought to ask Harrison about Randolph's intent, but found her guard had changed. Harrison's jarvey friend Sullivan was to deliver her to the dowager. Thank God, she would soon be with the Furies. Perhaps they would know what she should do.

She set her head back onto the bench and listened to the shouts, and clanks, and squeals of the street. She had missed the city. Here, she was not so exposed. In London, *everyone* carried scars made by the vast, lively churn of life. Wounds too deep and raw to be hidden were so common, they carried no shame. The city was unpredictable, a never-to-be-solved-mystery whose only permanence was impermanence. Mired in the mess of her feeling for Randolph, she found the swirling chaos comforting.

As the carriage slowed, the scent thickened, the heavy ache in her heart eased.

Made safe from prying eyes by the high garden wall, the carriage entered the old Wynchester mansion mews. Sullivan dropped the stair, and guided her, cloaked and veiled, to the servant's entrance.

As she entered the stairwell, a squeal erupted from above. Sophia looked up to see Lavinia descending in a thunder of footfalls. With joyful exclamations, Lavinia bundled Sophia in her arms.

"I have been so worried," Lavinia said as they climbed the stairs.

A near-mad laugh gurgled up Sophia's throat. "So have I."

"And yet, you are here." Lavinia opened the door to the bedchamber containing the secret passage between the old Wynchester mansion and the Dowager's home. She turned and placed her cool palms on Sophia's cheeks. "Oh, love. You look worse than I feared."

"You needn't say," Sophia replied. "If my outside reflects my inside, I look a hapless mess."

Lavinia bit her lip. "Have you forgiven us, though?"

Sophia frowned. "Forgiven you?"

"Randolph did not tell you?" Lavinia felt the bookcase for the latch.

The door snapped open and swiveled.

"Lavinia," Sophia did not follow her friend into the passage, "tell me whatever it is you wish to confess. Now."

Lavinia's look was long and searching. "I am *so* sorry. Thea and I told Lord Randolph about the mail coach."

"Lavinia! How could you?"

Lavinia went pale. "Your life was in danger. Randolph insisted you did not understand the extent. He seemed…" she swallowed.

"He seemed *what*?"

"He seemed to genuinely care for you." She bit her lip. "Can you forgive us?"

Love shone through Lavinia's pleading eyes. Uncomplicated, thorough, committed love. Sophia knew Lavinia—and Thea—would do anything for her happiness and protection, even act contrary to her wishes. How could she not forgive her friends?

Sophia sighed. "I understand, dearest. Randolph used your worry to his own end."

A crease appeared in Lavinia's brow. "We would not have betrayed your confidence for anything less than risk to your life. I swear Randolph cares for you, Sophia. He *begged*."

Sophia's heart did a moth-to-a-flame flutter... Which she immediately stomped. "What do you mean, *begged*?"

"I mean," Lavinia leaned forward and lowered her voice, "throat cracking, skin flushed, muscles tensed, down on his knees *begged*."

"Impossible." He was a heartless, self-appeasing, laudanum-slinging wretch who had stolen her gown.

"I would not lie." Lavinia said.

"*He*, however, would. He would do anything to get what he wanted."

"What if what he wants is you?" Lavinia asked, in the same quiet voice.

"Then he is as ignorant as he is untrustworthy." Her quick quip hid the question's deeper effect.

Baneham was a friend. You are a friend. Randolph had said those words before they'd met each other in the depths of an almost mythic passion.

What if, like Lavinia and Thea, he thought he acted in her best interest when he had given her the laudanum?

Impossible. *Or was it?*

"Come," Lavinia pulled her through the passage, "Let us go find Thea and Emma, you can tell us all that transpired— and we can tell you what has happened here."

Bewildered, Sophia followed Lavinia into the Dowager's

home.

"I just had hot water prepared for tea," Lavinia said.

As Lavinia poured over already-prepared leaves, Sophia half-heartedly laughed.

"Will you taste it first? I find myself suspicious of tea."

Lavinia gave her a curious expression and she handed her a cup. "I took the leaves from my locking cabinet."

Sophia inhaled the richly complex scent. Fine dark tea, heavily sugared and topped with a dollop of fresh cream. *Just as she preferred.* She indulged a long draught; the tea slid over her tongue, sweet and bitter at once.

"I take one taste of what I have been without and everything I learned disintegrates."

Lavinia lifted a brow. "Are you talking about the tea?"

"Not just." Sophia's droll smile felt heavy on her lips.

The door swung open, revealing the duchess and the dowager. Sophia set down her tea as Thea rushed toward her with open arms.

"Dear, dear Scandal," Thea said, drawing Sophia close, "you have returned."

"To hear," Sophia said, "you betrayed my trust."

Thea drew back and eyed Sophia with her haughtiest Duchess expression. "As you are breathing and in one piece, I would say we did the right thing."

Emma, the Dowager Duchess and kind, former-madam, drew Sophia into a second embrace. "Harrison wrote you'd been hiding among Quakers." Emma laughed. "Now that is what I call a scandal."

"One former Quaker." Whose presence she already missed. "The others were a mottled collection of humanity."

"Fascinating." Emma invited them all to sit. "Tell us more."

Sophia made a quick tale of her flight—the disguises, the stops, the encounter with Polly.

"Yes," the dowager said. "Polly has been acting as Thea's maid."

"Thank you." Sophia exhaled. "At least *someone* has benefitted from my folly."

She went onto describe the farm, the attack, and her unwilling ingestion of laudanum. When she finished, Thea and Lavinia exchanged glances.

Lavinia cleared her throat. "Are you sure you've told the whole?"

Sophia nodded.

"Well," Lavinia said, "What happened between you and Randolph before the attack and the laudanum is not quite clear."

Sophia raised her brows. "I know."

"Leave her be." Thea shook her head at Lavinia. "Not every man can be your Max. Randolph is a lying rogue and he deceived her—what more do we need to know?"

Lavinia folded her arms. "Do you not remember Randolph's expression? He loves her—I would swear on my life."

Thea flashed an annoyed expression. "I will only admit he displayed genuine distress."

"I fear…" Sophia dropped her eyes to her lap. What, exactly did she fear?

"No matter what you fear, you are the bravest woman I know," Lavinia said. "You always said the earl wouldn't allow—"

"*Goddamn* the earl." Years of carefully locked frustration snapped.

Lavinia drew back in surprise.

"Sophia," Thea asked, "what aren't you telling us?"

"How much did Hugh" —Sophia cleared her throat— "Randolph reveal?"

Lavinia and Thea exchanged a raised-brow glance. "He said the man they called Kasai had agents seen in London and they would come after you."

Sophia rose from her seat and walked to the window. The bustle down below soothed. "True. The earl used his talent for ruthless diplomacy for the East India Company. He made enemies. What is more, Randolph trained under the earl."

"Ah," Thea said. "When Randolph said your father was in diplomatic service, he meant your father was a spy—and Randolph is a spy as well."

Sophia nodded. "I shackled myself to the embodiment of everything I loathe."

"Oh, Sophia," Lavinia said.

Sophia held up her hand. "No pity. *Please*."

"If pity you reject," Emma said, "How do you feel about action?"

Sophia turned. "I am listening."

"Wynchester's brother is alive," Thea said. "And Wynchester does not yet know."

Sophia cocked her head. "Lord Eustace? Alive? But how?" And why the hell hadn't Randolph told her?

Lavinia explained. "Max and Sullivan recognized Lord Eustace when they saw him at the brothel the night I went to confront that bastard who accused me of killing my husband. Lord Eustace was traveling as translator with an emissary of Kasai's. The emissary was later found dead."

"*Traveling* with Kasai's emissary? No one simply travels with an emissary of Kasai."

"Especially," Lavinia said, "when the emissary was the guard Max thought he had seen murder Lord Eustace."

"Staged death." Sophia's neck tingled. *If* Kasai was English, who was to say Lord Eustace was merely a translator…

"Will you tell me what you know of Lord Eustace's character?" she asked Thea.

Emma and Thea mirrored one another's dark expressions.

"Wynchester," Thea said, "was blind to Eustace's nature; I was not. Lord Eustace is without conscience or shame."

Sophia returned to the grouping of chairs to kneel eye-level with the duchess and dowager. "Is Lord Eustace smart and brutal enough to take on the identity of a butchering mercenary?"

Thea blinked, and then blinked again. "What are you saying, Sophia?"

"I am not saying; I am speculating." Her heartbeat sped nonetheless.

"There were," Emma wrapped her arms around her waist, "stories about Lord Eustace. Accusations made by the village children." Her eyes shadowed. "Horrible accusations, but never any proof."

"I knew none of that," Thea said.

"My duke," the dowager said, "paid reparations and asked for silence."

Thea took a deep breath and turned to Sophia. "Lord Eustace subjected me to sly taunts and subtle slander. One night, after I suffered a spectacular gaming loss, Lord Eustace accused me of theft—his word against mine. The theft was severe enough to force Wynchester to choose between his one, living heir, and the wife who could bear him his next. He sent Lord Eustace to India. But Wynchester never fully believed me—his choice was solely calculated on propagation of the name. Lord Eustace's death has haunted him."

"If Lord Eustace returns," Sophia said, "Wynchester will have his much-desired heir."

Thea nodded. "Between Wynchester's guilt about sending his brother to his death and the joy of his brother's miraculous restoration, I fear Lord Eustace will have Wynchester utterly at his mercy."

"And Lord Eustace," Sophia added, "will have access to the highest levels of government."

"I cannot allow Lord Eustace to influence Wynchester," Thea said. "We've been devising a way for me to return without thoroughly sacrificing my pride."

Sophia grasped Thea's hands. "Would you do that?"

"Should anything happen to Wynchester, Lord Eustace will become the Duke and both Emma and myself will be at his mercy."

"Yes, I understand," Sophia said, her gaze boring into Thea's. "But are you willing to return—for Wynchester's sake?"

The resolve in Thea's eyes dissolved. She looked as lost as Sophia had ever seen.

"Many would suffer with Lord Eustace at the helm of the dukedom. My fear cannot be the reason he wins." She swallowed. "I must try."

Sophia had always believed Thea and the Duke would come back together. Just a few days ago, her reaction would have been hopeful joy. Thea's bleak look was one she now understood. She'd felt the same the moment she'd become aware of the laudanum.

"I should tell you something." Thea took a deep breath. "The day the duke and Max dispersed the rioters outside

Vaile house, we kissed. It was" —she cleared her throat— "pleasant. But too much had happened for me to return. He acceded almost against his will to my request we stay with Emma. If I arrived, baggage in tow, a few days—or weeks— before he finds out about Lord Eustace, he would be more than a little suspicious."

"So," Lavinia picked up Thea's trailing explanation, "our idea is a Fury soiree. The duke will be invited and Thea will challenge him to a wager. She will do everything she can to let him win."

Sophia closed her eyes and leaned back against the chair. "I believe I should acquaint you with a pair of my father's dice."

The discreet knock of Emma's butler sounded on the door.

"Enter," Emma called.

"An afternoon report on His Grace has been delivered."

Thea straightened her skirts. "Go on."

"A morning appointment with his secretary. Entertained a minister of Parliament from Blackwood. Spent the afternoon at his club, and returned home" He cleared his throat, "readied for sleep."

"Drink," Lavinia mouthed.

"His plans for tomorrow?" Thea asked.

"A meeting with Lord Randolph is first on his schedule."

Randolph's name was a hot rod to Sophia' spine. "A meeting with Randolph? When?"

"Do not," Lavinia said, "even consider confronting Randolph. Wynchester will find out Thea is getting reports on his whereabouts."

"I've always received reports—to prevent the scandal of a public meeting. I've merely asked for more detail." Thea turned to the servant. "To know who is coming and going in your own house is only natural. Is it natural?"

The butler exchanged looks with Emma before answering. "No, Your Grace."

"That will be all for now," Emma said.

The butler nodded and backed out of the room.

"Do you wish to confront Randolph?" Emma asked.

Sophia sipped her tea to stifle an over-fast answer. He'd given her laudanum and sent her away without warning. Did she need any more evidence to prove he had not fully remade himself in Earl Baneham's image?

On the other hand, he'd taken her gown—a gesture revealing a surprising predilection to sentiment. What exactly was going on in his devious, plotting, unscrupulous, magnificently dear mind?

Lavinia turned back to the duchess. "Thea—if someone asked you a month ago whether or not Randolph would spend nearly a month on a Quaker farm, what would you have said?"

"I would have suggested the person toddle along straight to Bedlam."

"Randolph is a master of lies and subterfuge," Sophia said. *And tenderness and passion.*

Lavinia chimed in. "Perhaps he *had* to play a part for his mission."

Thea leaned forward. "Having good reason for an action, does not excuse a lack of character."

"I," Lavinia said quietly, "have actions to my name I would like to disown. Don't you?"

"We all do, dear," Emma said, patting Lavinia's knee.

"Your situation is different," Thea said.

"Different how?" Lavinia asked.

"Just different."

"Different," Lavinia challenged, "because you love me and because you seek to understand why I made the choices I made."

Why had Randolph made the choices he had made? Sophia felt a prickling feeling on her forearms. In her mind, she heard Randolph as if he were seated at her side: *I am in unchartered waters*. Perhaps he did not share the earl's bad qualities, but he shared the earl's weakness. She sat down her cup. *Her*.

Could it be—her heart swelled full and painful—Randolph had fallen in love? Could it be that by drugging her and sending her back to the Furies he thought he was answering her plea to let her go?

"I don't like the look in your eye," Thea said.

Emma glanced to Thea with a scowl. "Because you have not forgiven Wynchester, does not give you leave to encourage Sophia to share the same burden."

"Enough, Emma." Thea rose. "Excuse me."

Emma prevented Lavinia from rising as Thea left.

"I will go," Emma said. "If her return to Wynchester is to succeed, she must face things she has kept locked away." Emma turned a knowing gaze on Sophia. "To you, I will say love is a great deal of trouble. You are only in true trouble if love comes without challenge and sacrifice."

Sophia slumped back in the chair. If only she'd been right from the start. If only love did not exist at all.

Chapter Fourteen
Baneham's Rules for Winning
"ALWAYS LISTEN. ESPECIALLY WHEN THE ENEMY IS UNAWARE."

By Sophia's calculation, Randolph would be occupied with Wynchester for at least three hours. She had timed her visit to her home on the Thames accordingly. She'd come by barge, and two hulking footmen were stationed just inside the servant's entrance while the boat and oarsmen waited on the shore. Even if Kasai was watching, he would take no note of a grey-clad servant.

Her precautions had been unnecessary. The house was quiet and sealed. If her father's enemies intended to search the house again, they had not yet bothered. And, since her servants were to return tomorrow to begin soiree preparations, now was all she had. She shivered. Despite the outside warmth, weeks of neglect had taken their toll. The house was dark and damp.

She had done a great deal of thinking in the night—and

a great deal of planning, too.

Randolph had been wrong to drug her. *Very wrong*.

As she had been wrong to run. But when confronted with her folly, Randolph had said, *I almost understand*. She had decided she owed him the same courtesy. Her talk with Emma and the Furies had set her on the journey to understanding.

…And, the sights, so far, had not been comforting.

The only thing her long, restless night had made clear was a resolution to do everything she could to bring the Earl's twisted game to an end. Which meant—she placed her hands on her hips—if Baneham had hidden something in this study, she would find it today.

She fixed her gaze on the elaborate ceiling. When the earl had commissioned the house, cherubs were common décor. The earl had requested gargoyles. They grinned down in evil glee. After Baneham's death, she had been able to change the furnishings, but not the essence. The Earl was in every part of this house.

Every arch, every brick.

She had been so certain she would never leave this house. But was a home built to the earl's vision the legacy she wanted to give her heirs?

If she could create a home, it would be light and airy, comfortable and warm. And it would have nothing of the earl built into its walls. She felt the earl's house releasing its grip on her imagination. In its place floated the serenity she hadn't known she lacked.

Exorcising the earl, however, couldn't be fully accomplished with plans and resolutions. The hunt must commence. She worked the tinder and stone until sparks lit the char cloth within the small tin. She lit her candle from the flame and re-sealed the tin to smother the flame.

Strip by strip by strip she tested the floorboards—every one of them solid. She moved onto the window seats, the desk, the bookcases—nothing. She blew her hair out of her eyes and groaned. Hands-on-hips, she turned in a slow circle. What had she missed?

Her gaze shifted to the fireplace.

She tapped the wood around the mantle—it *sounded* solid. She leaned back and bit her nail. Baneham had designed this study. Wouldn't he have created an egress in case of danger? A hiding place, at the very least. She knocked against the wood, slowly making her way down the side—and, for an infinitesimally small space between the paneling and tile, the sound changed.

With some effort, she found the trick and opened the panel. On her knees, she could barely duck within. She frowned, uncertain she wanted to know what was beyond.

Then, the distinctive sound of horse's hooves sounded outside. Careful to keep herself hidden, she glanced into the courtyard. Charlemagne…and Randolph.

Her heart sunk.

…*so much for Thea's report.*

He dismounted, tied his horse, and strode toward the entryway. He walked with purpose, a man of specific intent.

Though curious why he had intentionally concealed his schedule, she was not ready to face him. She blew out the candle and set the holder back on the desk. Making herself as small as possible, she crawled into the hole. She took a deep breath and replaced the panel.

She would be fine so long as no one started a fire.

She would be fine, so long as she didn't sneeze from the dust.

She would be fine if she convinced herself the tickle against her arm was a stray hair and not a spider.

She closed her eyes hard, though the small space was already pitch black. She swallowed, straining to hear. Darkness flattened seconds into hours. When muffled voices approached, she wondered at first if she were imagining them.

But no. *Two voices*. The second was unidentifiable, but there were definitely two.

With silent breath, she pressed her ear to the panel. Randolph's companion, whoever she was, was female. *Helena*? What would Randolph be doing with Helena?

Closer. She willed. *Closer*. In her mind, she reeled them in as if on a string—a tenuous connection between her and them. *Concentrate. Concentrate…*

Then, the door gave a telltale swish over her new wool rug. The clear sound of Randolph's voice inviting Helena to enter rung in her ears.

• • •

Baneham's Rules for Winning
"IGNORE THE SPECTER OF YOUR SIN, NO MATTER HOW PERSISTENT."

Randolph sighed with relief when Helena's hack stopped beyond Sophia's gate. Until she emerged and began to move like a wraith through the slight mist, he had not been sure Helena would answer the summons he'd left with her former landlady.

Helena—Baneham's bastard daughter. Although they

had worked together, he saw her in a new light. Seeing her was like seeing a ghost…in more ways than one.

For a long moment they remained fixed in their respective positions—she at the foot of Sophia's entry, he at the top. Rage emanated from her like soot from a chimney. She lowered her hood.

"Helena," he greeted.

"Helle," she answered. "I have grown to like the name. Brings to mind the place my father sent me."

He swallowed, internally shaking off her accusation. His guilt had made him vulnerable to her deception. He could not allow guilt's gateway to open again. He had brought Helena here so the loss and speculation would keep *her* off balance, not him. And he had brought her here to force her assistance.

"Shall we go in?" he asked.

She swept past him as if she owned the place. And, had Baneham married her mother, she may very well have. Her attempt to dominate the space revealed much.

…A deal could still be made.

He turned to find her staring up the stairs to the balcony above. The morbid glint in her eye revealed the nature of her thoughts.

"Yes," he said. "As I understand it, this is where Baneham died."

She inhaled quickly, and then exhaled long and slow. "Pity."

"Shall we proceed to his study?"

An unholy ice-smile graced her lips as he led her to Baneham's study. He used the tinder he carried to light candles, one by one. Something in the air was off—but he could not place his unease. The window vestibules were empty—no one hidden in the curtains. Surreptitiously, he checked beneath the desk. *Nothing.*

"I am waiting," Helena said.

"Come, Helena," he said softly, seeking a way to soothe her hate. "Let us come to an accord."

"Randolph, Randolph, Randolph." Her voice transformed to a cat-like purr. "How quickly you have forgotten your training. You are supposed to court the enemy, draw them under your spell."

"I have forgotten nothing," he said flatly.

"I hope"—she circled him while running a finger across his chest and back—"that includes what you did to me."

"I followed orders." The excuse was not enough to save his soul, but it let him sleep.

Helena snorted. "At first, Baneham's games were fun, weren't they? You had the world at your fingertips. Money. Power."

"I had both before Baneham. I have both now he's gone."

"One can never have enough. *Never.*"

Once, he might have agreed. But if Sophia were happy and safe, he swore on his soul he would not ask for more. His eyes wandered to Baneham's portrait. By placing Sophia in his care, had Baneham known Randolph would ceaselessly continue the fight against Kasai?

Of course Baneham had. He, too, had been Baneham's pawn.

"I serve his majesty," Randolph said. "*Ideals*, Helena. Not wealth. Not power."

Her laughter trilled, high and bitter. "You serve yourself, as do all of Baneham's boys." She crossed her arms. "I suppose you have a proposition for me. What, I wonder, will you propose in service to your *ideal*? From my vantage, you have nothing to bargain. You want my records—the real ones I took from the brothel."

"*Your* records? They were the property of one Lord Montechurch and, since the man is deceased, they are now the property of the crown."

Her eyes flashed. "They are mine."

"How so?"

She lifted her chin. "Debt paid."

"Did Montechurch owe you a debt?"

"Montechurch sold those records to Kasai's emissary. *He* owed me a debt."

"So," Randolph said, "you took the emissary's life and his papers?"

She lifted her brows and he realized, too late, his mistake. She had not been the killer.

"Bloodthirsty and greedy." She looked down at her gloves and smoothed the fitted leather over her fingers. "All in the work of a day."

She would dance this little dance until he could no longer remember his purpose. He began to slice to the heart of the matter.

"Who murdered Baneham? And do not tell me you don't know."

"Of course I know." Helena tilted her head to one side. "You killed Baneham."

He sucked in through his teeth. "You know that is not true."

"What happened is irrelevant. What's in the records is what matters."

Randolph frowned. "The brothel records?"

"Those…and more." She grinned—a fiendish version of Sophia's light-hearted smile.

"I *never* went to the brothel. Not as a customer."

"Oh but you were there, weren't you?"

He snorted. "I was there because the Under Secretary asked me…" *Ahhh.* The truth slid through him cold and serpentine. "The Under Secretary asked me to watch Montechurch's movements."

"You are starting to understand now, aren't you?" She made a pitying face. "That's not what the records say. You know, the records you paid me to steal. The Under Secretary is anxious for you to face retribution for your treasonous acts."

Randolph's cold blood rushed in his ears. "The Under Secretary is the rat. I never paid you."

Her lips spread; her eyes twinkled. "Perhaps you should have."

"What do you want, Helena?"

"Why should what I want make any difference?" she asked.

"You can help me," Randolph stated calmly. "While you still have the real records, you can help."

"Tell me—in detail, mind you—what you will risk for the real documents?" She lifted her head and her gaze locked on his. "You and Baneham took my life, Randolph. So your offer had better be commensurate."

"I tried to free you," Randolph said. "Over and over I tried."

"Forgive me for not being overwhelmed by your kindness. After all, you delivered me in the first place."

Randolph side-stepped the rush of guilt and fixed his mind to his end. "Helena, you were a willing participant in

Baneham's game."

"Is that what Baneham told you? Or is that what you told yourself to ease your conscience?"

Both. "You are hale."

Her eyes flashed. "How would you like to be forced to serve in Kasai's private harem?"

"Harem?" He chuckled. "You and I both know Kasai is English."

Helena eyes grew wide, then she smiled. "Clever. But late. The records say you are Kasai."

The sensation within was like nothing he'd ever experienced. Life, draining through a sudden chasm in the earth. Garrett's voice echoed in his ears.

…it is already too late—for me, for you, for Baneham's daughter and for England.

He grabbed Helena by her shoulders. "Another *lie*."

"Yes," she purred. "And don't think I fail to recognize the murderous glitter in your eyes. Killing me will not stop what Kasai has planned."

He lowered his lids. He settled his breath. She was toying with him.

He'd watched Baneham burst with firework-rage more times than he could count. With each spitting performance, Randolph's resolve to command his person at all times had grown. *The greater the threat, the greater the calm required.* Randolph's rule number one.

He steadied his breath. He lidded his eyes. He engulfed the churning puddle of rage and fear with a deeper sea. He could contain the tide. Control it with a subtle pull, like the moon commanded water.

"I grow tired of your games, Helena," he said. "You

aren't working toward Kasai's ends. If you were, you would not have come. And if you were, you would not have tried to shoot your sister."

A growl-like hum emanated from Helena's throat. "That coddled bitch is *not* my sister."

Randolph stretched the silence like netted cloth. Hands clasped behind his back, he circled Helena as she had circled him. "You and she share Baneham. You inherited his guileful cunning, she his fortune and this house."

"She is nothing," Helena said.

"Nothing to you. Everything to Kasai. To Kasai she is *entre* into society…wealth and connections and this magnificent city mansion."

"He wants me, not her."

"Perhaps. But he will act according to his greater advantage." Randolph stopped at the point in his circle where he had started—directly in front of Helena. He tilted his head. "He may bed you, but he will marry her fortune."

"He will *not*." Helena slapped the table so hard it rattled.

"You know he will, Helena."

She gritted her teeth. "He cannot. Not if she is dead."

He *tsked*. "Remember the rules. Keep the larger objective in sight. You want Kasai. He wants," he spread his arms wide, "all of this." He fixed on her eyes. "Both of you can get what you want. Sophia does not have to die."

Helena squinted. "What could you possibly offer me?"

"You have not been listening," he said. "I can give you all that should have been yours."

"For what?" she asked.

"For Sophia's life. And for the real records."

She became far too still. "Kasai would kill me."

"Yet you tried to kill Sophia the other night. Would he welcome that bit of news?"

Her eyes flashed, but she remained silent.

"He wants Baneham's fortune. If Baneham's fortune were in your hands, you would have power over him." He tilted his head. "That is what you truly want, isn't it? You don't actually *care* for Kasai—you just do not want to be discarded when the time comes. Relinquished without a second thought—just like what happened before."

She inhaled. "How are you going arrange to give me all of this?"

How did one trick the devil's handmaiden? With the truth. "Kasai has planned for me to take the fall because he has discovered that I now stand in his way."

"Because you are a brilliant spy?" Helena asked derisively.

"No. Because Sophia is my wife."

He reached into his pocket and took out his copy of the special license. She examined the paper, frowning. "Everything she owned now belongs to you?"

He nodded. "Helena," he said, "understand this: I will bring down Kasai, I do not care if he is, as I suspect, the Under Secretary himself. This desperate attempt to frame me will fail. And you will suffer for your complicity. I am offering another way—help me and not only will you remain free, you will have your father's legacy."

"All this?" she asked. "For the real records?"

"All this," he answered. "All that should have been yours."

"If you believe Kasai's plot against you will fail, why offer me this?"

"Because," Randolph said, "with your help, I can put a quick end to the threat against Sophia."

Helena's gaze scoured his eyes. "Good God, Randolph."
A look of horror froze her features. "You *love* her."

"Yes." The truth was, this time, his final resource. "I love my wife."

She eyed him as if he were a grotesque fiend on display for her pleasure. Perhaps he was. He hadn't been truly surprised that Kasai planned to frame him. When he'd married Sophia, he'd become a target.

What Kasai had not anticipated were the Furies...their devotion to each other and the devotion of the men who loved them.

"Baneham called love weakness." His voice started low but grew in strength and power. "Love is the opposite. I have the strength of a legion of mercenary bastards. I will be *damned*," the last word echoed out into the empty halls, "before I let *anything* happen to Sophia."

"I hate Sophia," she said.

"So give her the worst punishment you can imagine—a life with me."

She snorted—harsh and unwilling—before shaking her head in disbelief.

"*If*," she said, "I decide to take you up on your offer, where would I deliver the records? And when could I expect the deed?"

"Deliver the records here—tomorrow night, just before dawn, and you will have your deed at once."

"I will consider your offer."

She lifted her hood back over her head and disappeared back into the growing gloom.

He shivered with his proclamation's force. He did have the strength of a legion. He would match Kasai wit to wit, sinew to sinew. He would win.

He set his hand down onto the desk and jerked back when his finger sunk into a spot of still-warm wax…beside a candle he had not lit.

• • •

"When nothing makes sense, reach out from your heart."
~Sophia Baneham Countway, Lady Randolph

Sophia remained within the secret panel longer than necessary. Nothing but darkness existed, eyes open or shut. Curled into a ball and resting her cheek on her knees, she had no cue for direction but the unseen floor. There, in the dark, she examined the puzzle pieces she possessed.

One. Kasai—whoever he was—planned to lay ignominy and ruin at Randolph's feet.

Two. To save himself, Randolph had offered all that was hers.

Three. Her sister, however wronged, was as soulless and ruthless as her father had been.

This grouping of three called out for her anger, distrust, and fear.

In Cimmerian solitude, she started a shell game with those pieces. Carefully, she felt rather than thought through each, one at a time. And then she rearranged, and felt through the pieces once again. An answer eluded.

She wove in three more pieces to her dark game.

Four. Randolph had given her laudanum and sent her away.

Five. Randolph had stolen her nightgown.

Six. Randolph had admitted he loved her—*to someone*

else.

Together, her mind-shells made a six-pointed star, a distant light to guide her through the darkness. *Love at war with darkness.*

But was the North this grouping led to true or false? What did she or Randolph know of love? She thought of her mother, waving Sophia away, to pine in wasting solitude for Baneham. She thought of Baneham warning, *Kasai will come for you*, his eyes crazed and fingers biting into her arms.

She laid these images aside and chose the shell that hid her pearl.

Randolph declaring, *I love my wife.*

Love *did* exist. Not the kind of selfish love that had caused her mother to wallow. Not the kind of possessive love that caused Baneham to stutter and rage. Sophia's love was a coin stamped on one side with Emma's challenge, vulnerability and sacrifice, and on the other, with Elizabeth's soul-healing light. *Thee will remember what thee has learned.*

She remembered. She remembered the idea that had taken hold just before the laudanum. She need not be taken back down into Baneham's darkness; together she and Hugh could be lifted by love.

"Hugh," she whispered into the gloom.

She started the game again.

One. Hugh loves me.

Two. I love Hugh.

She stitched both ideas—bright and pulsing—into and around her heart until the perception taken from her returned. She saw Hugh through her heart: flawed, passionate, arrogant, and yet beautifully, consummately devoted.

She lifted her face. There was hope.

She stretched out her arms and pushed open the panel. A familiar face was silhouetted against the light.

"What an interesting place to rest." Hands on his knees, Hugh peered inside her hiding place. "Come out so we can have a proper row."

As always, she could not read his intent.

"I'll emerge with pleasure." Rather inelegantly, she scooted from the crawlspace. "A moment, please."

As her eyes adjusted, she shook out her skirts. A cloud of coal soot misted down over her lovely carpet of pink, ivory, and gold. It didn't matter. Nothing mattered but Hugh's answer to the tale she had promised to tell the day he'd gone to the madhouse.

Bring him home so *I may tell him the truth about our wager and show him I care.*

Hugh. Her North. Her star.

She would have preferred to wait—wait until the transformation had become solid, wait until her senses and her wit sharpened. But she had only now. Now, when he expected *a proper row*.

Not quite ready to face him, she used her foot to swing the panel closed.

The latch failed to click; the panel bounced back. She swung it again. The latch failed a second time. She kicked yet again. *Hard*.

A nasty, screeching noise sounded above her and the gargoyles' leering face broke free.

Hugh's arm hit her chest and she was yanked back. The gargoyle smashed the spot where she had been standing. Hugh held her back to his chest, both of them breathing heavily. She blinked to clear her confusion.

"Look." He released her and pointed to the ceiling. "Something is there."

Even at his height, he could not reach the opening.

"Lift me," she said.

His features knit into an expression of concern.

"I won't fall," she assured.

"*That*," he replied, "was not my primary concern."

Reluctantly, he put his hands to her waist and lifted. Steadying herself with a knee to his shoulder, she grasped the piece of panel and pulled—the panel extended into a box. When she had the box grasped against her chest, he lowered her slowly and gently to the floor.

"You can let go," she said.

"Right."

She placed her prize on the desk. Flushed from exertion, they both stared at it as if they had found a living creature.

"Deeds, perhaps," she said, knowing it was not.

She retrieved a book page cutter from her desk and worked to open the lid. Sheaves of paper curled like bonnet ribbon within the box. Hugh lifted one out and let the scroll fall to the floor. It was dotted with letters and numbers, seemingly at random.

"What is it?" she asked.

"A code. I won't know what it says until I find the key."

"It's written in his hand," she said.

"Yes." He squinted. "Yes, it is."

"His notes perhaps?" she asked.

He nodded. "All I can make out are dates. Is there anything else in the box?"

Sophia carried the box to the window to better catch the

fading light. She examined the stitching in the velvet lining. Poorly done. She loosened the thread and carefully picked out the stitches. She lifted the lining and gasped. The most beautiful jewels she'd ever seen lay within.

"Sapphires," she breathed.

Randolph joined her at the window. "Have you seen them before?"

"No." She frowned. "They are very good quality—I've rarely seen the like. They must be worth a fortune."

"May I take them?"

She eyed him askance. "So you can give them to Helena?"

He grimaced. "So I can show them to Harrison."

"To Harrison, not to the Under Secretary?"

"The Under Secretary could be Kasai."

She raised her brows. "Lord Eustace could be Kasai."

He audibly inhaled. "Damn." He bit his bottom lip as he considered. "Lord Eustace *could* be Kasai. The fact remains: I cannot trust anyone but Harrison."

"Does that," she asked softly, "include me?"

Her heart beat in her throat while she waited for his answer. The moment was a boulder in the sand. With the right strength, the mottled footprints the past few two days could be covered.

"No," he said finally. "Despite your coal-cupboard theatrics, I trust you."

She placed the box on the settee where Hugh had so often lounged, watching her work with his wolf-eyed stare. She prepared to confront him. If she did not do so now, she would lose her courage.

"Please," she gestured to her desk chair, "sit."

He hesitated.

"I have a few questions I would like to ask." She smiled sweetly. "I won't bite." Remembering his shoulder's taste, she swallowed. "I won't bite, right now."

He flashed a wary look and sat.

"You bargained for your life with what is mine," She tapped her finger against his lips in a gesture that silenced anything he would have said. "If you were a man like Baneham, I would believe you married me to deliver Baneham's legacy to Helena…, not just to save your life, or mine, but to assuage your conscience."

"You knew about Helena," he said.

"Yes," she replied. "Though I did not know for certain that the two of you were acquainted. I am disappointed you did not confide in me."

He flashed a guilty glance. "I should have told you. Regardless, you must realize I made a false bargain with Helena. Our marriage documents are clear—I cannot dispense of your property without the express permission of your trustees, and you know they would never grant permission without your leave."

She ignored the obvious. "If you must have one of Baneham's offspring, why not choose her? She knows, plays, and loves, your game."

He frowned in a way that communicated just how absurd he thought her suggestion.

"Baneham's game is not my game."

"Isn't it?"

He shook his head no. "Helena is a means to an end."

"Am I also," she swallowed, "a means to an end?"

He ran his hand through his hair. His incredibly thick, soft hair. "No. The reason," he flushed, "I gave Helena was true."

He loves me.

The confirmation of her suspicion rushed around her like warm water. Ah, but she wanted to tell him she loved him, too. She took a deep breath and forced herself to be coolly rational.

"There is," she said, "a craggy path between here and there."

He could not give away what was hers by right; she had realized that in the process of her shell game—just as she had realized so much more.

"What are you going to do?" he asked.

She leaned back and drew her finger across her lip. "I will trust you with Baneham's notes and the sapphires, only if you continue to answer me honestly."

He agreed with a slow nod.

"All of Baneham's men committed some atrocity. What was yours?"

His brow furrowed in honest befuddlement. "Baneham sought me, not the other way around. He required no test."

She voiced the suspicion that had been growing for some time. "So, Baneham meant you, from the start, for me."

With a groan of reluctance, he nodded again. "…But then he discovered you had secretly married. I proved myself valuable when Kasai's attacks grew worse. He kept me on."

She closed her eyes. *Oh, Father.*

An ache throbbed in her chest—an ache not hers but Baneham's. She'd been his unintended weakness. A weakness he did not understand and could not afford. So, he'd plucked her a shiny soldier and had planned to plant him at her door.

She opened her eyes. Hugh came into focus in a new light. He'd never been one of Baneham's boys. He'd been the wall Baneham had built between his daughter and his enemies.

Ridiculously, she wanted to laugh.

She and Hugh had been brought together by Baneham's darkness. Could they still be joined together by Elizabeth's light?

"Have you spoken to Harrison this morning?" she asked.

Randolph shook his head no.

"Tomorrow evening," she continued, "the Furies will hold a Soiree."

"Here?"

She nodded.

"I presume," he said, "this has something to do with the duchess's intended return to Wynchester?"

Sophia kept a close eye on her husband. "Thea challenged Wynchester to a wager. The game will involve four throws of a single pair of dice. When she loses, she will return home for the summer. If all goes well, she will stay."

"Dice? You said *when* not *if* the duchess loses…?"

"I did," she confirmed. "Which brings me to the crux. You told me Baneham was a man of honor."

"I confess," he sighed, "discovering Kasai was his creation has tested my trust. But the ends *can* justify the means."

"So you still believe he lived by his own sense of honor?"

"Yes."

"A man of true honor would never cheat."

"No."

She stopped speaking and listened to the silence. No fire. No servants. No one to break the moment but she and Randolph. The hush gave her courage. Most of the crucial moments in her life had not been of her choosing. This one, she would force.

"Open the top drawer on the right. You will find a pouch with Baneham's dice."

He retrieved the pouch and tossed contents on the table. Frowning, he lifted them and tossed them again. And again. And again.

"Weighted," he whispered.

"Yes," she confirmed. "The odds of rolling a seven are quite good."

"These belonged to Baneham?"

She nodded. "He bid my first husband to use them the night he was killed in a duel."

Randolph rolled the dice in his palm. "Corruption, lies, and blood."

"On every level," she added.

"He used me." Randolph's frown deepened. "He knew I would not let his fight rest."

"He used you." Her eyes softened. "His only act for which I am grateful."

He looked up. His intent gaze quickened every sense.

"Allow me," she continued, "to paraphrase another ruthless man: to estimate the intelligence of a ruler, look at the men he has around them."

"Is that a compliment?"

"That depends," she stood and reached out, "on you."

He stared at her hand as if she held poison. "Please don't."

"You don't want me?"

"I want you, sweetness. But I cannot have what I want." His voice cracked. "You were right. A return to Baneham's world would destroy you. I cannot drag you there."

Her heart turned to liquid—soft, hot and churning. "Why

did you fill my tea with laudanum and send me away?"

His eyes went to his hands. "Because you deserve better."

Ah. The dear man. The dear, stupid, terrified man. "Who will I find better than a man who finds me the most desirable woman in the world?"

He leveled his gaze. His eyes had grown red. "You heard Helena. *She* is a child of *The Ruthless*. If you stay with me, then you—"

"If I stay with you," she interrupted, "I will be as I always have been…and possibly even more."

His jaw flinched, but he made no other movement. "Sophia… the Under Secretary is Kasai or he is working for Kasai, but," he inhaled sharp and quick, "before we take him down, you can use his influence to your benefit."

She did not like his tone. "What do you mean?"

"The Under Secretary *offered* to have all evidence of our marriage removed. You could be free of me. The records would simply disappear."

"I see." Sophia's throat dried. "And if the Under Secretary is Kasai, he will come after me as soon as I am free."

His eyes grew dark and fierce. "I will keep you safe, no matter what."

"And if," Sophia said slowly. "I do not wish to have all the records disappear?"

His red eyes blinked. "Are you with child?"

"It is still too soon to tell." She watched him—God help her—with hawk eyes. "Would you like it to be so?"

His shoulders slumped. He turned away. She summoned all her strength to keep herself from kissing the wet mess that leaked from the corners of his eyes.

"I should not want it to be so." His voice was hoarse and troubled. "I *have* to leave so you can have a chance at happiness."

Thea was right. Men were thick as a medieval Scotland keep's walls. She walked to his chair and gripped each arm, hovering above him like, well, a vengeful Fury.

"I forgive you for the laudanum and the deception. But underestimating my character and intelligence? Now that is truly beneath you."

He looked up, wet eyes so deep she could swim.

"I love you," he whispered.

Her heart cracked. "The Randolph I know would not give up with such ease," she said, rephrasing the words he had used against her. "The Randolph I know would fight for me."

"How?"

"Publicly claim our marriage and protect us from those who would see us divided."

He whetted his lips. "What if I destroy you?"

"Damn Baneham. I give you Machiavelli: never was anything great achieved without danger." She smiled, faint and small. "Even ruthless bastards have occasional insight."

"You cannot," he said, "convince me you wish to be shackled to me for life."

"Can't I?" She lifted the dice from the table opened his palm, and placed them within. "You have seen these dice before."

He frowned. "Did the Furies use these at your soirees?"

She smiled and stepped back. "Ask the right questions, Hugh."

He looked up into her eyes. "Have *you* ever used these?"

"Only once." She inhaled. "To lose a wager so that I

could win you, instead." She picked up her cloak and wound it around her shoulders. "I thought marriage would protect me. My mistake was believing my ravenous needs were only of my body. They are also of my heart." She tied her cloak at her throat. "My mother withered as she fed false hope to a loveless marriage. I am not like either of my parents. And yet I am like them both. I expect you to choose me, Hugh. I demand all of you. Understand?"

He nodded in awed silence.

She leaned down and inhaled. She drew her cheek close enough to his for the warmth beneath his skin to demand a corresponding blush in hers. His scent coiled through her chest and held her still as if he were burning frankincense and she in prayerful contemplation. Her body had chosen him first, then her heart, then her mind. Now, she wanted to wrap them both together in a marriage beyond earthly vows.

She exhaled.

Every part of him pulsed his answer. *Love*. Pure and heartbreaking, an abrasion with the pain and power to heal.

He had chosen her body, heart, and soul—but his mind continued to wrestle for the most noble and poignant of reasons: He wanted better for her.

"Claim me, Hugh. Claim me so we cannot be undone."

She would have to leave him in the darkness to grapple with uncertainties in a shell game of his own. Her eyes had grown as wet and red as his. She pressed her lips against the stubble-laden skin beside his ear.

"Goodnight, dearest," she whispered.

Chapter Fifteen
"No matter the heartbreak, hold your head high."
~Thea, Duchess of Wynchester

Sophia's white petticoats were encased in cerulean skirts tucked up in a la Polonaise fashion and edged with a thin strip of indigo silk. Her back-laced bodice had gloves and fichu to complement, and into the ribbons of her hair she'd donned her version of *a fanciful array of ostrich plumes*.

…A fine ensemble for triumph or for heartbreak, whichever was to come.

Hosting a soiree when Lavinia had not yet observed the full year of mourning for her estranged husband *could* have been perceived by the Furies guests with disdain. Instead, the crowd was jovial and the coin flowing. No one, apparently, missed the late Lord Vaile.

Donning a slightly more respectable air, the Furies forwent the winged-costumed maids. And, in addition to the usual refreshments, footman served sugar-paste baskets with jewel fruits.

Sophia had not thought of Hugh's weakness for all things sweet when she'd ordered the fruits. Not at all.

…Just like she was not thinking of him now.

She glanced again to the door. Where *was* he?

As if called by the uncertainty expanding like a rising loaf of bread inside Sophia's mind, Lavinia appeared at her side.

"Here you are," she said with excessive cheer. "A refreshing draught of champagne for my sweet Scandal."

Sophia grasped the glass and drank deep.

"Huzzah to our Scandal!" A man yelled from a nearby table. "Drink to her health."

Sophia lifted her empty glass in acknowledgment before placing it on the tray of a passing footman.

"Another?" she asked.

"I think not," Lavinia answered.

"Drink does not affect me," Sophia said.

Lavinia raised her brows. "Because you are not prone to drinking full glasses all at once." She patted Sophia's arm. "I know this is difficult, but, for Thea, you must remain strong."

Sophia bit her lip. "How is our Duchess Decadence?"

"Showing an appalling lack of decadence, as a matter of fact."

They leaned to the side in unison, to get a better look at Thea. The duchess dominated the space with a coral-red gown embroidered with black beads. The beads shimmered when she moved. Her smile was serene…and completely faked.

"Oh dear," Sophia breathed. "Is she losing?"

"In buckets," Lavinia replied.

"We must step in."

Lavinia sighed, "I suppose we must."

Bronward, who was playing Thea, let out an ungentlemanly whoop. Thea sat back into her chair, pale and shaken. That she'd even deign to let her back touch a chair in mixed company was troublesome indeed.

"Come Lady Vice," Sophia took Lavinia's arm, "let us rescue the duchess." Sophia swayed her way through the crowds—pausing to give particularly loyal guests a watered version of her famous smiles. Her heart was no longer into mindless flirtation.

They arrived at Thea's table. Sophia congratulated Sir Bronward on his win, while deftly evading his questions and maneuvering an unwilling Thea to her feet. "Come, dearest, I would like your opinion on the most delightful figurine Lavinia has given—"

She lost her words as two new arrivals paused on the threshold.

"The Duke of Wynchester," her butler announced, "and Mr. Maximilian Harrison." The duke had forgone his usual wig, and his black locks hung in wild disarray. He leaned heavily on Harrison's arm.

An expectant hush came over the assembled men.

"Where is she?" Three, short words and the duke could not hide his slur. A moment later he gestured in the Thea's direction. "There she is!"

"He is drunk," Lavinia spoke in an astonished whisper.

"How," Thea breathed, "how the mighty have fallen."

"Let us hope," Sophia modified the rest of the verse, "his weapons of war also perished."

Grim-faced, Harrison led Wynchester to Thea.

"You, duchess," the duke said, "promised me a game."

Thea blinked rapidly, but flashed a duchess-y smile. "Indeed I have," she replied. "We shall retire to Sophia's study to play."

A murmur of disappointment swelled within the room.

Sophia assessed her guests with a stern expression. "Oh come now. Duchess Decadence has already provided ample entertainment for one evening."

She turned to heed an amusing exchange between the duke and duchess and smiled. She kissed Thea's cheek and whispered, "Good luck, dearest."

Thea returned the kiss with a *well-here-I-go* look in her eye. "Randolph will come," she assured. "Shall we, Duke?" Thea took a deep breath, threaded her arm through Wynchester's and led him toward the study.

"Do not think," he slurred as they disappeared into the crowd, "my state will give you an advantage."

Sophia glanced back to Harrison and Lavinia. "I don't like this."

Harrison made a low sound between a growl and a groan. "Agreed."

"I will stand by the door," Lavinia said, "in case she needs help."

Harrison gave Lavinia his arm. "I will join you."

Lavinia looked up at her lover, with an expression of gratitude and love so pure, Sophia's eyes smarted. She turned back to her guests and forced a smile. "Play on, Gentlemen."

The level of noise slowly resumed—not much could keep these men from their play.

"Scandal," the man who had toasted her called, "what do you say to a game?"

"Not tonight," she turned away from her fruitless stalking of the door and offered the man a conciliatory hand.

"You are stunning," the man grasped her fingers and kissed, "as always."

"Thank you." She retrieved her hand, uncomfortable with the gleam in the man's eye. "Now I really must be—"

"Come now, Sophia. Why not *play* with me." His tone suggested more than cards. "You played freely with Randolph."

A mortified blush crept up into her cheeks.

"Your expression confirms. But have no fear, consolation is my specialty." He lowered his voice. "And I assure you, my rod is as good as his."

"I do not," she said with a glacial glare, "appreciate your insinuation."

The man drew back. "I intended no offense."

Sophia swallowed her shock and lifted her chin. If Randolph chose not to claim her—she realized with a sinking sensation—this man's vulgarity was the least she should expect. Sly looks at best, and, more commonly, overt offers such as this. Her stomach lurched. How could she have been so careless?

She settled her shoulders. *Hugh will come.*

Then, as if by magic, the butler announced, "The Earl of Randolph and the Dowager Countess of Randolph."

Sophia's skirts swished as she swiveled.

Hugh appeared, as she had not seen him for weeks—a perfectly turned out courtier. He'd donned a gold-embroidered regal coat of red. Matching velvet breeches hugged his muscular thighs. On his arm, stood grace personified. Stately, tall, and dressed in the height of fashion, the matron's eyes—a perfect match to Randolph's winter-grey—searchingly swept the room.

Hugh leaned down and whispered something in her ear. Immediately, her gaze settled on Sophia. The man who'd propositioned her stiffened. Sophia's feet had grown roots;

she could not move as Hugh guided his mother across the room.

The lady lifted her quizzing glass and inspected Sophia.

Sophia turned her wide eyes on Randolph. "What are you doing?" she said under her breath.

"Fulfilling your command, my wish," his eyes twinkled, "and my duty. Once I told her of our marriage, her ladyship would not be denied."

The countess cleared her throat.

"Mother," Hugh said, "allow me to introduce my wife. Lady Randolph, my mother."

Chatter rose through the crowd as the implications of Hugh's announcement spread through the room. Sophia ignored the whispers and looked into the woman's eyes. Remembering how Thea held herself when she was uncertain, Sophia looked past the woman's stiff haughtiness. Within those eyes beat the heart of a mother. *A deeply apprehensive mother.*

"I have concerns," the countess said to Sophia. "Is there a need?"

Sophia wetted her lips and curtsied.

"No, my lady," she said softly.

The countess nodded and released Randolph. "Excellent choice, Randolph."

"Thank you." Hugh's lips broke into the widest grin Sophia had ever seen. "I will endeavor to deserve her."

The countess sighed. "I have been promised entertainment. You," she pointed to the man with whom Sophia had been speaking. "Escort me to the Faro table."

"Yes, Lady Randolph."

The countess turned her eyes on Sophia. "The *dowager* Lady Randolph."

The man guided the dowager countess away. Sophia nearly laughed aloud at the quake in his step.

"Ah, Hugh," Sophia smiled up at her husband, "that was…"

"Definitive?" he supplied.

"Very much so." She lifted a brow. "One might almost call it shocking."

"Another point for me," he quipped, refitting his gloves. He tilted his head and lowered his voice. "I am sorry to say, you have witnessed the countess at her most genial."

Sophia glanced to the dowager countess and back to Randolph, her heart as light as it had been in years. Perhaps even a decade. "I like her."

"Good." His eyes warmed. "You cannot change your mind now."

As a footman passed, he plucked a sugared basket from a tray.

"Sweets," he said. "You must have known I would come."

A blush crept into her cheeks. "I had hoped."

He placed the basket on the table and, heedless of chatter and shock, he took her into his arms. Her eyes fluttered closed, she lifted her lips…and then froze as the duchess's wail cut through the room.

Her eyes flew open. "Thea!"

The duke stalked past, knocking chairs, and people, and tables aside—his arms full of his furious wife.

"Put me down." Thea beat the duke's back to no avail. "Help!"

"You lost," the duke said. "That means you're mine—no negotiation."

"He has lost his *mind*," Sophia gasped and gave Randolph an urging push. "You must help her! Please!"

"Wynchester!" Harrison yelled.

Hugh sprinted toward the couple, reaching them inside the entry hall, just beyond the doors.

"Wynchester," Randolph said with dark intent, "The duchess has requested you *unhand* her."

"The duke," Wynchester replied, "declines."

"Wynchester," Harrison skidded to a stop on the hall's marble floor. "You are not yourself."

Sophia and Lavinia paused at the door, and continued a silent approach behind the duke.

"Put down your wife," Hugh growled.

Wynchester swung around, knocking Sophia off her feet. Lavinia caught the slipping Thea and drew her away. Hugh threw a neat punch; the duke went down with a stone-heavy thud. As Harrison bent over the duke, Hugh exhaled, straightened his coat, and attended a bemused — and perfectly hale, if rumpled — Sophia.

"A moment, sweetness." He turned to address the room beyond. "We request discretion," he said to the stunned guests, "A gentleman must defend his wife."

"Hear, hear," the dowager Countess of Randolph called as Hugh closed the doors.

Harrison and the butler bundled the duke and took him back to his carriage as Hugh helped Sophia up off the floor.

"How was that for an announcement?" he asked.

She smiled. "Splendidly scandalous."

"No," he said, "This is splendidly scandalous."

His lips moved over hers, hot with the promise of a lasting love.

• • •

Randolph and Harrison stood back while Sophia, Lavinia, and Thea conferred beside the duke's carriage.

"Well," Randolph said wryly, "wherever Lord Eustace is, he will know the duchess has returned home by morning. I daresay the duke will not remember very much."

Harrison snorted. "He will have half of London to remind him. I don't doubt this will make Grub Street. His drink had gotten heavier of late, but I had no idea. If I had realized how far gone he was…"

Randolph raised his brows. "…You would have called off the evening?"

"No." Harrison sighed. "I suppose it is for the best. If I know Wynchester, his mortification will override all other feeling. He prides himself on his level and steady reputation."

"That horse, I am afraid, has left the stall." Randolph stepped closer to see if he could discern what the ladies were saying. "The duchess at least, will have an easier time."

Thea raised her voice to speak to the duke's coachman. "Before he wakes, I want all spirits removed to the cellar and the cellar locked."

"With due respect, Your Grace," the coachman said, "there is none."

"Oh?" Thea asked. "I find that hard to believe." She leveled her gaze at the coachman. "I am mistress of the house, and I will find out if you are covering for him."

Randolph smirked. Thea in full duchess splendor was quite the thing.

"Yes, Your Grace," the coachman replied. "Will you be riding back?"

"No," she replied. "The dowager's carriage will bring me round in the morning."

They all fell silent as the coachman lifted himself up onto the carriage and cracked his whip. Wynchester's carriage rolled forward toward the gate. The coachman, Randolph surmised, was carrying the duke back to a house he knew but a life he would no longer recognize.

The ladies joined them in the relative privacy of the garden.

"So, you are still determined to go back to Wynchester?" Lavinia asked.

"Yes." Thea inhaled. "But that wasn't the Wyn I know."

"I should say not," Sophia said.

Thea tilted her head to one side. "In some ways, I like him better."

Lavinia stifled a giggle. "You are mad, you know."

"Unfortunately," Thea said, "not half as mad as the duke's brother."

"We are but a message away," Sophia said. "If you need anything."

The duchess placed one arm around Sophia and one around Lavinia. "You can count on me doing just that."

Randolph exchanged glances with Harrison, and they fell back.

"Any sign of Lord Eustace or Helena?" Harrison asked under his breath.

"No," Randolph said. "I placed agents among the guests, just in case. Sophia believes Lord Eustace is the one who is pretending to be Kasai."

Harrison stiffened. "If Lord Eustace is Kasai, he's played a brilliant part." His jaw twitched. "Any proof?"

"No. The Under Secretary seems the most likely candidate. But I intend to ask the Dowager Duchess of Wynchester about the man Lord Eustace had been before he disappeared into

Kasai's ambush." He was missing something very important, he was sure.

"Excuse me," Sophia interrupted. "I would like to speak with my husband."

"Of course," Harrison said and he slipped away.

Sophia took his hand, ran her fingers over his knuckles, and looked him in the eye. "Are you hurt?"

"From a single punch?"

She smiled. "So, it takes a great deal to topple the Earl of Randolph, does it?"

"You may rely on that." Randolph checked himself. "With the exception of one, petite countess with the voice of a temptress, the face of an angel, and the body of Venus."

Her dimple briefly graced her cheek, but her fingers tightened around his hand.

"What is it, Sweetness?"

"I…I have a gift."

"What kind of a gift?" he asked pulling her close.

"Not that kind," she said. "I am serious, Hugh. …I thought through this last night, and had the papers prepared this morning." She looked up over to her home with a wistful expression on her face. "The deed is in the top drawer of my desk. I want Helena to have Baneham's house."

Her gesture was unexpected, to say the least.

"Why?" he asked.

"Because it will save you," she said running the back of her hand over his cheek. "And because after what Baneham put her through, she deserves a part of his legacy."

"It is," he frowned, "more than generous of you."

"I do not think so," she whispered, lifting her lips to his. "I have *my* prize."

Chapter Sixteen

Earl Baneham's Rules for Winning

"THE FINAL RULE: CLEAN UP LOOSE ENDS."

Weary of congratulations, Sophia sank into her study chair and closed her eyes. Randolph had volunteered to assist the departure of the last of her guests so she could have a moment alone.

She had done the right thing, both by claiming Randolph and by signing over the deed. She only hoped she'd made the right wager—that Helena could be fully won to their side.

"Hello, Sophia."

She had only heard her sister's voice twice, but she recognized Helena immediately. She turned. Uncanny how the same almond-shaped eyes she saw in the looking glass stared back at her now. But Helena's jaw was from the Earl, while Sophia had her mother's cheekbones.

"Stop," Helena said, "looking at me that way."

"I see our father in you."

"There is certainly more of him in me than in you." Helena snorted. "You are weak. You take in strays. You never did learn the ways. I am the true daughter—heir of his legacy. Why he loved you and hated me…"

"Truth is," Sophia said, "I would have gratefully ceded his love."

"Easy enough to say when you have everything."

Sophia held her sister's gaze and poured the truth into her eyes. "I mean every word."

"I will give you one thing." Helena tossed back her hair. "You do not seem afraid. I could kill you."

She kept her gaze fixed on her sister, trying to read the calculations as they happened. "You would never make it out of the house."

"Your friends have hidden talents?"

"Lavinia was once suspected of murder, so not so hidden." She shrugged in Gallic fashion. "My death would not make a difference. It won't justify your suffering. Your chance at true vengeance died with Baneham." She rose out of her chair. "But Helena, your chance for justice has not."

"Stay back," Helena said.

"I am offering you your place," Sophia said.

"Randolph already made that bargain."

"No, he offered you my house." Sophia paused for effect. "I offer you not just the house, but acceptance. Acknowledgment of you as my sister."

Helena frowned. "Why?"

"Because I am not Baneham. *I* believe in justice. And, I believe you will do the right thing and tell Randolph that Kasai and Lord Eustace are one and the same."

Helena paled. "If I did that," she said, "Lord Eustace

would have me killed."

"He will not have that power. You can take it from him."

She groaned—a low and gritty sound stocked with fear. "You have *no idea* what he is capable of."

"Which is why *you* must be the one to tell the truth. You, who have suffered at his hands. Take your place, Helena. Protect yourself."

Hope dawned in her sister's eyes and Sophia's heart lifted. For a brief, shining moment, Sophia thought justice would win. For a brief and shining moment, she truly believed she could save them both.

…And then the shot rang out.

• • •

White light flashed from beneath the door as a deafening boom clanged in Randolph's ear. He kicked open the door.

Helena lay crumpled on the floor. Lord Eustace stood in the doorway opposite, skin flushed. His glittering gaze was fixed on Sophia. Though pale, Sophia held what must have been the world's smallest flintlock pointed directly at the traitor's heart.

Randolph held out his arm, preventing his men from entering the room.

"You bastard," Sophia spoke to Lord Eustace. "She was about to tell the world what you are."

"Was she?" Lord Eustace asked. "What do you truly know, Lady Randolph? She was Kasai's most trusted confidant."

"I know," Sophia said, "you are supposed to be dead."

"Yes." Lord Eustace lips curled around his teeth. "Helle was my jailer, not my unwilling accomplice."

"Sophia," Randolph called softly, "put down your gun. My men will attend to Lord Eustace."

She remained frozen. "He shot her. Right through her heart."

"I know," Randolph said. "Let us take him."

Sophia shook her head no. "You will take him but there will be no justice. There *must* be justice."

Ache curled like smoke around Randolph's heart. "Your part in this is over."

"What of Kasai? What of his vengeance against my father?"

"The records she carries," Lord Eustace said, "will show the true nature of the Under Secretary's character. Baneham created Kasai. The Under Secretary used Kasai to his own end—and had Baneham killed. Once the Under Secretary is arrested, Kasai becomes, once again, a figment. He will be no threat to you...nor to anyone else. She," the duke's brother gestured to the body on the floor, "is the one who wanted you dead."

"I don't believe you," Sophia said. Her cheeks slowly darkened—an awful color speaking of anger and vengeance. "Why would she kill Garrett?"

"She was protecting the Under Secretary—they have been working together all along. Garrett is the only other person who could testify of Kasai's crimes against me—against the others he released from imprisonment."

"Your crimes, you mean," Sophia said. "The story works just as well with you as the mastermind."

"Who are you going to believe, a bastard whore like Helle or the son of a duke?"

"There is only one way to tie up all the loose ends." Sophia placed her finger on the hammer.

Randolph whispered fiercely, "You don't need to do this, Sophia."

"She's mad," Lord Eustace said.

Randolph took a step toward Sophia. She did not flinch. He took another step.

"The final rule," she said brokenly. "Clean up loose ends."

"You don't need Baneham's rules any longer. *We* don't need them."

"This is so *touching*," Lord Eustace said.

Randolph motioned to his men. They took aim at Eustace. "My men will take care of him." Randolph drew close to Sophia and whispered, "Only us."

Sophia blinked. Slowly, she lowered her weapon. "Only us."

"Secure," Randolph called out.

Harrison swung into the room, holding the doorframe.

"Sophia is fine," he called over his shoulder. "The Furies are worried."

"Oh God, the Furies," Sophia said, as if just waking. "… and Helena." She dropped on her knees beside her sister's body.

Harrison's gaze moved from Sophia to the body on the floor to the man in the doorway.

"Eustace," Harrison's voice was flat, his expression unreadable.

"Harrison," Eustace replied.

The acknowledgment was all that verbally passed between the two men.

"Bind him," Randolph ordered.

"I demand to see my brother," Lord Eustace said.

"That would be Wynchester to you." Thea stood in the doorway, arm and arm with Lavinia. "And he is indisposed."

"Duchess," Eustace said with a mock-bow. The word was laced with hate.

"Take him below," Randolph ordered.

"You know your duty," Lord Eustace said to Thea as the men led him past.

"Of course. Wynchester will come for you," she answered with a chilling smile. "But he will not be alone."

"*Now* you are the devoted wife," Lord Eustace called over his shoulder. "Wynchester may have chosen you the last time, but you have since betrayed him. He will choose differently this time."

"Just wait and see," Thea whispered.

"What next?" Harrison said.

"The Privy Council will want to question him."

"Do you believe his story?" Sophia asked.

Harrison and Randolph exchanged glances. "It doesn't matter what we believe. The Duke must be informed."

"Lord Eustace is after the title," Thea said.

"Or," Randolph replied, "he could be the one wronged, and will recover."

"He cannot," Harrison said, "make an attempt on Wynchester's life in the open."

Thea set back her shoulders. "If he wants to get to Wynchester, he will have to get through me."

"You won't be alone," Lavinia said.

"No, you will not," Harrison said, threading his arm through Lavinia's.

Thea flashed a tight smile. "Thank you."

"I'll take him to my house," Harrison said. "Duchess, Sullivan can take you and Lavinia to Wynchester house. I'll leave the duke to you."

"Excellent plan," Randolph said.

"I will send for a coroner," Harrison clapped his hand on Randolph's shoulder. "You, I take it, will see to Sophia?"

"Of course." Randolph crouched beside his wife. "You cannot help her now."

"I know," She glanced up. "You are taking a chance on Lord Eustace."

"We cannot keep the duke from his brother, you know that."

She sighed.

"And," he continued, "Lord Eustace could be telling the truth."

"I said to Helena, 'Lord Eustace is Kasai.' She responded 'Eustace will kill me'. That is proof enough for me. I am worried for Wynchester. And for Thea."

"We will decipher Baneham's notes and discover the significance of the sapphires. As Lavinia and Harrison said, Thea will not be alone."

Sophia's expression softened. "None of the Furies are alone any longer, are we?"

"No," Randolph said.

"Helena, on the other hand, *was* alone." Sophia looked down at her sister. "She will be buried in the Baneham plot."

Randolph nodded. "Whatever you wish. I am at your service."

"Thank you," she said.

"Come Sophia, let us go home."

Her brow furrowed. "Where is home?"

"Anywhere you'd like."

She sunk against his chest. "When you pursued me, was it just because the earl intended me for you?"

He closed his arms around her and held his precious love. "It started out as a mission, but you—you stole my heart."

"Why?" she asked in a whisper.

"Society said you were nothing more than an Earl's daughter, capable only of cementing male alliance. You spurned that. Chance made you a widow, but you didn't seek protection—no, you offered your protection to others in even more need. You thought your enemies would come, so you invited them into your home and put them in your debt. I respect you, Sophia. Your spirit leaves me awed."

"Oh Hugh," she said. "I haven't told you, have I? Have I left it too late?"

"Left what too late?"

"Telling you I love you."

Some punches one expected, and some punches came from beyond one's vision. Randolph expected her confession, but he hadn't expected the crack in his heart…nor the blinding light shining from beyond.

She loved him. *Why?*

She looked up, blue eyes more beautiful and more vulnerable than he had ever seen them before and he thought only a fool would question a gift freely given.

"It's never too late," he said.

Her lip trembled. "Well then, I love you."

He brushed her sweet lips with his. "And I love *you*, now and forever."

Epilogue

Sophia traced her finger over the lines of an arched window that would form the conservatory in the new townhome Randolph was building. They were going to build a home of light and peace together…quite literally, in fact. A place where friends would always feel welcome.

"Are you as excited as I am?" She asked him.

"Until the bills come in, of course."

She frowned but he dropped a kiss on her forehead and said, "We can more than afford what we've planned. Our new house will be the talk of London."

"Finally, I can be a topic without being a scandal."

He laughed. "We're a love match, Sophia. That alone is scandal enough for some."

She rested her chin on her hand. "We've been very lucky haven't we? The past is truly behind us."

"We worked for our luck. As for the past…"

He wandered to a shelf, opened the door, and pulled out

a thin book bound in dark brown leather. His expression shadowed as he thumbed through haphazardly cut pages.

"Is that what I think it is?"

"Baneham's book of rules." He snapped the book closed. "I was so excited when he gave me a copy I rushed to slice the pages."

She held out her hand.

"Are you sure you want to look?" Randolph asked.

"Baneham can't hurt me now, can he?"

Reluctantly, Randolph gave her the book.

It had been so long since she held an actual copy of the rules. She hadn't realized any still existed.

"He believed in those rules," she said, "He died believing the rules protected him."

"They did, though they created most of the hardships from which he needed protection."

"Do you still believe in those rules?"

"I believe they are a good foundation, but, like many rules—the broader concepts need to be better understood before following them blindly."

"And the broader concept is…?"

"You always have something to fight for, but everything need not always be a fight."

She smiled.

"Shall I dispose of this copy?" he asked.

She sighed and closed the book. "Do as you wish."

He lifted a quill from his desk. "How about an edit, or two?"

He opened the page and then dipped the pen in ink. He scratched, blew, and then handed the book to Sophia.

"Rule One: Never underestimate your ~~opponent~~." In

Randolph's even scrawl she read "wife—for she is wise in all things." She shook her head and laughed, closing the book. "I think I am finished with rules."

"Including ones about studies, and daylight, and kisses?"

Her lips turned up. "Definitely including those."

He walked to the door, turned a key, and tossed the book into the fireplace.

"Well, Lady Randolph. Let's create a real scandal."

And, artfully employing her fichu, he proceeded to seduce his wife—thoroughly.

Acknowledgments

Having a Historical Romance published was a life-long dream. The experience exceeded my expectations. I cannot thank the readers who took a chance on *Lady Vice* enough, nor can I say how much Elizabeth Essex's amazing cover quote and Gaelen Foley's endorsement meant to me. I'd especially like to thank bloggers Kimberly Rocha (and BOC Janet Rodman), Kim Lowe, Melanie Friedman, PJ Ausdenmore, and every blogger who kindly hosted me or reviewed *Lady Vice* for their enthusiasm and kindness toward a debut author. More thanks to Danielle Gorman at Author's Pal for organizing my tour, Debbie S. at Entangled for her amazing support and every single reader who took the time to write a review on Goodreads, Amazon, B&N or elsewhere. Thank you, thank you, thank you.

I'd also like to send a special shout out to the people from my childhood and my family who went out of their way to show their support, especially Helen Wahrenburger,

Johanna Schmutz, Emily Gorsuch, Jennifer Rawls, Shannon Nolley, Sheila Holliday, Buddy & Nadine Stango, Natali Wicklund, Prim LaCapra, Alice Dent, & Helen Feinstein.

And I couldn't have gotten through this book without writer friends Katrina Snow, Stacey Agdern, Kiersten Hallie Krum, Stacey Reid, Erica Monroe (and the PastThrills.com ladies), Sue McGee, Sally Mackenzie, Talia Surova, Mary Behre & Beppie Harrison (hear, hear, Beppie!), Madeline Martin (spreadsheet genius) and my weekly check-in friend, Madeline Iva.

Firebirds and LaLas, you rock.

Richard & Debbie you are essential.

Erin Molta you are a sentence genie extraordinaire.

If I've missed you, let me know...*Duchess Decadence* is still to come!

Two final footnotes: Friend Elizabeth is my thank you to the amazing Quaker teachers who lit my way (particularly Dwight, Mrs. Smith & Margaret Barnes). Thank goodness plain speech is no longer the custom among Friends. And, on a completely different note, although Randolph and Sophia share little more than a pet name and a height difference with the daytime super couple Patch and Kayla, they are, in part, my homage to Stephen Nichols and Mary Beth Evans and the staff writers who brought those characters to life.

Sweetness, indeed.

About the Author

Wendy LaCapra has been reading romance since she sneaked into the adult section at the library and discovered Victoria Holt & Jane Aiken Hodge. From that point on, she dreamed of creating fictional worlds with as much richness, intrigue, and passion as she found within those books. Her stories have placed in several contests, including the 2012 Golden Heart®. She lives in NYC with her husband and loves to hear from readers. You can read about her books on her website at http://www.wendylacapra.com.